"A riveting beginning and a nicely complex plot make DANGEROUS CURVES a compelling read. Kristina Wright skillfully combines romance and suspense in this fine debut."

—*New York Times* bestselling author Tess Gerritsen

"You don't have a plan, do you?"

Samantha asked.

Jake shot her a hard look tempered with a halfhearted smile as they pulled into the congested traffic. "Planning is highly overrated. But I do know one thing."

"What?" Sam asked.

"Kissing you quiet was definitely better than shaking you would have been. And you know what else?"

Sam shook her head, feeling her cheeks grow warm.

"If you do anything so stupid as try to run off without me again, I may not stop at just kissing you."

"Is that a threat?" she asked hoarsely, her mouth going dry.

Jake's voice thrummed with emotion. "Oh, no, sweetheart. It's a promise." He sent her a quick sideways glance. "One I wouldn't mind keeping."

Dear Reader,

We've got a special lineup of books for you this month, starting with two from favorite authors Sharon Sala and Laurey Bright. Sharon's *Royal's Child* finishes up her trilogy, THE JUSTICE WAY, about the three Justice brothers. This is a wonderful, suspenseful, *romantic* finale, and you won't want to miss it. *The Mother of His Child,* Laurey's newest, bears our CONVENIENTLY WED flash. There are layers of secrets and emotion in this one, so get ready to lose yourself in these compelling pages.

And then...MARCH MADNESS is back! Once again, we're presenting four fabulous new authors for your reading pleasure. Rachel Lee, Justine Davis and many more of your favorite writers first appeared as MARCH MADNESS authors, and I think the four new writers this month are destined to become favorites, too. Fiona Brand is a New Zealand sensation, and *Cullen's Bride* combines suspense with a marriage-of-convenience plot that had me turning pages at a frantic pace. In *A True-Blue Texas Twosome,* Kim McKade brings an extra dollop of emotion to a reunion story to stay in your heart—and that Western setting doesn't hurt! *The Man Behind the Badge* is the hero of Vickie Taylor's debut novel, which gives new meaning to the phrase "fast-paced." These two are on the run and heading straight for love. Finally, check out *Dangerous Curves,* by Kristina Wright, about a cop who finds himself breaking all the rules for one very special woman. Could he be guilty of love in the first degree?

Enjoy them all! And then come back next month, when the romantic excitement will continue right here in Silhouette Intimate Moments.

Yours,

Leslie Wainger
Executive Senior Editor

Please address questions and book requests to:
Silhouette Reader Service
U.S.: 3010 Walden Ave., P.O. Box 1325, Buffalo, NY 14269
Canadian: P.O. Box 609, Fort Erie, Ont. L2A 5X3

DANGEROUS CURVES

KRISTINA WRIGHT

Published by Silhouette Books

America's Publisher of Contemporary Romance

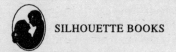 **SILHOUETTE BOOKS**

ISBN 0-373-07917-6

DANGEROUS CURVES

Dear Reader,

What a difference a day makes.

I have always dreamed of being a novelist. I decided at a very young age that I would rather write about a princess than be one. But the night I won RWA's prestigious Golden Heart Award, I felt like royalty. The only thing more exciting would have been George Clooney as my escort. (Sorry, hubby.)

The Golden Heart let me know I was on the right track on days when my dream seemed just out of reach. I never could have guessed how one day would change everything. When it happened—"the call" I had been waiting for—all I could think was, "Do they have the right person?" It took a few days to realize I had finally achieved my dream. And now, thanks to Silhouette, I get to share my stories with you!

I hope you enjoy *Dangerous Curves*. It was written from the heart, and I offer it to you with warmest wishes.

Sweet dreams,

Kristina Wright

P.S. I would love to hear from you!
You may write to me at: P.O. Box 50385, Summerville, SC 29485-0385 (Special note to George Clooney: My phone number is…)

To Jay, my husband, my hero, my technical support guy.
I love you bunches.
Annette, Mary, Joan and Phyllis, thanks for sharing the
brain. Who wants it next?
To the special friends I've met on the side trips of my
life...love, hugs and chocolate kisses! :)

Prologue

If they caught her, they would kill her.

The swamp grabbed at her legs and tried to pull her into the muck. Unfamiliar and unfriendly terrain stretched endlessly in all directions and she didn't know how much farther she could go. Her lungs strained painfully and the stitch in her side had her doubled over. But the thought of death kept Samantha Martin running.

Her breathing sounded ragged, harsh and impossibly loud. A wave of panic threatened to pull her under and she fought to control it with a mind clouded by drugs and fear.

She should have waited a few more days. But she knew she wouldn't have gotten another chance to escape unnoticed. She was pushing her body harder than she ever had in her life, demanding more than she had a right to expect, considering the shape she was in. She couldn't let them take her back there.

The desolate landscape was awash with the shimmering brightness of a full moon. Saw grass swayed eerily in a light breeze that did nothing to lessen the effects of the oppressive humidity.

The droning of cicadas and crickets flooded her senses while the mangroves loomed like ominous prehistoric monsters. Shadows clung below every surface, absorbing the silver moonlight.

Moisture seeped through the ill-fitting nurse's uniform and she shivered, but not from cold. Her canvas sneakers were soaked with swamp water and she could feel the muck oozing out over the tops of her feet. She tried not to imagine what might be living in that watery slime. Mosquito wings beat a delicate tattoo against her bare legs but she couldn't be bothered with brushing them away.

It wouldn't be long before they noticed her missing. She tried to calculate how long she'd been gone, but without a watch it was impossible. It felt like forever. Determined to put as much distance between the hospital and herself, she had run until she couldn't run anymore.

Out of shape and out of breath, she cursed herself. She should have been better prepared. Hysterical laughter bubbled up from deep within her as she remembered some science-fiction movie. The heroine had pumped up before her big escape from a mental institution. But that nutcase had been trying to save the world. She was only trying to save her own hide.

Gasping for air, Sam crouched low and rested in the tall grass, smacking her hands together and making as much noise as she dared to drive away potential predators. She hadn't escaped from hell only to get eaten by an alligator—although being some big lizard's dinner was preferable to being at the mercy of the reptiles back at Sunlight and Serenity.

As her pulse slowly returned to normal, Sam looked over her shoulder at the glow of the hospital security lights in the distance. She hoped she was heading east. The drugs they'd given her had fogged her mind and made her question her own judgment. She'd stopped taking them days ago but her mind still played tricks on her when she needed it most. She remembered traveling west from Interstate 95 when they'd brought her to the hospital. They'd crossed the turnpike and then driven at least an hour into this wilderness. If she could hike to the interstate she could hitch a ride. She knew where she had to go from there.

Climbing an embankment, Sam was finally free of the swamp water that filled the air with a stench of decay. She tripped over something and realized it was asphalt as she hit the ground on her hands and knees. It wasn't the road to the hospital, so it had to be the highway to the interstate.

Wincing at a sharp pain in her palm, Sam pushed herself into a kneeling position and examined the damage in the bright moonlight. Her hand was bloody, with small bits of gravel embedded in the torn flesh. She hissed in pain as her knees pressed into the rough roadway. She'd have the scars to show for her escape.

Picking the sharp stones from her hand, she wondered if the distant hum in her head was a side effect of the drugs. Her brain felt fuzzy, not all there. She looked up to see the source of light that was beginning to blind her.

Headlights.

And they were coming right at her.

Chapter 1

Jake Cavanaugh knew State Road 84—Alligator Alley to the locals—like the back of his hand. He'd been coming up to Lake Muskogee to fish for more years than he could remember but now it unnerved him to be out here at night. The unrelenting darkness closed around him, making him claustrophobic. The irony was, the Florida Everglades provided more wide-open space than most places he'd been. Still, he drove with the windows of his sport utility all the way down.

He didn't even know why he was out here. He should have stayed at the cabin until morning. But the silence, the never-ending quiet, had been more than he could take. These days he slept better with a little traffic noise, the television on—anything except relentless silence. When it was quiet like this, his mind tried to fill the void with reruns of the past.

A snuffling sound from the back of the truck brought a smile to his somber features. Lately, he hadn't even been a fit companion for a dog. He flexed his left knee out of habit and felt the familiar twinge as the scar tissue stretched over muscle. The sensation brought it all back in vivid Technicolor—the alley, the flash of gunfire, Charlie's cry; a scream, followed by his own low moan of agony.

The dull pain in his knee was nothing compared to the agony he went through, reliving that moment. In the aftermath, his senses had been dulled by a different kind of pain. The humiliating pain of losing his job and losing his wife. Margo's accusation that he loved his job more than he loved her cut deep—mostly because it was true.

Wrapped up in the suffocating blanket of the past, Jake barely had time to react to the pale form on the road in front of him. He slammed on the brakes, thankful that it was his left leg that bore the damage of that long-ago night. His right leg functioned on instinct borne of training and experience. He gripped the wheel as the tires grabbed the road, lost purchase and then held. He was vaguely aware of the smell of burning rubber as he watched the object in the road get closer and closer.

Just when he thought his luck had deserted him for good and impact was inevitable, the truck came to a shuddering halt. Jake closed his eyes and exhaled a breath he hadn't realized he'd been holding. He blinked. He would have laughed if he hadn't thought he was going crazy.

An angel knelt in the middle of the road, her eyes closed and her hands raised as if in prayer. Illuminated by the harsh glare of the headlights, she looked beautiful and fragile. And definitely out of place.

It took a minute for the truth to register. This sure as hell wasn't his guardian angel sent to watch over him. And if it was, she'd come about two years too late.

The woman opened her eyes and squinted into the brightness. Cursing under his breath, Jake found the knob on the dash and killed the lights. It took his eyes a moment to adjust to the sudden darkness. In her white clothing that reflected the moonlight, the woman was like an apparition in a horror movie. Jake felt fingers of dread travel up his spine. Something was wrong here. He'd bet his pension on it. Of course, his pension was long gone anyway, so it wasn't much of a bet.

He opened the door and slid out of the seat, never taking his eyes off the figure in the road. The crunch of gravel under his boots was a comforting sound in this surreal situation. He approached her as cautiously as he would a strung-out junkie.

She looked like she'd been through some disaster. Her shoulder-length blond hair was a tangled mass, dirt streaked across one rounded cheekbone. Her clothes, which hung loosely on her, looked wet and her eyes were wide with fear. Jake took his sweet time getting to her—he didn't need a knife in the ribs for his efforts.

"Ma'am? You all right?" He kept his voice low, trying for a soothing quality he didn't think he had. When the only response he got was wide green eyes staring at him in terror, he tried again. "Lady, are you hurt?" Maybe she didn't speak English. "*¿Se habla inglesa?*"

Blond hair partially covered her face as she shook her head. "N-no. Not hurt."

Relieved he wouldn't be called upon to demonstrate his limited bilingual abilities, Jake didn't argue with her. He could see the dark stains of blood and he slowly reached out a hand to her. "Let me help you up."

Hesitantly, as if she expected him to pull away at the last second, she put her small hand into his. He was surprised at the strength he felt in the cold, narrow fingers. She unfolded from the ground and stood beside him, her eyes not quite focusing on his chin. He guessed her to be in her late twenties. Despite her ragged appearance, Jake didn't peg her as a transient. He suddenly realized what she was wearing.

"You're a nurse."

The woman hesitated again, then nodded slowly. Jake knew there was some kind of hospital on the edge of the glades. He racked his brain to remember.... Sunshine, Sunnyvale... Something like that.

"What are you doing out here?"

She shook her head and looked up at him. Moonlight illuminated her pale face and Jake felt pain twisting in his gut. She reminded him of another woman—a younger woman, to be sure. But the hair, the wide eyes filled with fear and mistrust, the feminine softness of her features... It shook him to the core. Then she spoke and the spell was broken.

"I—I have to get to the interstate. Can you take me?"

Jake wanted to say no. He knew it was stupid to even think about picking up a stranger. It didn't matter that she looked harmless. Sometimes the most innocent-looking people were the most dangerous predators. But something about the raw emotion in her voice, the way she held on to his hand like it was a lifeline, made him ignore the voice of caution.

"Sure, just tell me where you need to go." The words were barely out of his mouth before she flung herself at the sport utility, tearing on the passenger door in frustration.

"Wait a second. I have to unlock it," Jake said. He climbed behind the wheel and reached across to the other side to open the lock. As soon as he did, she was huddling in the seat beside him.

"Where do you want to go?" He watched her push the mass of blond hair back from her face. Her hands were trembling.

"Just to Interstate 95." He stared at her until she glanced up at him. He was rewarded with the barest shadow of a smile. "Thanks."

"To the interstate," he muttered under his breath. What did she intend to do once she got to the interstate? He didn't ask. It wasn't any of his business.

When Jake gunned the engine he felt rather than saw the woman flinch. She didn't like the noise. Funny, it somehow comforted him in this strange situation. He flicked the headlights back on and slipped the sport utility into gear, wondering for a moment if maybe he'd just made the biggest mistake of his life.

As the miles rolled out behind them, Jake could feel the tension easing out of the woman beside him. He cast a sidelong glance at her, curious in spite of himself. He wondered what her story was. What was she so afraid of that she'd risk hitching? He caught her eye and smiled in what he hoped was a nonthreatening way; he didn't want her to think she'd traded in one bad situation for another.

"You okay? Want anything? I've got some sodas in a cooler in the back." Jake watched her shrink away at the sound of his voice. "Hey, I'm not going to hurt you. You're safe."

She gave him a haunted look. "Not yet."

Before he could ask her what she meant, a piercingly familiar wail filled the air. Reflexively, Jake checked the speedometer. He was over the limit, but not enough to get busted in the middle of the night in the middle of nowhere. He wondered if it was one of the local yokels or a state trooper. Either bet was a good one.

He gave the woman an apologetic look. "I have to pull over."

"No!" Her whisper might as well have been a shout for all the terror it held. "Please! If they take me back there, they'll kill me!"

That feeling of dread came back even as Jake was easing off the gas pedal and steering toward the side of the road. He flipped his lights off and turned on his hazards. "Are you in trouble with the police?"

The woman grasped his hand before he could pull it back from the dash. "Please! I'll explain everything! Just don't tell them I'm here—" Her voice broke on a sob as she glanced out the tinted back window. The police car pulled off the road behind them. "Please," she whispered again as she threw herself over the bench seat and into the back of the truck.

Reacting on gut emotion, Jake said, "There's a tarp back there. Cover up with it and keep quiet." She didn't respond but Jake could hear the rustle of the tarp as she got into place.

Jake rolled down his window as the officer approached him. The uniform wasn't familiar. A local. Maybe his luck was changing after all. "Evening," Jake said.

The officer nodded, shining a flashlight into Jake's face. "Sir, do you realize you were speeding?"

Jake nodded. "Sorry about that." He looked at his badge. Officer Barnell. The name was familiar but it was a long shot. "Barnell? You ever work down in the Metro-Dade area?"

The officer nodded. "Back in '92 for a while, until the wife decided she was tired of the tourists and the crime." He peered at Jake. "Do I know you?"

"Our paths probably crossed. Jake Cavanaugh, Metro-Dade drug task force."

"Part of the Dream Team, huh?" Barnell asked, referring to the group of top-notch detectives Jake had headed up. "I'm sure I saw you around. What're you doing in this neck of the woods?"

"A little fishing. Decided to cut out early and head home."

"Catch anything?" Barnell leaned against Jake's sport utility, apparently content to pass the time talking to another cop.

Jake thought of his stowaway. "A little something. But I'm wiped out and ready to hit the sack." He hoped the guy would take the hint and let him get going.

The radio in the patrol car squawked and Barnell raised his hand. "I'll be back in a minute."

When the trooper was out of earshot, Jake said over his shoulder, "Hang on, we'll be out of this in a minute." He didn't know why he was helping this woman. Maybe it was because she reminded him of someone else whom he hadn't been able to help.

Barnell double-timed it back to the truck. "Hey, Cavanaugh, you seen anyone out this way?"

Jake's senses went on red alert. "Vehicles?"

"Naw, someone on foot." He glanced at the clipboard in his hand. "Female, Caucasian. Five-six, about a hundred and thirty-five pounds, blond hair."

Jake forced a laugh. "I wish I had seen someone like that. Would have been a nice break in the monotony."

"Trust me, you don't want to run into this broad."

"Why?" The hair on the back of Jake's neck stood up. "What's she done?"

"She's a nutcase from Sunlight and Serenity."

"Sunlight and Serenity?"

"Private psycho ward for the criminally insane who have the money to buy themselves out of the state facility."

"Criminally insane, huh?" Jake's senses were in overdrive now, screaming at him to give up his passenger before he got himself killed. "What did she do to land there?" The way Jake's luck had been going, he should have expected the answer.

"Murder."

Before Jake could decide to go with his instincts and turn Little Miss Psycho over to Officer Barnell, the radio crackled to life again.

"Guess I'd better get going. She's probably lost out in the swamp somewhere. Maybe if we're real lucky she'll be gator bait before morning."

Jake watched as Barnell got back into his patrol car and pulled around him with a wave of his hand. He was alone with a murderer. Aiding and abetting a known felon. Jake Cavanaugh had sunk lower than he'd ever thought possible.

"You can come out now." The words were cold and harsh. Sam wanted to stay put, but the tarp smelled of fish and felt oily. As if she had any reason to complain. She threw the tarp off and something yelped.

"What the hell?" A wet nose followed by a wetter tongue touched her cheek and she pressed against the back of the seat. She could make out a dog in the darkness—a decidedly large dog. "Why didn't you tell me there was a dog back there?" she asked as she climbed over the seat.

"That's Fletcher. He's my fishing buddy." A low woof from the back of the truck confirmed that Fletcher knew they were talking about him. "He'll sleep through anything."

"I could have given myself away," Sam grumbled.

The man's brown eyes met hers in the gloom. She'd heard every word of his conversation with the cop. She was in trouble. But for the first time since she'd left the hospital, she wasn't afraid. This guy had helped her—for whatever reason.

"Lady, you're damn lucky I didn't turn you in."

Sam watched his large hand flick on the headlights and start the engine. Losing some of her newfound confidence, she whispered, "So why didn't you?"

The look he gave her was unfathomable in the darkness. "I don't know."

"Then you'll take me to the interstate?"

Pulling back onto the road, the man nodded curtly. "Yeah."

Sam sighed.

"But I want to know who I'm helping and why. According to Officer Barnell you were in the psych hospital for murder."

Sam nodded, staring straight ahead. She didn't want to rehash the story, but if that was what it would take to get this man's help, she'd do it. The thought in the back of her mind was that only a crooked cop would help her. Only someone who worked for *them* would do something illegal. Maybe he wasn't her savior after all. Maybe he was delivering her to the very people she was trying to escape from.

"Well?"

Startled, Sam jumped. "What?"

"Are you going to tell me who you are?"

"Sam."

The man snorted. "Not good enough. What's your whole name?"

"Samantha Martin." Regaining a bit of her courage, she asked, "And you are?"

"You heard me before. Jake Cavanaugh."

"Officer Cavanaugh," she said, emphasizing the word *officer*. Tension crackled in the air between them. Sam glanced out the window and saw the interstate sign. Five more miles.

"Detective. And it's ex-Detective Cavanaugh." The cop threw another odd look at her. "Now I'm just Jake."

"Still, you were a cop."

"Yeah." Was that regret she heard in his voice?

"And you didn't turn me in."

"Nope."

"Want to tell me why?"

Sam was jolted out of her seat when he jammed on the brakes. Without a seat belt on, she slammed into the dash and ricocheted back into the seat.

Jake's arm shot out to keep her from sliding to the floor. There was a yelp from the back as the dog bounced around. Pushed sideways on the bench, Sam looked up into eyes that were filled with concern—and something else she didn't quite recognize. She pulled herself into a sitting position and scooted away from him.

"Sorry, Fletch," Jake called out before turning his penetrating gaze on her.

"What the hell did you do that for?" she demanded.

"Look." He gestured beyond the windshield.

Sam stared out in front of them. A dark object stretched across both lanes. It looked like a log. But there were no trees on either side of the road, only a ditch that disappeared into murky swamp. "What is it?"

"Gator."

Sam shuddered. This is what she had been out in the swamp with. "Can't you do something?"

Jake shrugged. "What do you want me to do?"

"Go around it." Sam realized even as she said it that he couldn't. The alligator took up most of both lanes, his rounded snout jutting into the lane on their side of the road while his jagged tail reached well into the middle of the other lane. To bypass it, they would risk toppling into the swamp.

"Sorry, lady, I'm not in that much of a hurry." Jake shut off the engine and settled back into his seat, arms behind his head.

"He'll move when he's ready. Why do you think they call this Alligator Alley?"

Alligator Alley. Sam shuddered. Had she been that close to danger? "Can't you honk the horn or get out and scare him off?" Her frustration grew as she stared at the monstrosity that lay between her and freedom.

"You really are nuts. That tail has more power in it than three men. One swipe and you'd have to drive yourself to the interstate because I'd be on the way to the morgue." Jake glanced at her. "And don't be fooled by that large, slow body. That guy there can outrun a horse if he's motivated. I don't plan on giving him any motivation."

Sam bit her lip. "How do you know so much about alligators?"

"Used to wrestle them."

She stared at him, wide-eyed. And he thought she was crazy! "What do you mean you used to wrestle them?"

Jake shrugged. "Put myself through college working down at the Seminole Indian Village in Miami. Wrestled gators for the tourists. Course, we had a few tricks we used. And the gators knew me."

"There's got to be a better way to earn a paycheck." Sam had a faint recollection of the Seminole village. Her father had taken her there when she was four, maybe five. She'd been more fascinated with the bead crafts than with the alligator wrestlers.

"My grandmother was full-blooded Seminole. I spent a lot of time at the village when I was a kid. My great-uncle taught me to wrestle and I liked it."

Sam shook her head. "Sounds like being a cop is the least dangerous thing you've done."

Jake's eyes pierced through to her soul. She could vaguely make out the Native American features he had inherited from his grandmother—the high cheekbones, the straight, powerful nose. Her gaze traveled past the neck of his white T-shirt. His lean, well-muscled torso looked capable of wrestling a gator. Or anything else, for that matter.

"Lady, danger is what I do best. Always has been."

"Is that why you're helping me? Because you like the danger?"

"Maybe." Jake suddenly started the engine and Sam realized that their friendly neighborhood gator had slithered off into the primordial ooze. "Or maybe I'm the dangerous one."

Chapter 2

"Here we are."

Sam looked around. They were stopped at an intersection, the streetlight flashing yellow at this hour. The sign for the interstate was straight ahead, beckoning her. A darkened strip mall squatted on one corner and an open-all-night gas station sign announced two-for-one chili dogs on the opposite corner. They were alone. But what had she expected? A welcoming committee? The cavalry?

"Thanks, I'll just get out here." Sam's hand was already on the door handle.

"Wait a minute. Where are you going to go?" Jake asked. "Do you have a ride?" He sounded like a Boy Scout, ready to do his duty but anxious to get back to the campfire.

"No, but I'll be fine." She smiled at the man who very well might have saved her life. "Thank you." She opened the door.

Jake's hand touched her arm and she stilled, feeling the warmth of him penetrate the damp material. It was, quite possibly, the first gentle human touch she'd had in over a month. It held her in place with more force than if he'd restrained her.

"Look, this isn't the best neighborhood to be wandering through at two o'clock in the morning. Isn't there someplace else I can take you?" His voice was low, soothing. It reminded her of those late-night radio deejays. Familiar. It made her feel somehow less alone.

"There's only one place I can go."

"Where's that?"

"Key West."

Unspoken questions were etched on his face. "Sorry, that's a little out of my way. Besides, you haven't told me what this is all about."

"Mr. Cavanaugh, you don't want to know." She stared out the window, hesitating for a moment too long.

"Maybe I do," came his quiet reply. "You look like you could use a good meal. Why don't we go somewhere, get a hot dinner or breakfast, whatever you want. And you can tell me your story."

Sam knew she didn't look like she was starving. A month of confinement had added several extra pounds to her usually lean frame. Luckily, the stolen uniform was several sizes too large. "Thanks, but you've done enough. What I don't understand is why you want to help me."

"Me, neither, but I've taken you this far. You've got my curiosity up. Come on," he cajoled.

Sam's stomach growled in answer and she suddenly felt light-headed. When had her last meal been? Yesterday? "All right. Just for a little while." Her eyes surveyed their surroundings. Theirs was the only vehicle on the road. "Where can we go?"

"I know a couple of all-night diners. Nothing fancy—" he glanced at her "—but then you don't look like you're up for a four-star restaurant."

The fact that he could joke about where she'd been should have had her warning signals going off like crazy. Instead, she relaxed. She was out of the worst danger. All she had to do was get to

Key West. She'd think about the rest later. In the meantime, a meal—a real meal, not hospital food—sounded pretty damn good.

Big Louie's Diner was less than a mile from I-95. The narrow gravel parking lot was partially roped off and in the process of being resurfaced. A bright red sign announced a newly paved parking area in back. Jake drove behind the diner and parked next to the two other cars there. "Sit tight, Fletch," Jake said before coming around to Sam's door and helping her out. His arm stayed on her elbow until they were inside the diner, as if he was afraid she would run off.

Whatever her misgivings before, Sam felt some of her tension drain away as they settled into a booth near the back. Fatigue was wearing her down and the smell of comfort food warmed her from the inside out.

A short-order cook and a tired-looking waitress in a pale pink uniform were the only people in the place. The waitress took their orders and shuffled away, not seeming to notice Sam's ragged appearance.

"Will your dog be all right out there?" Sam didn't have a particular fondness for dogs, but it seemed like a safe topic.

"Fletcher is tired. That's why he didn't notice you at first. But he's better than a car alarm. As long as I bring him something to eat, he'll be happy to take a nap until I get back."

"Oh." Sam stared out the narrow opening in the red checkered curtains. The lights inside were dim enough that she could see part of the empty gravel parking lot and a discount department store across the street. The squeak of the waitress's shoes announced her approach. Sam tilted her head toward the window, letting her hair fall limply across her face as the waitress put their drinks on the table.

"So how did you come to be in the Everglades?" Jake asked when the waitress retreated to the front counter.

Sam sipped her cola and stared at the scarred Formica tabletop. How much should she tell him? He knew she was wanted for murder and that hadn't scared him off. Maybe he was a sicko, feeding on death and horror stories. Didn't some cops burn out and turn bitter about the world? He had said he wasn't a cop anymore.

Sam traced the initials carved in the table, feeling very old. She looked up at Jake and realized that his eyes were blue, not brown as she'd originally thought. Dark blue. Her gaze shifted away as she read the questions in his eyes—questions she wanted to answer.

"I was accused of murder and sent to Sunlight and Serenity." She spoke the truth, but it barely scraped the surface of her month-long ordeal. The words sounded like they were coming out of someone else's mouth. This wasn't her life. Was it?

"Isn't this the point where you tell me you didn't do it?"

Sam tilted her head, the corner of her mouth edging up in a self-deprecating smile. "Would you believe me if I said I didn't do it?"

"Did you?"

"No."

"Really." His tone was neutral—one she was sure he reserved for criminals. She expected no more.

"I know it's difficult to believe. But I've got something somebody wants. And they're desperate enough to have me framed for murder and put away until they get it."

Jake pushed his glass around on the table, leaving a trail of moisture. The glass looked dainty in his large hand. He seemed to be thinking about what she had said. "Who framed you?"

"I don't know."

"What do you have that they want?"

"Film." She felt like she was back in the interrogation room—except then, she had lied.

"Pictures?"

"Just negatives."

Jake's gaze was inscrutable. "What's on the negatives?"

Sam squirmed under his gaze—not because she had anything to hide, but because the questions he asked didn't have answers.

Yet. "I'm not sure. Pictures of people who didn't want their picture taken—I think."

"You think?"

The blandness of his tone was getting to her. "Look, you wanted to know my story and there it is. I'm sorry if it's not tied up in a neat little package. If it were, I wouldn't be here." Conscious of the waitress's curious stare, Sam lowered her voice. "I told you you didn't want to know."

Jake's eyes never wavered from her face. "I want to know. It just seems your story is full of holes."

"Tell me about it."

"Can I ask you one more question?"

Sam sighed and tucked back a stray piece of matted hair. With the way her day had been going, she'd probably get some weird swamp disease. Her hands were trembling and she folded them in her lap, staring down at her ragged, dirt-encrusted nails. "Sure."

"Who was it you were supposed to have murdered?"

Cringing inwardly at the most obvious question, Sam braced herself for his reaction and looked him in the eye. "A federal agent."

His eyes registered surprise, then became guarded. "I see."

"Do you?" Sam asked, unable to hide her bitterness. She'd been through hell. Alone. She didn't ask for understanding or help. But it would be nice if someone would just believe her.

"Okay, so I don't. You caught me by surprise, that's all." Jake smiled, but his eyes remained guarded. "Why don't you go get cleaned up a little and we'll eat."

Sam nodded slowly. "All right." This was too easy. He wasn't going to let her off the hook—was he? She slid out of the booth, wishing for a clean change of clothes. She shivered from the arctic blast of the air-conditioning vent and wrapped her arms tightly around herself. "I'll be right back."

The rest room was no cleaner than she felt, but at least there were plenty of paper towels and a full soap dispenser. Sam scrubbed her face, hands and arms until her fingers puckered, but the blood was gone. Reluctantly, she stared at herself in the mirror. The fluorescent light made her look sickly. She looked better than she had, but she still didn't feel clean. Dizziness blurred her image in the mirror and she had to grip the basin until it passed.

The hand dryer was a luxury. She stood in front of it until the nurse's uniform felt less damp. She still smelled like eau de swamp, but it was an improvement. Aware that time had passed, she left the bathroom with some reluctance and headed back to the booth.

Jake was gone.

Startled, she looked around the deserted diner and spotted him by the door. The small entryway was crowded with a phone booth, cigarette machine and newspaper stand. Jake had his back to her and she couldn't tell which convenience he'd been using. If he was making a phone call at this hour, he could only be calling the police. Panic clawed at her insides, holding her in place for a moment too long; he turned to her as she started to back away.

He moved quickly down the aisle toward her. "Wondered what happened to you." He had a newspaper tucked under his arm. "I've been up at the lake for a week and thought I'd catch up on what's been going on in the world."

"I think it's too soon to be seeing my picture in the papers." Sam glanced back toward the rest room, trying to remember if there had been a window. She couldn't recall. Her memory felt fuzzy around the edges.

"You're probably right," Jake answered, sitting down at the booth and looking at her expectantly. She settled back in the booth and watched his face. Maybe he was telling the truth. Maybe he really did want to help her.

"You look better."

"Yeah, a real beauty queen, I'm sure." She pretended a keen interest in the saltshaker to avoid meeting his eyes.

"So where do you go from here?"

"I told you, Key West."

"Figure you need a vacation?"

"That's where the film is."

He didn't respond, and for that she was grateful. He almost seemed to want to believe her. The silence dragged out and she watched the window, feeling his eyes on her. She wanted to say something, to thank him for his help. But this sort of thing wasn't covered by Emily Post and the words stuck in her throat.

The waitress squeaked over just then, weighed down with two large platters heaped with hamburgers and fries. The amount of grease alone could kill her, but Sam dug into her meal with gusto.

"I guess you were hungry," Jake said, his own burger disappearing at a more leisurely rate.

"Starving." Sam glanced up at him and saw him looking out the window. From his side of the booth he had a better view of the parking lot. Sam tensed. "What is it?"

Jake tried to smile at her but he couldn't shake the feeling that he was a rat. He had nothing to feel bad about. She was a murderer and probably insane to boot. It was his duty to turn her in. "Nothing. Just another late-night diner."

"Oh," Sam mumbled around another bite of burger. He watched her bent head and felt bad anyway. Then he turned his gaze back to the window.

Two cars had pulled into the roped-off parking lot. One man got out of the light-colored Ford while two others exited a dark sedan. Jake recognized Greg Tilton as the first man. He'd called Greg while Sam was in the ladies' room. He didn't recognize the two guys in suits—and that didn't sit well with him at all.

They weren't in uniform and they sure as hell didn't look like feds. He'd warned Greg that Sam was likely to bolt and he didn't want her to get hurt, no matter what she'd done. He glanced across the table, but Sam was busy mopping her fries in a puddle of catsup.

When he turned back to the window, something was wrong—

seriously wrong. Greg was struggling with one of the men. Jake's
hand automatically went to his side, but his holster wasn't there.
Before he could go to Greg's aid, he watched his friend crumple
to his knees. The man Greg had been struggling with stepped
away, the dark silhouette of a gun in his hand. It must have been
equipped with a silencer because Jake hadn't heard a shot. Greg
slumped to the ground and the two men turned toward the diner.

Jake's mind raced. A silencer on a police weapon? Not likely.
Every instinct in him screamed to get the hell out of there, even
as his mind told him he couldn't leave Greg. Instinct won out.

"Let's go." Jake stood and reached for Sam's arm.

"Now? Why?"

"I said, let's go." Jake pulled her up and headed to the counter,
pulling a crumpled ten-dollar bill out of his pocket. "Is there a
back door?" he asked the waitress.

The sleepy-eyed waitress looked at him suspiciously.
"Through the kitchen. But why—"

Jake didn't let her finish. He dragged his protesting companion
behind him, his mind churning with questions. What the hell had
he gotten himself into?

The cook was dozing in a corner of the kitchen and jerked
awake at the intrusion. "Don't mind us," Jake said, pushing open
the wide metal door and slipping out into the darkened parking
lot, Sam tripping on his heels.

"What the hell was that all about?" she complained, putting
some distance between the two of them.

"Just get in." He opened the passenger door and shoved her
in. "And stay down."

Jake climbed behind the wheel and started the engine. The two
goons in suits had to be in the restaurant by now and would
realize any second that they'd lost their target.

He eased out of the parking lot and onto the highway, checking
his rearview mirror. The cars were still there and so was Greg's
body. Jake wished for a police radio. He floored the accelerator,
adrenaline coursing through his veins as steadily as the hum of

the engine. They were eating up the highway, heading for the interstate. Within moments, he saw headlights bearing down on them.

"Are you going to tell me what's going on?"

"Someone just got killed back there," Jake ground out, watching the rearview mirror. He pushed the accelerator to the floor, taking the on-ramp at a dangerous speed. The squeal of tires on the pavement filled the dead, humid air.

"What? Are you sure?" Sam clung to the seat with one hand while hurriedly fastening her seat belt with the other.

"I'm sure. A cop—a friend of mine—just took a bullet in the chest."

"This isn't real," she moaned.

"Believe it. It's real."

Fletcher hung his head over the seat and slurped at Jake's ear. "Sorry, buddy, forgot to get you something," Jake said. The car was gaining on them.

Sam turned in her seat and looked out the back of the sport utility. "Who is that?"

"Why don't you tell me?"

"You called the police." Her voice was flat. Jake felt that rat feeling again and the gut-shot realization that he'd gotten Greg killed.

"Yeah."

"I thought you wanted to help me."

He couldn't take it. "Look, lady, what did you expect? You killed a fed and escaped from a mental institution! Did you think I'd just drop you off on the corner and tell you to have a nice day?" He glanced over at her, but she was staring straight ahead, her arms wrapped around her.

"Now my friend is dead," Jake finished, conscious of the car coming up fast behind them. They'd passed three exits on the interstate as they headed south. Only a couple more exits and he could lose them.

Their wheels screeched as they careened around the curve of

the off-ramp and for a moment he felt a weightless sensation as his stomach caught up with him. The four-lane divided highway didn't give them the safety they needed. Jake had to get off the main roads if he had any hope of losing their pursuers. Now the sedan was riding their bumper, a menacing shadow in the darkness. A noise ripped the air and the tinkling sound of glass made Jake slide down low in his seat.

"What was that?" Sam yelled, sinking lower in her own seat. Fletcher whined and Jake took a corner on what felt like two wheels. They were in a neighborhood subdivision now—not one that Jake was very familiar with.

"They're shooting at us. Stay down!"

Jake saw the next corner coming up and reflexively braced his body in the seat. Two cars parked on either side of the road narrowed the two-lane street to barely one, but he managed to squeeze past them. In the rearview mirror Jake watched the sedan overshoot the turn and slam into the front fender of one of the parked cars. Before Jake even had a chance to get his bearings, the sedan jerked into reverse, straightened and then was on them again. But at least they had nearly a block lead now.

"Can't you lose them?" Sam asked, her voice absurdly calm under the circumstances.

"I'm trying!" Jake jerked the wheel to the left, flying around another corner. This time there were no parked cars to impede their pursuers and the sedan's headlights appeared around the corner behind them.

"Well, try harder!"

"If you think you could do a better job, you're welcome to it!" Jake turned the wheel at the last minute and flew around another corner. Sam slammed into the passenger door and Fletcher skittered across the back of the sport utility.

"If they don't get us killed, you will!"

Three more corners later, the sedan didn't reappear. "I think we lost them." Jake looked over at Sam.

"Great." She rested her head against the back of the seat.

"Only one problem."

"What now?"

"We're lost."

Sam groaned. "I thought cops didn't get lost. I thought cops knew where everything was."

"I'm not lost-lost. I just don't know how to get out of this neighborhood. Why don't they number the streets anymore?" Jake peered out the windshield at the street signs. "Everything has to have a name. Oakview. Oak Place. Oak Root. I've lived in south Florida all my life and I've never seen an oak tree."

Shaking his head, Jake maneuvered through the darkened streets, past a community swimming pool and playground. There was no sign of the sedan and he relaxed a little. Finally, he found the road back to the main highway. All the lanes were empty.

"Leave it to me to find a cop with a lousy sense of direction," Sam grumbled as they sped down the highway going away from the interstate. She should just get out now. The only problem with that was she'd never been fond of jumping from a moving vehicle.

"Ex-cop."

"Whatever."

"Hey, I saved your butt back there. The least you could do is thank me."

"Thanks, but no thanks. You were going to turn my butt in, if you recall," she reminded him. "Now, if you don't mind, I'd just as soon take my chances with the criminals on the street."

"Out here, you're more likely to get adopted by a senior citizen than mugged by a criminal," he said.

"Are you going to let me out or not?"

Jake turned into another subdivision, and she tensed. Where was he going now? "Yeah. In just a minute."

They drove down a couple of streets, then Jake turned into a cul-de-sac of similar-looking houses. As they pulled into the driveway of one of the houses, he turned off the headlights.

"Where are we?"

Pushing the button for the garage-door opener, Jake eased the sport utility inside next to a pale blue minivan. "Home."

Sam reached for the door. "No way. Uh-uh. If you think for one minute I'm going to—"

He grabbed her arm in a vise-like grip. "You're not going anywhere."

Fear had her heart trip-hammering in her chest. "Wh-what?" She'd been right the first time; the guy was some nut. As the garage door closed behind them, taking the last thin strands of light cast by the streetlamp, Sam trembled. When the door finally creaked shut and they were plunged into total darkness, she knew that the worst was not behind her. Not by a long shot.

"Stay here. The light is burned out and I don't want you to trip over something," he ordered, leaving her alone. The dog whined from the back seat. She felt like doing the same, huddling in the oppressive darkness that left her helpless. He'd told her to stay, but she couldn't have found her way out of the sport utility if she'd tried.

A fluorescent light flickered on over a workbench, illuminating the garage. Shelves lined the walls, piled high with assorted tools and other guy stuff that Sam didn't have the vaguest clue about. She did recognize a table saw in the corner and shivered. What had she gotten herself into this time?

Jake stood at a door leading into the house. "Come on in. I won't call the cops again. Not until I figure out what the hell just happened."

It wasn't the most comforting thing he could have said, but it didn't sound like he intended to cut her up into little pieces—yet. She opened the door and stepped into the garage, inhaling the scent of wood and grease. She started to close the door behind her when the dog barked.

"Sorry," she mumbled as the large brown mutt squeezed out of the back seat and trotted to his master.

Jake scratched his ears and then patted him on the rump.

''Come on, Fletcher. Let's get you some dinner.'' He looked over his shoulder as he disappeared into the darkened house. ''You coming, or would you rather sleep in the garage?''

Sam wanted to answer but a black wave of dizziness and nausea swept over her again. This time, it won.

Chapter 3

Jake watched Sam with equal parts fascination and dread. His heart had nearly stopped when he saw her lying on the garage floor. Checking her pulse and determining she wasn't dead, he'd carried her into the house. He cleaned up the scratches on her hands and knees. Tremors periodically racked her body and her skin had the pasty green look of someone who had been ill for a long time.

She belonged in a hospital, most likely. He kept telling himself he needed to just wash his hands of this whole situation. But the image of Greg being gunned down in cold blood kept him from making any calls. Somebody wanted this woman badly and they didn't care who died. Jake had to find out exactly what was at stake before he did anything.

He applied another cool compress to her forehead and was rewarded with a groan from the unconscious woman.

"What—?" Weak as a newborn kitten, she lifted a trembling hand to push him away.

"You passed out." He restrained her gently, reapplying the damp cloth.

"Oh." Her eyes focused on his face. "Where am I?" She gestured around the room with its pale lavender walls and four-poster bed draped in yards of white eyelet fabric.

"You weren't in any condition to walk and the garage floor isn't the most comfortable place to spend the night."

"This is your bedroom?" she croaked, her eyes going wide at the lacy white curtains and the white wicker furniture.

"Doesn't it look like me?" He would have laughed if the situation hadn't been so strange.

Sam shook her head and winced in obvious pain. "No. But your wife did a nice job with the decorating. Very feminine."

It bothered him that she thought he was married. He didn't know why. Of course, if he'd been married he probably would have caught all kinds of hell for picking her up in the first place. "Sorry, no wife."

He watched her gaze travel from his eyes to his mouth. He grinned and she frowned. "So, you like lavender?" she asked finally.

"Can't stand it, actually. But this isn't my room so it doesn't matter."

"Then would you tell me whose bed I'm in?"

The exasperated tone of her voice coaxed a full-fledged smile from him. She was one tough little cookie. "It's my sister's room—her house, for that matter."

"Where is she?"

"Paris. Annie's a French teacher at Coconut Springs High. She's spending a year in France as part of an exchange program. I'm supposed to make sure no unsavory characters get in. Looks like I failed." His attempt at humor only brought another dark look to Sam's face.

"I didn't ask you to. For that matter, I didn't ask you to get involved."

"Funny, you seemed pretty intent on involving me when you asked me to hide you from that cop," Jake said, all traces of humor gone.

"Fine. Whatever. Just let me rest for a while and I'll be on my way."

He watched the way her hands trembled as she pushed back her hair. Realization struck him like a blow. "What are you on?" His voice was harsher than he'd intended and she recoiled from him, fear in her eyes. He tried again. "What are you taking?"

"I'm not 'taking' anything!"

The sarcasm in her voice rankled on his nerves. He grabbed her wrists and held her hands at eye level, watching her fingers twitch uncontrollably. He could feel her whole body quake beneath his touch. "Don't lie to me. You've got the shakes, sweetheart. What is it? Drugs or alcohol?" Not waiting for a reply, he pulled her hands toward him, looking at the pale blue veins running up her arms. No track marks.

She jerked from his grasp, her eyes sparkling shards of emerald in her pale face. He didn't know why he felt bad to have made her cry. God knew, he'd seen enough substance-abuse problems in his life to recognize a pitch for sympathy when he saw it. But he was a sucker for a sweet face and big green eyes.

"Drugs."

He'd wanted her to deny it, he wanted her to be different. He slammed the door on his feelings. "What kind?"

She shook her head and met his gaze, her eyes steady even while her body trembled. "I—I don't know," her teeth chattered and he watched her fight for control. "Whatever they use at mental hospitals. Tranquillizers, I imagine. Strong stuff."

He took her at her word. For now. "When did you stop taking them?" If she'd been on heavy doses of tranks, the withdrawal would be hell.

"Th-three days— No, four days ago," she whispered, her arms wrapping around her to control the shivering.

"Did this just start?

She shook her head. "No. I was feeling sick yesterday and the day before."

"Terrific," Jake muttered to himself. To her, he said, "You're in for a bumpy ride, lady."

She favored him with a cutting look and a smirk. "Thanks for the warning, officer."

"Hang on to that sense of humor—you're going to need it. You ever been on drugs before?"

"No." Her eyes dared him to doubt her.

"The withdrawal will be worse than anything you felt while you were on the drugs. There will be this uncontrollable trembling," he said, gesturing at her shaking hands. "Dizziness. Nausea. Blackouts, if you're lucky. Maybe hallucinations. Probably some other stuff I'm forgetting."

"Thanks for the pep talk," she replied, struggling to sit up on the bed. "I've already had most of that. No blackouts until now."

"Then you should know what you're in for. You can't quit cold turkey like that and expect no side effects."

"I didn't have a choice. Those damn pills made me crazy. I couldn't think straight." Sitting up, she cradled her head in her hands. "I still can't think straight."

"How did you stop taking the pills without anyone noticing?"

She shrugged. "They were too busy to watch me. I stuffed them in a hole in my mattress so the nurses wouldn't find them."

Jake shook his head in amazement. She was one gutsy chick. "If you're up to it, maybe you should take a shower. It might make you feel better."

Sam stood with his help, swaying against him. From the stricken look on her face, he knew what was coming.

"I don't feel so good," she whispered, clutching her stomach.

Jake wasted no time in hustling her through the adjacent bathroom door. He flipped up the lid of the toilet and eased her to her knees. "Go ahead and get it over with."

Her retching brought a sympathetic pang of nausea to Jake's stomach. Pushing it back, he knelt beside her and pulled her hair away from her face. She clutched the edge of the commode, her

knuckles white. When it was all over, she sat back on her heels
and wiped the back of her hand across her mouth.

"Finished?"

She nodded, head bowed. "Thanks." The whispered gratitude
was more than he could take.

"Don't thank me," he said, standing and retreating to the bathroom door. "Just take a shower and get cleaned up. There's probably something in Annie's closet that will fit you. When you're
done, we'll talk." Cursing his softhearted foolishness, Jake fled
the bedroom, the hounds of hell—or his past—hot on his heels.

Jake's sister hadn't left much behind in the closet. Most of what
was there was two sizes too small. Sam picked out an oversize
denim shirt and a pair of faded jeans that looked like they might
fit. The dresser had more to offer. Sam borrowed some athletic
socks and a pair of panties, feeling a little weird about wearing
someone else's underwear. After everything she'd been through,
it amazed her that something that insignificant would faze her.

The shower had been a blessing and she'd stood under the
spray until the water turned cold. Her hair felt clean for the first
time in weeks. She hoped her host didn't intend to take a shower
before morning. The thought of Jake brought a frown to her face
as she buttoned the borrowed shirt. He was a contradiction, that
one. He seemed interested in helping her one minute, then ready
to throw her to the wolves the next. She wondered what his sister
would say about him bringing home a fugitive. Judging by the
decidedly feminine surroundings, Annie Cavanaugh wouldn't like
it one bit.

The jeans proved to be a tight fit and Sam groaned as she got
them zipped. Maybe Annie had some sweats lying around. She
didn't think she'd be able to breathe in these painted-on pants.
Before she could explore the possibility, she heard Jake calling
her from somewhere in the house.

She pulled her hair into a ponytail and opened the bedroom
door. The sounds of a television pointed her in the right direction.

She found Jake standing in what looked like a combination family-room/office, his back to her as he watched the TV. Shelves lined the walls, haphazardly filled with books and knickknacks. Pictures jockeyed for space on an end table and Sam recognized Jake in several of them.

Sam glanced at the television, the centerpiece of a large entertainment center. She caught her breath. There, in full color and looking ten years younger, was a picture of Jake Cavanaugh.

"What—"

"Shh! Listen!"

From his tense stance, Sam knew it wasn't going to be good. She moved forward to stand beside Jake and turned her attention to the TV. The picture of Jake had been replaced by a perky blond newscaster wearing her best this-is-serious-news look.

"Once again, tonight at approximately 2:00 a.m., shots were heard at Big Louie's Diner on Pebble Road in Hollywood," the blonde said, glancing at her notes. "Officers arriving at the scene found three bodies, one of them identified as an on-duty detective from the Hollywood Police Department. The other two victims have not yet been identified, but it is assumed they were employees of Big Louie's Diner. A vehicle leaving the scene has been identified as belonging to Jake Cavanaugh, a former Metro-Dade detective. Cavanaugh is considered armed and dangerous. If you have seen this man, the police are asking that you contact them immediately. We will have more details as they develop."

Jake clicked the remote and the television went dark. Stormy eyes met Sam's across the narrow room. "What the hell have you gotten me into?"

Sam shook her head. Somewhere in the house a clock chimed four times. "I don't know. It's all a misunderstanding. Just call the police and explain to them—"

"Explain what? Yes, officer, I was there. Yes, I called my good friend Greg, and yes, I saw him get killed. But no, I didn't think I needed to call the police because at the time I was being chased by a couple of killers with guns. No, I don't know who they are, but maybe you'd like to ask my companion, here.'' He raked a hand through his dark hair, giving it an even more disheveled appearance.

Sam sat down on the edge of the brown tweed couch, feeling weak in the knees. ''But you used to be a cop. Surely they'd believe you.''

''Don't bet on it, sweetheart. I left the force with a less-than-stellar record. I'm the last person they'd believe.''

''Oh.''

''Why don't you tell me what's really going on here? This isn't about some pictures you took. You must have really pissed somebody off good if they want you dead—bad enough to kill three people to get to you.''

''Three?'' Sam suddenly recalled what the news reporter had said. Her stomach turned over sickly. ''The waitress and cook?''

''That's my guess. Innocent people are getting killed here, Sam. Because of you.''

His words battered her, making her feel raw inside. But he was right. This was her fault. A nightmare that kept getting bigger and bigger. ''I told you. Somebody wants the pictures I took in Miami.''

''Start from the top. Who are you? What were you doing in Miami?''

Sam answered him by rote: ''I'm Samantha Martin. I live in Atlanta.'' She paused for a moment. That wasn't quite true. ''I guess I should say I used to live in Atlanta before this nightmare started.''

''Go on.''

''I'm a photographer for the Atlanta travel magazine *Hit the Road*. I was doing a pictorial on Miami Beach—pictures of cafés, the beaches, hotels, that sort of thing.''

''So far, this all sounds pretty harmless,'' Jake said, his voice laced with impatience. ''Get to the part where the killers with guns start chasing you.''

''I was on my last day of the shoot. I was going to spend a

few days in the Keys before heading home. I was taking some pictures downtown. Architectural stuff.'' At his questioning look, she explained, ''I do some freelance work on the side.''

''And?''

''I was in the alley behind the courthouse. I'd just switched to my telephoto lens,'' she said, recalling the play of shadows across the immense building. ''Several men came out as I was snapping off the last of the roll.''

''Who?''

''Nobody I know,'' Sam replied. She'd asked herself this a dozen times. She had a vague recollection of having seen one of the men before but didn't think it was worth mentioning. ''Anyway, I'd clicked off a few shots when a security guard came running across the street saying I couldn't take pictures of the courthouse for security reasons.''

Jake paced the length of the room. ''Who could have been there?'' he asked, almost to himself. ''Then what?''

Sam closed her eyes, recapturing the memory like a photo in her mind. ''I took off. My car was parked at the corner. As I was pulling out, two men came up beside me. One reached into the driver's side and tried to grab my keys and the other one tried to get in the passenger door. I thought it was a carjacking. But then the guy trying to take my keys said something about film.''

''The guys at the diner?'' Jake had ceased his pacing and stood in front her.

''I didn't see them,'' she said.

''Whoever they are, they're pros. Mob, maybe?'' Jake fell silent for a moment. ''Then what did you do?''

Sam looked up at him. ''What else could I do? I hit the gas and got the hell out of there.''

''They must have gotten your license-plate number and run a check on it. Rental?''

Sam nodded. ''I knew something was wrong. At that point, I was feeling pretty paranoid.''

Jake sat on the couch beside her. ''I can imagine. Then what?''

"I stuck the film in an envelope and mailed it, figuring if they followed me or found out where I was staying, I wouldn't have the film on me."

"Good job."

The compliment steadied her nerves. "Thanks. I sent it on to where I would be staying in the Keys, intending to pick it up when I got there."

"But you never got a chance."

She shook her head. The dizziness was starting again. Her stomach was empty but it roiled in protest. She leaned over, clasping her knees. Taking slow, deep breaths, she tried to get herself under control.

"You okay?"

"Could I have some water? I'm feeling a little light-headed."

Jake went into the kitchen. She could see him at the sink through the pass-through counter that served as an eating area. When he returned, she took the glass gratefully. Sipping slowly, she willed her stomach to calm down. "Thanks."

"So you mailed the film," Jake prompted.

Sam sighed, nodding in resignation. He was going to get the whole story out of her whether she felt like reciting it or not. "I went to the police and filed a report. They called it an attempted carjacking. When I went back to my hotel that evening, the room was trashed and somebody was there. They hit me over the head and I blacked out. When I came to, there was a dead man in my room and a gun on the floor beside me."

"It was probably the same guys as at the courthouse. And I'd bet a dozen doughnuts it was the same guys tonight."

"What is that—police humor?"

"There's nothing funny about this. People are dead."

She winced at the onslaught of memories.

"And you called the cops and they found your prints on the gun," Jake guessed.

"No. Before I could even call the police they were pounding on the door. Someone else must have called them." She hesitated.

Jake's relaxed posture on the couch didn't fool her. He was the interrogator here and she was definitely on trial. Would he believe the truth? "It gets pretty strange after that."

Jake rolled his eyes at the understatement. "Tell me."

"They locked me up, questioned me for hours about the federal agent. I kept telling them I didn't have anything to do with it."

"They didn't believe you?"

She shook her head. "They threatened me, saying they could put me away for a long time. They wouldn't let me make any phone calls. I know enough about police procedure to know something was terribly wrong."

"Good guess."

"I spent the night in a cell in Miami. Next thing I knew, some men claiming to be federal agents showed up. They were more interested in my film than in the other agent they thought I'd killed. When I wouldn't tell them anything, they took me to Sunlight and Serenity."

Jake shook his head. "No attorney, no hearing? Nothing?"

"Nothing," Sam repeated.

"Weren't there people expecting you? How did they just make you disappear without causing an uproar?"

Sam's head was beginning to throb. She didn't want to remember anything about what had happened to her, but it was still happening and she didn't know how to make it stop. "I don't know."

"Come on. This is like something out of the *Twilight Zone.* One minute you have a life and the next you just disappear? How is that possible?"

"I told you, I don't know!" She trembled with anger, fear, helplessness. Then the dam broke and the tears started flowing. Her body began shaking violently and she wrapped her arms around herself to control it. "I don't know."

She could feel Jake watching her. Helpless to stop the torrent of emotion and pain, she sobbed into her chest. She felt his breath on her cheek for a moment before she felt the support of his arm around her shoulder. It was comforting, but her body shook harder.

"Shh. All right, you don't know. It's okay. We've got something to start with now," Jake soothed her. "How did you get out of the nut farm?"

"They send the laundry out every week. The truck doesn't come until late," she said haltingly. "They didn't lock my door because they thought I was sedated. I waited until after lights-out and hid in the laundry cart."

Her teeth were chattering and she bit the inside of her mouth to control it. It felt as if she had razors underneath her skin, scraping away at her insides. Her joints ached, her head hurt and she felt nauseous again.

"Smart thinking," he praised.

She let his comfort wash over her as she finished the story. "There's a train crossing right outside the hospital. Luckily, a train came by as we came to the intersection and I jumped out then."

"Why not wait until you got back to civilization?"

She relived the terror of that night. "I was scared they'd find me."

"You're safe now." His arm tightened around her. "Were you— Did they do anything besides drug you?"

His voice sounded low, dangerous. But Sam wasn't afraid of him. "N-no. They kept me isolated, but they didn't hurt me. But the longer I was there, the more likely it seemed I'd never get out."

"Why did they go to all the trouble of keeping you drugged? There are easier ways to get information out of someone."

"They tried sodium Pentothal. Apparently I'm allergic. I was sick for days. One of the men said it didn't matter, it would all be over soon."

"Meaning?"

Sam shrugged. "I took it to mean they were going to kill me. Now I'm not so sure."

Jake's hand made soothing motions over her arm. "Why not?"

"Well, at first they just kept me separated from the other patients. When I started demanding to see someone—the police, anyone—they started giving me the tranquillizers."

"They wanted to keep you quiet."

She nodded. "I lost track of time after a while. I knew where I was and I knew if I didn't stop taking those pills I'd never get out of there."

"Well, the worst of it's behind you. You'll get through the withdrawal in a few days."

"But what do I do now?" she whispered against his shoulder. He smelled faintly of sweat and sunshine and she allowed herself to pretend that he cared; that somehow he could help her get her life back.

"We are going to get some rest. Then we're going to get the hell out of here before they track me down."

Sam trembled weakly in his arms. *We.* He'd said "we." She wasn't alone anymore. It was almost enough to make her feel better. Except her body ached so badly she wanted to go to sleep and never wake up again.

Jake shifted beside her, pulling away to look down at her. "I know this is rough for you. Hang tough. Don't let it drag you down. It'll take a couple of days, but you'll get through this."

She tilted her head up to look at him and gave him a weak smile. "I guess your job taught you a lot about drugs and withdrawal."

He brushed a tendril of damp hair from her cheek, his blue eyes as dark as a thundercloud. "That. And personal experience."

"You?"

"Booze," he answered. "Been there. Done that. Threw up on the T-shirt."

Sam shook her head. "What a pair we make, huh?"

"Yeah. A regular Bonnie and Clyde."

"Why are you helping me, Jake?" His name was as familiar on her lips as if she'd known him all her life.

His dark eyes lost the sympathetic softness of a moment ago. "They think I killed three people, remember? The only way to clear my butt is to get you out of your mess."

"Oh." Silly her, thinking he cared. With a tremendous amount of effort, she broke free of his arms and stood. Turning her back on him, she carefully put one foot in front of the other, hoping she could get back to the bedroom without falling down.

"Where are you going?"

"To get some sleep. Wake me when you're ready to leave." Fighting back tears and forcing herself to keep walking, Sam reminded herself that she had always been alone, and that nothing had changed.

Chapter 4

Jake jerked awake, disoriented, struggling out of the snare of a dream. His heart hammered in his chest as he tried to figure out what had woken him up. Then it came again. A scream.

Sam.

He bolted out of bed, fumbling for his jeans and dragging them on as he stumbled to the door. The sun was starting to come up, which meant he hadn't been asleep for more than a couple of hours. "Fletch?" he called softly. Fletcher always slept by Jake's bed, if not *in* Jake's bed. The dog wasn't there.

He paused at the door and listened. Except for the scream that still echoed in his head, he heard no unusual sounds. He eased the door open, wincing when it gave a protesting squeak. Annie's room—Sam's, now—was at the end of the hall around a blind corner. Moving quietly, Jake edged down the hall, his shadow cast on the walls by the night-lights Annie had a fondness for. He rounded the corner in a crouch, wishing for a gun or a baseball bat—something, anything to fend off this sudden sense of helplessness. But his gun was back in the bedroom and he didn't know if he could use it even if he had it.

Jake tripped over something and caught himself on the edge of the wall. Instead of the platoon of bad guys he'd imagined, Jake's nemesis came in the form of one very large canine sprawled in front of Sam's room, his nose pressed to the bottom of the door. Sniffing out danger, no doubt. "Damn dog!"

Fletcher looked up at him in the darkened hall, his sad-hound eyes beseeching in the glow of a night-light. He whined and Jake retracted his curse. The brave police dog was nothing more than a terrified scaredy-cat. "Sorry, buddy. What's going on in there?" In answer, Fletcher pressed his nose back to the bottom of the door, his ears pricking up as another wail ripped through the silence.

Jake maneuvered around the animal and slowly opened the door. He could make out Sam, huddled up against the headboard. He turned on the light and approached the terrified woman. Her eyes were wide-open and wild looking, her hair mussed. She'd slept in the shirt she'd been wearing earlier, having tossed her jeans to the end of the bed. The sheets were twisted around her body and her hands fluttered like agitated seagulls around her head. The exposed skin of her neck and upper chest glistened with a sheen of perspiration.

"Sam?" Jake crossed to the bed and sat down on the edge. She didn't acknowledge him. "What's wrong?"

"Bugs," she moaned, clutching the sheet to her chest. "Bugs!" The last was followed by a scream sure to wake the neighbors.

Jake gently took her in his arms and rocked her, feeling the way her body trembled. The hallucinations had begun. "There aren't any bugs, Sam. It's the withdrawal. Hang tough."

"No! Don't you see them? They're everywhere! They're all over me!" Her hands came up between them, batting at her imaginary tormentors.

Jake turned her around in his arms, so that her back was pressed to his chest. He hauled her onto his lap and edged back on the bed until he sat leaning against the headboard. "There are no bugs, Sam."

She cried out again, her head jerking in fear and clipping him hard on the chin. "Make them go away! Make them go away!" She turned and burrowed her face into his chest, seeking refuge from the terrors of her mind.

Jake shook her roughly, tasting blood on his lip. "Listen to me!" he yelled over her cries. "Listen! There aren't any bugs! It's in your head! Look, Sam, look!" He held the back of her neck and forced her to look up, keeping her steady when she tried to pull away. "See? No bugs."

She whimpered as she looked around the room, her erratic movements slowing. "Bugs," she whispered expectantly.

"No. No bugs. See? It's a hallucination. It's not real."

"Not real," she repeated dully.

"Right. Not real. It's okay. It means you're getting the drugs out of your system."

She shook all over, as if rejecting the nightmare. "I was hallucinating?" she asked in her own voice.

Jake nodded against her hair. She smelled like the night-blooming jasmine that grew by the lake. Her body relaxed in increments against him and he felt the soft swell of her breasts under her shirt. Realizing he was still holding on to her, he let go. She didn't seem in a hurry to move.

"It's the withdrawal. It'll pass," he said, blaming the huskiness of his voice on sleep.

The violent tremors subsided. She turned in his lap, the movement bringing an involuntary groan to his lips. What the hell was wrong with him? He didn't need this. He didn't need to get involved in her problems.

"Did I hurt you?" Her hand, still trembling slightly, came up to his jaw. The scrape of her nails against his stubble was an uncomfortably intimate sound. He snapped his head back, cracking it against the headboard.

"Son of a—" he cursed, rubbing his scalp. "I'm fine. You can get off my lap now."

Color came into her pale cheeks. "Sorry," she mumbled, sliding sideways onto the bed.

She gathered the sheet around her like a child with a favorite blanket, protecting herself—from the nightmares and hallucinations, or from him? He wondered which was the lesser of the two evils. Determined to put some distance between them for his sanity's sake, Jake stood and turned away. She'd shaken something loose inside him—something he'd kept tightly bound for a long time. Before he was halfway to the door, her voice called him back.

"Jake?"

He turned to her, trying to ignore the soft vulnerability in her eyes. She had the tranquil, doe-eyed look of a satisfied woman. Except he knew better. "Yeah?"

"Uh— Could you, would you—"

"What?" he asked, impatient to get out of the room, his jeans feeling a size too small all of a sudden.

"I mean, I was wondering if you would stay with me," she said, adding quickly, "Just until I fall asleep."

"In here?" Jake asked, hoping she hadn't noticed how his voice cracked like an adolescent schoolboy's.

Snuggling down under the covers, Sam gave him a sleepy-eyed grin. "Yeah, in here." She patted the space beside her. "Please? It's a big bed."

"Not big enough," he whispered under his breath, walking toward her beckoning hand like a man heading for the electric chair.

Jake sat gingerly on the bed, resting his chin in his hands. His lip throbbed and he touched it, wincing. How in the hell had he gotten himself into this?

"Aren't you going to lie down?" Sam's voice was husky, but one look at her told him it was sleep—not lust—that pulled at her. "Come on," she said. "I don't bite."

Stretching out on top of the sheets, Jake muttered, "But I might." Fletcher approached the bed with a tinkle of metal dog tags and heaved a sigh as he stretched out on the floor next to Jake.

"I know you're a nice guy under that tough exterior."

Jake stared at the ceiling. "Yeah. You also said the drugs made you crazy."

"I'm not crazy."

"I know that."

He did know it. Whatever she was, it wasn't crazy. He'd heard plenty of sob stories in his time—hundreds of innocent pleas from lowlife scum trying to avoid prosecution. But he'd also seen innocent people accused of crimes they hadn't committed. It didn't happen often, but it did happen. Wrong place, wrong time. Maybe that was the case with Sam. He'd like to believe that. Her voice swept over him, shaking him from the past.

"Tell me something, Jake."

"What do you want to know?"

He felt her shift beside him on the bed, turning so that she could look at him. He kept his eyes on the ceiling, tracking the faint fingers of light that wended their way through the room. Common sense told him to get out of the bed but it felt good to lie in the darkness with someone. With her. His gut tightened expectantly.

"What do you do, now that you're an ex-detective?"

He exhaled a breath he hadn't realized he was holding. "I run a charter service, piloting tourists down to the islands. I have a couple of partners who take care of things when I'm not around."

That reminded him. He'd have to tell Brian and Mac something. The truth was so bizarre that even he had a hard time accepting it.

"Do you enjoy it? I mean, more than being a cop?"

He thought about that. Being a cop had been his life for thirteen years. He'd felt like someone had cut off an arm or a leg when he'd turned in his shield. When Margo had served divorce papers

on him a year earlier, it hadn't hurt nearly as badly. But being a
pilot gave him the freedom and independence he craved. No more
red tape. No bureaucracy. No unwritten codes.

He'd wanted to get away from the stress of police work. Flying
charters for tourists was about as far from being a cop as he could
imagine. No one counted on him. He couldn't let anyone down.
Every day wasn't a life-and-death adventure. The only one he had
to look out for was himself. And he liked that just fine.

"It's different," he said finally. "When you're a cop everyone
is a little afraid of you. Even if they haven't done anything wrong.
You see it in their eyes, hear it in their voices. You feel like the
enemy when you've made the vow to serve and to protect."

Sam watched the angular contours of Jake's face as the shadows played across them. The husky tone of his voice matched the
dawn—steel gray and uncompromising, but laced with golden
tendrils of hope and promise. She hadn't even known he was in
the room while the hallucination had her under its power. It had
been his voice—powerful, encouraging, utterly masculine—that
had driven the demons away. His voice soothed her weary spirit.

"But being a pilot, well, everybody likes you. Everyone wants
to know you. Work is like going to a party."

"That doesn't tell me if you like it better," she persisted. She
watched the emotions play across his face and resisted the urge
to run her fingers through his dark hair. She sensed that this man
didn't give freely of himself and she wasn't yet ready to break
the spell of intimacy that wrapped around them like a warm cocoon.

"I miss being a cop," he said simply. "But it wasn't in the
cards, so I enjoy being a pilot. I like the freedom."

Freedom. It was a word she'd dreamed about for a month. It
had taken on new meaning when the walls had closed in on her
and someone was controlling every aspect of her life—what she
ate, what she wore, when she slept. Freedom meant something to
her now. But even being out from behind those hospital walls

didn't give her freedom. Someone still owned her soul and she wouldn't be free until she found out who. And why.

"You'd better go to sleep. We have to get out of here before they find us."

"Do you think they know where we are?" Her pulse picked up, destroying the calming effect Jake had had on her nerves.

"Probably not. Not yet. I have a town house in Miami, they'd probably go there first, which is why we're here." He shifted, his arm barely brushing hers. "But whoever killed Greg had an inside connection to the police department. It's only a matter of time before they track me down."

The words were practical, but their ominous tone made Sam shiver. They would find her. Whoever they were, they'd invested too much in keeping her quiet, keeping her hidden. They wouldn't just let her get away. "Then what?" she whispered.

"Then I figure out who is after you and why they're dragging me into it."

He'd said that before, in the living room. She knew he had personal reasons for wanting to help her. But his voice and his hands had soothed her and somehow she knew he wouldn't let her down. It was irrational, really, this need to trust him. Her mind argued that he'd tried turn her in to the cops already. But her heart tugged when she recognized the familiar ache of loneliness in his eyes, in his voice. He was all she had.

"Jake?"

"Yeah?" His voice had dropped an octave, sounding low and gruff.

"Thanks." She leaned in toward him, not giving herself time to hesitate, and gently kissed lips that were warm and pliable. It was a featherlight touch, hardly a kiss at all. She felt his breath on her cheek like a sultry tropical breeze and she trembled for a whole new reason. When he didn't move, she whispered, "Jake?"

He didn't seem to hear her. His eyes were closed, his breathing even. She realized he was asleep. A moment later she realized something else.

He snored.

"Get up."

The voice came from a long distance away and Sam resisted it. She needed to sleep, dammit. When someone prodded her sharply in the ribs, she groaned and rolled onto her side, pulling the comforter over her head.

"I said, it's time to get up," the voice spoke again.

A more insistent prod—and the suffocating thickness of down—brought her out of her burrow. She sat up, running a hand through her hair and wincing as it snagged in the tangles. "What?"

Jake stood by the bed, fully dressed in jeans and a white shirt that accentuated his tan. And his muscles. He had shaved and he smelled like soap and woodsy cologne. His dark hair was wet and tousled, curling slightly at his collar. In the bright morning light she could see that it was dark brown, not black, and shot through with deep russet highlights. She felt at a definite disadvantage as he towered over her, his muscular thighs and lean hips hugged by faded denim.

"Come on. We're burning daylight. Get a move on," he said again, his hands on his hips. His dog—Fletcher, was it?—sat behind him, tongue lolling out of his mouth as his tail thumped the floor.

Sam snapped a mock salute in Jake's general direction. "Yes, sir."

"I want to get out of here in thirty minutes. Think you can manage that?"

Rubbing the sleep from her eyes, Sam stretched. Every muscle in her body protested, feeling taut and bruised. She still had a sensation of light-headedness but the nausea seemed to have subsided for the time being. "Sure. What time is it?"

"Nine. I don't want to take a chance that someone's going to find us here."

The panic of the night before hit her full force. Unmindful that she was only half-dressed, Sam pushed the covers back and hauled herself to the edge of the bed. "Right. Just let me shower and I'll be ready." She needed another shower just to wash away the sleep and take the ache out of her muscles. When he didn't answer, she looked up and caught him staring at her legs. "Yoo-hoo." She wriggled her fingers at him.

His eyes went two shades darker as he glared at her. "Just hurry up," he said, stalking from the room before she could respond.

Fletcher turned to watch his master go, then looked at her, clearly more interested in seeing what she might do. His ears were two sizes too large for his head and they flopped back and forth as he turned his head from the door to her, torn by doggy indecision.

"Come on, Fletcher!" Jake called.

His tail wagging excitedly, Fletcher went to the door, then glanced back at her. "Better go," Sam said. "No reason why both of us should be in trouble."

The dog went and Sam wondered if talking to animals meant she was losing her mind. "Too late," she said aloud, heading for the shower.

Twenty minutes later, judging by the alarm clock beside the bed, Sam was ready to meet Jake on his own turf. She'd unearthed another shirt from the closet—dark green this time—and put on the same jeans she'd worn last night. A futile search hadn't turned up anything larger. She'd just have to grin and bear it. And hold her breath.

Following the noises coming from the garage, Sam ventured out of her room and found Jake putting a duffel bag in the back of the minivan. From her vantage point by the door she had a nice view of his backside. Preoccupied with her thoughts, she didn't hear the jingle-jangle warning until an overzealous dog's nose had lodged itself in the seat of her jeans. Her yelp brought Jake around with an amused look on his face.

"It's not funny," she fumed, reaching behind to push the dog away and trying to maintain her dignity at the same time.

"Sure, it is. You were watching me and Fletcher was watching you," he said, summing up the situation. So much for dignity.

"Uh, would you mind calling off your dog?"

His infuriating grin never left his face. "Fletcher, down."

Sam felt the dog drop to the floor behind her and she relaxed. "Thank you."

"Do I get another kiss?"

Sam knew her face must be flaming beet-red. "You were awake?"

"Sweetheart, it's not often I get kissed by a beautiful woman these days. I make it a point to stay awake if at all possible."

Make that fire-engine red, Sam thought. Bright and hot. She changed the subject. "What are you doing?"

"They'll be looking for my sport utility. They won't be looking for Annie's minivan."

"Where are we going?"

"Key West."

She hadn't expected him to say that. Whatever her thoughts the night before, she hadn't really expected him to help her. That he even believed her about the film left her feeling a little giddy. "Oh."

"You might want to grab a couple of changes of clothes out of Annie's closet."

That didn't seem likely, given the slim pickings. "Uh, do I have time to wash my clothes?"

He shook his head. "We need to get going. Besides, that nurse's uniform isn't in any shape to be worn again. Why would you want it?"

"No reason," Sam replied, thinking about sitting in Annie's tight jeans. "I'll have to see if she left any shoes that might fit me." The canvas sneakers she'd been wearing were still on the bathroom floor, caked in mud and gunk from the swamp. She'd go barefoot before she'd put them back on.

"Hurry up, then," Jake said, following her into the house. At the bedroom doorway he left her and disappeared down the hall, Fletcher trailing behind him. "Ten minutes!"

Sam went through Annie's closet and bureau, piling some socks, panties, a couple of shirts and a pair of athletic shorts on the bed. She struck pay dirt in the shoe department, finding a pair of battered Nike running shoes only a half-size smaller than what she wore. She carried her borrowed clothing back to the garage, not sure what to do with it. Remembering the duffel bag, she climbed into the back of the van.

In the kitchen, Jake stacked cans of dog food in a cardboard box. He added a few other provisions for Sam and himself. Sam. She'd surprised him last night, and that wasn't something that happened to him often. Even in the middle of a drug-induced hallucination she exuded an inner strength he couldn't help but admire. The illusion of fragility was only superficial. She was tough. He counted on her staying tough for whatever they were up against. The last thing he needed was a hysterical female.

He wondered what Charlie would have made of her. He thought about his partner with a mixture of fondness and grief that never seemed to fade completely. Charlie had been a world-class cop and a hell of a friend. And Jake had let him down. Bad enough to let a friend down, but his mistake had cost Charlie his life.

"Woof!"

Distracted from the path his thoughts were taking, Jake gave Fletcher a halfhearted grin. "I promise I won't forget you, buddy."

He threw Fletcher's spare water bowl into the box, along with a flashlight, a roll of duct tape and a portable radio/tape recorder. He felt like he was preparing for a hurricane, and his paranoia bothered him. "Better safe than sorry," Charlie had always said. And look what it had gotten him.

Margo used to accuse him of being paranoid. She hadn't understood that it came with the territory. A cop couldn't afford to trust anyone. But she'd resented his job, resented his partnership with Charlie. She was an uptown girl and he'd convinced himself that he could make her happy because he'd loved her. He bit back a bitter laugh. Hell, he missed his job more than he missed his marriage. What did that say about him?

Jake didn't hear anything as he carted the box of supplies to the garage. He hoped Sam hadn't fallen asleep again. That woman was hell to wake up. He grinned to himself. He'd been surprised by the kiss but had recognized it for what it was and decided to ignore it. In times of crisis, people's hormones kicked into overdrive. Survival instinct, pure and simple—only his thoughts about Sam were far from pure and not nearly as simple as he pretended.

He nudged the van door open with his hip and found the woman in question. Sam sat cross-legged in the back of the van, a pile of clothing beside her and his duffel bag in front of her. He felt his grin slip away.

"Sam?"

She looked up at him.

"Get the hell out of there!"

Chapter 5

"What's the matter? Afraid I'll find your smiley-face boxer shorts?"

"Just get out of there. Now, Sam!"

"Jake?"

He could hear the hurt in her voice and he steeled himself against it. There was nothing he could say. Jake avoided her gaze, standing back to let her slide out of the van, grabbing the forgotten clothing on her way.

"Just stay out of my stuff and don't ask questions," he said when she stood beside him.

They were inches apart, but the chasm widened with every inane thing he said. He felt her withdraw, felt the fragile thread of trust shatter. He told himself it was just too damn bad. He even tried to believe it.

"I was just trying to find a place to put my clothes." She thrust the pile of clothing at him, letting it go before their fingers could touch.

He relented, his voice softening. It wasn't her fault he was a total jackass. "I think Annie has a spare bag in the hall closet. Why don't you get whatever personal stuff you need out of the bathroom and check the closet while I finish up here?"

She yanked the bundle from his arms and fled the garage before he could add that he was sorry. It was just as well, he thought. There was no point in letting her get too close. And no chance of it, after this. Fletcher pushed past him when he opened the passenger door of the van and vaulted up into the seat. In spite of himself, Jake smiled at him.

"In the back." Fletcher sighed like an angst-ridden teenager but obediently climbed in behind. He flopped onto the seat and turned his back on Jake. "Don't pout," Jake said. Fletcher let out another huge sigh. Great. He'd offended Sam *and* the dog. And Fletcher was even better at making him feel guilty. Jake wished fervently that if there was an afterlife he would come back as an overindulged mixed-breed mutt.

He heard Sam behind him and turned. She shifted from foot to foot, refusing to meet his eyes. Anxious or nervous? he wondered. She'd found Annie's bag and had it slung over her shoulder. When he reached out to take it from her, she flinched. The movement sparked white-hot anger in him and he took the bag off her shoulder roughly.

"Don't, Sam," he said again. "Nothing has changed. We're in this together."

She looked up then, her eyes burning like green fire as she stared straight through to his soul. "Are we?" she asked. Not waiting for an answer, she climbed into the van and slammed the door.

The air conditioner blasted out cold air, making the van a protective shell against the oppressive Florida humidity. Sam glanced over at Jake and wondered who would protect her from him. She could kick herself for being so wrong about him. Just when she thought she could trust him, he went strange on her. His grim features gave away nothing, shared nothing. He didn't want her

understanding and that was fine with her. But they were still together, still going to Key West. That had to mean something.

They left the tidy rows of cracker-box-style houses behind as
they merged northbound onto I-95. Traffic flowed like a steady
stream along all four lanes toward Fort Lauderdale.

Fletcher snored loudly in the back seat, the only noise in the
van besides the traffic sounds that filtered through the windows.
The silence agitated her, reminding her of the hospital. She sighed
and wiped her moist palms across the legs of her jeans. If they
were going to be together for a while, she had to talk to him.

"Where are we going?"

Jake glanced at her, a look of surprise in his dark eyes that was
quickly masked by some other emotion she couldn't read. "I have
to let my partners know what's going on."

"Oh." She couldn't tell him what to do or where to go, but
she hated him calling the shots. She hadn't escaped that cuckoo's
nest just to get sent back because he had to run some errands.

Twenty minutes later, Jake left the freeway and followed a
maze of numbered roads, finally stopping at the Fort Lauderdale
executive airport. A small plane taxied parallel to them and lifted
off with gravity-defying grace. As she followed the direction of
the plane, Sam could see the lights of a stadium to the south of
the airport.

Noticing the direction of her gaze, Jake said, "That's where
the Yankees used to spend spring training."

"You ever watch them play?" she asked, more for something
to say than because she loved baseball.

"Every year." The wistful tone in his voice vanished before
she could examine it. "Here we are."

They had pulled up to the rear of what looked like a bus station.
"Now what?"

"Now you go in there, look for the counter marked Particular
Harbor Tours and talk to Brian. There shouldn't be anyone else
there but him. Tell him—"

"Wait a minute! Wait one damn minute," Sam interrupted. "Why me? Why don't you go find him?"

Jake shook his head. "That won't work. My picture has been plastered all over the television and the newspapers, too, most likely. If there are cops still around, they're looking for me and this is a good place to look."

"The police are looking for me, too."

"Not this far south, as far as we know. They've got every reason to assume you've headed back to Atlanta. Or that you've been eaten by a gator."

She shuddered. "Don't remind me."

"Anyway," he went on, "they don't know we're together. Just tell Brian to come out here. Tell him I sent you." He reached behind his seat and pulled out an emerald-green baseball hat with the words Particular Harbor Tours emblazoned in hot pink across the front. "Wear this. He'll know you're with me."

Sam's stomach flip-flopped, but she put the hat on and tucked her ponytail up underneath it. She knew he was right, though she didn't have to like it. "Fine. How will I know he's Brian?"

A smile turned up the corners of Jake's mouth. "You'll know. Look for a guy wearing a Hawaiian shirt and belting out Jimmy Buffett tunes."

"Sounds easy enough," Sam muttered, opening the van door. Fletcher raised his head from the back seat at the sound. Jake touched Sam's hand and she looked up at him.

"Be careful."

"Careful is my middle name," she replied, feeling the heat of his touch even after he let go.

"Could have fooled me. I thought your middle name was Stubborn."

Jake's slow smile heated her insides in a way the Florida sun never could. She ignored that smile, refusing to acknowledge him, and strode to the narrow building. As she opened the door she hoped she wasn't walking into a trap.

The airport was nothing more than a row of counters with

various names stenciled across them. Sam spotted Particular Harbor Tours and swallowed her fear. Sure enough, a man in his late twenties wearing a bright pink-and-orange floral shirt was at the counter. He had shoulder-length black hair and the easygoing good looks of a surfer. But he wasn't singing "Margaritaville." In fact, he looked pretty down.

Sam walked purposefully toward the counter, careful to avoid making eye contact with any of the other people in the airport— mostly handfuls of tourists and the occasional pilot. Nobody seemed to take a particular interest in her and she didn't see any uniformed police officers. That had to be a good sign.

The guy looked up at her approach, smiling what she assumed was his best "Let me take you to paradise" smile. A month ago, that smile would have bowled her over. Right now, all she could think about was getting out of here without being caught.

"Welcome! Where can Particular Harbor Tours take you?" Then he noticed the hat. "Hey, that's—"

"Right," Sam interrupted. "Jake's out back. He needs to talk to you."

Without questioning her association with Jake, he followed her out into the bright sun, his lanky form casting long shadows over her. Jake had pulled the van into a parking space at the very back of the lot. He must have been watching for them because as they approached, the passenger door opened. Sam climbed in first and moved to share the back seat with an excited Fletcher, while Brian hopped into the passenger seat.

After greeting the hyperactive dog that was trying to climb over Sam to get to him, Brian turned to Jake. "Man! Where the hell have you been? Do you know what's going on?"

Jake nodded. "I know. The police been by?"

"Yeah. First thing this morning. I hadn't even seen the papers yet. What's going on, Jake?"

"Wish I knew. But until I straighten this mess out, I'm going to be laying low. Can you keep an eye on the place for a few days?"

Brian nodded. "Of course."

"What's the schedule like?"

"There's a group leaving for Saint Thomas tomorrow—that's under control. I booked two more for next week. I can call Mac in to fly the flights if you can't."

"Good idea," Jake said. "And would you keep an eye on Annie's place for me?"

"Where are you going to be?"

Jake cast a look back at Sam. "Key West."

Brian looked from Jake to Sam. "Are you going to introduce me to your friend?"

"This is Sam Martin. Sam, this is Brian," Jake said. "Now that those pleasantries are over, would you mind going back to work?"

Brian rolled his eyes at Sam. "He's a taskmaster. Yes sir, boss!" He gave Fletcher one last enthusiastic ear-scratching and climbed out of the van. He hesitated before closing the door and the happy-go-lucky persona faded. "Take care of yourself, buddy. Let me know what's going on."

Jake smiled and even from her vantage point in the back seat Sam could feel the strong bond between the two men. "Sure thing. Just don't drive us into bankruptcy before I get back."

Brian's laughter faded as he closed the door. Sam climbed back up to the front of the van, catching Jake's eye. "He's nice."

"Yeah, he's okay for a kid brother."

"He's *your* brother?"

Jake smiled at her astonished look. "Did you think I was hatched in a swamp or something?"

"You act like it sometimes," she answered. It made sense, though, the close bond between Jake and Brian. Still, they were as different as the clichéd night and day.

"Yeah, well, Brian got the charm and good looks and our older brother Mac got the brains and maturity."

"Let me guess. There wasn't anything left for you?"

"Very funny." Jake stared out the windshield, his body going as still as a granite sculpture.

"Now what?" Sam asked when the silence became unnerving.

"Hungry?" Whatever he'd been thinking, it wasn't about food, but Sam let it go. He wasn't her business. He'd made that very clear.

Sam hadn't thought about food since last night's rendezvous with the toilet. But her stomach rumbled hollowly and she nodded. "I guess."

"We'll grab some take-out and eat on the way, then."

Some of the tension between them had faded since Brian's appearance and for that, Sam was grateful. Whatever Jake had done or said really shouldn't matter to her. They had one mutual goal—to get to Key West, get the film and find out who was after them. After that they would go their separate ways, no questions asked. But some niggling doubt in the back of her mind whispered that it wasn't going to be that easy. He'd already betrayed her once. He could do it again.

Sam didn't think her stomach could handle burgers after last night, so they agreed on subs. While Jake and Fletcher waited in the van, Sam stood at the crowded counter of the sub-and-sandwich shop fighting back fear and another wave of dizziness. When it came time for Sam to place her order, the teenage waitress stared at her intently, snapping her gum with the enthusiasm of a cow chewing cud.

"You look so familiar," the girl drawled, her frizzy red hair bursting out from under her hairnet.

Sam resisted the urge to bolt. "Uh, yeah, I get that a lot," she mumbled, keeping her eyes down.

The girl peered at her, tapping her order pad. "No, really. You look like somebody." She snagged the shirtsleeve of another waitress walking by and pointed at Sam. "Doesn't she look like somebody?"

At this point, the customers behind Sam were getting impatient and Sam knew her face must as pale as an underexposed print.

She edged back from the counter slowly. Maybe she could get out before they called the police. One look at the door told her otherwise. Two motorcycle cops had just pulled up next to the van. She couldn't see Jake's face from here but he had to have seen them.

"Yeah, she does look familiar," the other waitress was saying.

"Look, I'm really in a hurry." Sam had one eye on the frizzy-haired waitress and one eye on the door. The cops seemed in no rush to join the crowd inside. Maybe they would decide to go someplace else.

"Hey! I know who you look like. That actress, what's her name? Meg Ryan," the girl said. The other waitress nodded in agreement and moved on.

A man behind Sam cleared his voice. "Now that we've taken care of that great mystery could we move it along while it's still lunchtime?"

The waitress smiled. "Sorry," she stage-whispered. "Now, what did you want?"

Sam felt faint with relief but managed to place her order and collect it without falling apart. But her timing was off; as she approached the door, the two cops chose that moment to come in. Keeping her eyes on the ground, she maneuvered around them. She sighed when she made it out the door without attracting their attention.

"What took you so long?" Jake complained after she got back into the van. "You're shaking like a leaf. Are you all right?"

The trembling in her hands wasn't just withdrawal anymore. "Didn't you see the cops?"

"They didn't even look at you. What happened inside?"

"Just a misunderstanding," Sam said as they got back onto the highway. She handed Jake his turkey-and-Cheddar sub.

Jake glanced at her. "All right. Just relax." Fletcher whined pitifully from the back. "I hope you didn't forget him. He's not very friendly when he hasn't eaten."

"I didn't forget him." Sam unwrapped the roast-beef sub,

broke it into bite-size pieces and spread the wrapper on the floor of the van. "There you go, big guy." Fletcher didn't need the encouragement—he inhaled his sandwich and was looking for more before Sam could get her veggie sub unwrapped.

The food was good, even if the motion of the van made it a little uncomfortable to eat. Sam and Jake shared an extra-large soda while Fletcher slurped water from the cup Sam held for him, sloshing it all over her and the seat. Funny, she'd never particularly liked dogs before. But with Jake the unpredictable as her human companion, she appreciated Fletcher's canine friendliness.

They were on I-95 again, headed south this time. Sam's sagging spirits were bolstered by her full stomach and the fact that her sub didn't show any signs of making a return appearance. "Do you think it will be safe to call the police once we're in Key West?"

"No," Jake answered. "Not until we know who's in those pictures. The fact that they knew where Greg was going means that they have someone on the inside. That means the Mob or a dirty cop. Until we find out how far their reach is, it's not safe to call anyone."

"So what happens once we know who is in the pictures?"

"Then we have something to negotiate with."

Sam shivered. It was like something out of a James Bond movie—only the end credits could very well be etched on grave markers for both of them. "What if they don't want to negotiate with us?"

He cast her a sidelong glance. "Then we'll have to find someone we can trust. And hope like hell we don't get caught by the bad guys first."

That put a damper on things. Sam sat back in her seat, content to close her eyes and visualize a peaceful place where she'd be safe. The steady hum of the engine and the motion of the van nearly lulled her to sleep. She snuggled down in the cushioned softness. When the van suddenly slowed, Sam cracked one eye open to see what the problem was.

Jake had pulled the van into the right lane, signaling as they approached an off-ramp to downtown Miami. Sam felt her pulse quicken, fear rising in her like mercury. All traces of sleep faded as she sat up. "What are you doing?"

The look he gave her was inscrutable. "Don't worry." He merged with the heavy line of traffic flowing onto Flagler Street. "I just need to make a couple of stops."

Sam caught a glimpse out her window of the formidable courthouse where her ordeal had started. She wondered what Jake needed to do and if it involved having her arrested.

Half of Jake's instincts told him to hurry it up and get the film. The other half, the cop half, told him he needed all the ammunition he could get. He listened to the cop half. He had a bad feeling about this whole thing. He didn't doubt for a moment that whoever they were up against would rather kill them than negotiate anything. He couldn't tell Sam that, of course. The woman was barely holding on by her fingernails—what was left of them.

"So, what do you have to do?"

He could hear the tremor in her voice, knew she didn't trust him. Hell, he couldn't blame her after that fiasco at Annie's. They'd just have to get past it somehow. "Go to the library."

"The library?" she repeated.

"Right." He pulled the van into the sprawling parking lot of the downtown library. He stopped under a clump of olive trees and turned off the engine.

"Do you mind telling me why?"

He hid his grin. Her indignation wiped away her fear. Good for her. He had a feeling she'd need that iron will before this was over. "You were arrested in Miami. You were accused of killing a federal agent. There has to be some record of it in the papers. If I can get an arresting officer's name, maybe some idea of the behind-the-scenes details, it could help us."

She nodded and he relaxed. He was sure it was going to be a battle all the way to Key West. He'd sensed her impatience back at the airport. He didn't give a damn what she thought, but he needed her cooperation.

Hell. Brian and Mac could be in danger. Jake hadn't considered that, but after what had happened to Greg, anything was possible. It made their mission all the more crucial. And Sam was going to help him if he had to tie her up and sling her over his shoulder all the way to Key West and back.

"It makes sense."

"I'm glad you agree. Let's go. I don't want to leave Fletcher out here for long." He looked around them. "And I don't like being this close to the enemy."

"You and me both," she muttered.

He rolled the windows down for Fletcher and they left the van, blasted by the unyielding heat even though it was only the first of April. Jake watched the beads of sweat pop out on Sam's forehead in the short trek across the parking lot. He knew she wasn't well yet but she was holding up better than he had expected.

The cool interior of the library was a welcome respite. Sam shivered and Jake laid an arm across her shoulders, thinking only to warm her up. But her startled look made him think twice.

"Over there," she whispered. Funny how people years out of grade school still whispered in a library, he thought.

No one was at the reference desk and Jake rang the silver bell on the counter. A portly woman with white hair and bad dentures came out of a rear office and smiled at them. "Yes?"

"We'd like to see the *Herald* from—" He turned to Sam for the date.

"February," she supplied.

The woman nodded and retreated into her office. She returned with a box of microfilm. "The machines are over there in the corner. Copies are twenty-five cents."

Jake took the film and they found an empty booth. "What was the date you were arrested?" he asked, threading the film through the reel.

"February twenty-sixth."

"All right, let's see what we can find." He scrolled quickly past the beginning of the month until he found the twenty-sixth. He slowly skipped through the frames until he came to the local news. Nothing.

"Try the twenty-seventh. It wouldn't have made it in the paper the same day."

Sam's fingers were wrapped around his arm as she leaned in beside him to view the screen. He liked the way her hand felt, warm and soft. Distracting. He could smell a faint floral scent of shampoo on her hair and it did funny things to his pulse. In the close proximity of the booth, his senses surged and he nearly missed what they were looking for.

"Wait!" Sam's voice pulled him back from his wayward thoughts. "I think I saw my picture."

She reached past him and scrolled the film back. Her hair was nearly in his face, and he inhaled her fragrance. Damn, he had to get a grip on himself.

She sat back in her chair. "Look."

He returned his attention to the screen. Sure enough, it was her. Her hair was styled, her face a little less rounded, but Samantha Martin had made the *Herald*. He glanced at her and noticed that all the color had drained from her features. Her hand clutched his arm reflexively.

"What, Sam?"

"Read the headline."

Her eyes never left the screen and he had to drag his gaze away from the haunted look on her face. But he did as she said and felt a shiver of foreboding coil down his spine. The headline was as grim as any he had ever read.

Chapter 6

Award-winning Photographer Found Dead.

Jake's eyes tripped over the words. He shook his head in amazement. This couldn't be happening. Something this sinister belonged in a John Grisham novel.

"Oh, my God."

Jake looked at Sam, hearing the agony in her words. He didn't know what to say. In all his police experience he'd never seen anything like this.

"How, Jake?" she asked, her voice rising shrilly. A white-haired man stared at them from a chair by the window.

Jake gently took Sam's hands in his, looking into her frightened eyes. He couldn't let her fall apart now. Not here. "Calm down, Sam. Don't make a scene."

"'Don't make a scene'? Did you read that?" She jerked her hands away and gestured at the shocking headline spread out in black and white on the screen. "They're saying I'm dead."

Jake captured her hands again. She was flying to pieces in front of him and he didn't know how to stop it. "It's a lie, Sam. It's how they kept anyone from looking for you. It's just a lie."

"Maybe it's a prediction," she whispered, her tormented eyes daring him to deny it.

"No way. We're going to get out of this. I promise you that." He shouldn't be making promises he couldn't keep. But the woman had a way of making him feel protective. *So did Margo,* he reminded himself.

She was shaking her head, mesmerized by the words on the screen. "They won't let me, Jake. Don't you see?" Tears glistened on her eyelashes like raindrops. "I'm as good as dead already."

"They're playing mind games with you, Sam. Don't let them win." He had to get her out of here. "Let me make copies of this and we'll go."

She stared at the screen, not seeming to hear him.

"Sam?"

The look in her eyes tore at his heart. She gave him a weary smile that did nothing to alleviate his concern. "Sure." She ran her hands over her face and wiped at her eyes. "I'm going to go wash up."

He didn't want to let her out of his sight in her condition, but he knew she needed to get herself together. "All right. I'll meet you by the door in a couple of minutes."

Jake watched her leave and then quickly scanned the rest of the paper. His search turned up another article—this one about the dead agent in Sam's room. He read through it and felt his blood run cold.

Looking up, he saw Sam crossing from the rest room to the front of the library. She moved zombie-like, not looking in his direction. He quickly made copies and returned the microfilm to the reference librarian. Not more than ten minutes had passed by the time he finished and walked out of the library. Sam wasn't there. He glanced across the parking lot and saw the van, with Fletcher's head hanging out the window.

"Dammit! Where did she go?" Jake jogged across the parking lot and opened the van door. She wasn't there, either. He snapped

Fletcher's leash on him and locked the van. "Come on, Fletch. We've got to find her." Surveying the parking lot, he added, "Before they do."

Sam walked, swiping at the tears that streaked her cheeks. It was over. They were going to catch her. She didn't know where she was going, but what did it matter? She was as good as dead. The headline echoed through her mind. *Dead*. Not even Jake could protect her now.

"Hey, lady, watch where you're going!" The angry cabdriver's voice broke through the numbness. She quickly stepped back on the curb. She bit back a bitter laugh. How ironic. It would serve them right if she got run over by a car.

She walked past the awning-draped stores that lined the busy road. Huge crucifixes shared space in shop windows with various voodoo paraphernalia. Signs peppered with Spanish phrases dotted the street. Sam kept walking. She didn't know where she was going, but she couldn't stop.

Her skin felt cold and clammy despite the humid warmth. She knew it was the withdrawal. She could feel the drugs working their way out of her system. She ached inside, wanting and needing something that they'd forced on her. Why couldn't they leave her alone? Why her?

She turned at the sound of pounding footsteps behind her. Fletcher leaped toward her. His front paws rested on her shoulders as he licked her face, his tail wagging furiously. Sam threw her arms up to protect herself from the excited mutt but she didn't miss the look on Jake's face.

"What the hell are you doing?" he growled. He pulled Fletcher back by his leash and took Sam by the elbow, guiding her into an alley between a Cuban restaurant and a floral shop.

"Let me go, Jake." She pulled away from him and stepped back against the warm stucco wall. "This isn't your problem anymore." Shadows played across his features, making his blue eyes as dark as storm clouds. The firm set of his jaw told her he wasn't going to give up so easily.

"What do you mean, it's not my problem?"

He moved until he was standing directly in front of her. He braced his hand against the wall beside her head and leaned closer. Fletcher danced nervously around their feet, dog tags jingling. The sounds of traffic filtered into the alley and the smell of fresh flowers and spicy food wafted on the air.

She avoided the dangerous look in his eyes. "Just let me go," she whispered.

"Go where, Sam?"

"I don't know! Just leave me alone."

He smacked the palm of his hand against the wall. She flinched. "Is that it, then? You're giving up?"

She met his gaze then. "What's my choice, Jake? Face it, I'm not going to make it out of this. They're going to catch me."

"Maybe. Maybe not. Why give them the chance?"

"Don't you see? If I get away from you, they'll leave you alone."

His eyes searched her face and she felt that connection with him again—what she'd felt back at Annie's house. It went deeper than physical attraction. Soul deep. It was basic, elemental, and it shook her to the core.

"That's it? You're doing this for me?"

Sam tucked her hands into the small of her back and leaned her head against the wall. Sunlight trickled down the side of the building and she closed her eyes, feeling the warmth of it on her face. "I can't do it anymore, Jake. I can't keep running. They've got everything covered. Even if I get to the film, who will believe me?"

"I will."

"No offense, but that doesn't mean much." She felt him shift closer but kept her eyes closed.

"Doesn't it?" he whispered in her ear, so close she could feel his breath against her cheek.

"Just let me go, Jake." The tears started again, squeezing out from under her eyelids.

"No way, Sam. No way."

She heard the slap of the leash hitting the ground and his quiet command for Fletcher to stay. She opened her eyes as he braced his other hand against the wall, bracketing her head. She swallowed hard and stared at the unyielding planes of his face. She could feel the heat radiating from him, the masculine strength coiled tautly inside him. She was trapped.

"Why?" she whispered.

In answer, his lips came down hard on hers, taking her breath away with their fierce passion. It was a hot, demanding kiss and after the initial shock of it, Sam found herself making demands of her own. She was open to him, vulnerable. Only their mouths touched, but the sensation coursed through her veins, setting her on fire.

She wanted to pull him closer, needing to feel his warmth, his strength. As if reading her mind, he obliged, stepping into the space between her legs as she sagged against the rough wall, his hands still framing her head. He pressed against her and she moaned deep in her throat, voicing their mutual need.

As abruptly as he'd kissed her, Jake stopped. He pulled back far enough to look at her. Her breath caught at the desire she saw in his eyes. She placed her hand on her mouth, still feeling the lingering touch of his lips.

"Why?" she asked again, though the question meant something altogether different.

Jake's lazy smile sent her pulse into overdrive. "It seemed like more fun than shaking some sense into you." He stepped away from her and bent to retrieve the leash. "Come on, before they catch both of us."

Sam followed him out of the alley, blinking at the brightness. "What are we going to do?"

He took her arm as they started walking back in the direction of the library. "Same plan as before. Except now we know what we're up against."

"And what's that?"

"Somebody who is damned afraid of you."

She would have laughed if she hadn't felt so scared. "Afraid of me?"

"Exactly. They're afraid of what you might know. You're their worst nightmare." Jake pulled her off the sidewalk and down another shadow-filled alleyway.

"Where are we going?"

"I need a drink," he said as he led her out of the alley and on to a small open-air café at the corner. "And I want you to read these articles and tell me what you think."

"A drink?" She remembered his confession from last night. "Is that a good idea?"

He gave her arm a reassuring squeeze. "Nothing alcoholic. I'm not ready to give in yet, even if you are."

His words stung. She'd never been a quitter. Maybe he was right. Maybe they still had a chance. Sam was silent as they walked past several empty tables and continued inside to the back of the café. The few patrons were dark-skinned older men, smoking cigars and engrossed in quiet conversation. Finally they entered an enclosed terrace draped in bougainvillea and shaded by palms.

"It's private back here. No one will bother us," Jake explained, guiding her to a small wrought-iron bistro table. Two elderly men played dominoes in the shade of a huge areca palm.

"What do you want to drink?" Jake asked after she sat down. Fletcher stretched out on the cool brick, his eyes on Jake.

"I don't care. Anything," Sam replied, realizing how parched her mouth had become.

Jake left and returned moments later with two large, frosty glasses. "Lemonade," he said, placing one of the glasses in front of her.

"Thanks."

"I found something else at the library." Jake fished some crumpled papers out of his back pocket and smoothed them out on the tile-covered table. "The federal agent you supposedly killed was listed as an accidental shooting in the paper."

Sam leaned across the small table to look at the photocopies. A picture of the man accompanied the article. "What does it say?"

"'Anthony Moreno was found dead in his home, the apparent victim of a self-inflicted gunshot wound,'" Jake read. "'It appeared Moreno had been cleaning his gun when the gun discharged. Foul play is not suspected.'" He looked up from the paper. "What do you think?"

Sam took a long drink of her lemonade, her hand shaking so badly she nearly sloshed the contents of the glass over herself. "I think this whole thing is crazy."

"That's the understatement of the year." Jake smoothed out the other sheet of paper. "The one about you is even more bizarre."

"Read it."

"'Samantha Martin, twenty-eight, a Pulitzer Prize-winning photographer, was found dead, the victim of an apparent suicide, in her hotel room in Miami Beach.'" Jake looked up at her. "You won a Pulitzer?"

Sam ducked her head. "Yeah. It's a long story." One she did not intend to discuss with him. She'd worked hard to put that all behind her and she had enough to deal with right now, without dredging up the past.

"Oh." Jake's eyes skimmed the page. "'Martin had been working for the magazine *Hit the Road* for the past few months and was on assignment. Co-workers described her as friendly, but Martin had been suffering from episodes of acute depression, according to one source.'"

"That's not true!" Sam slammed her glass down on the table, receiving startled looks from the domino-playing men.

"Since when have they been telling the truth? It works. Here's some loner photographer, off on her own. She ODs on drugs in Miami. Who's going to question it?''

"They knew just what to say."

"Do you have anyone who might have questioned you committing suicide? Friends?" Jake hesitated. "A boyfriend?"

Sam shook her head slowly. "I'd only been working for the magazine for a few months. I was friends with a few people, but I hadn't known them long." She met his eyes across the table. "And I wasn't involved with anyone."

"And before that?"

"I was living in New York. You don't make lasting relationships in New York. The friends I had there drifted out of my life when I moved to Atlanta."

"Family?"

Sam hesitated. "Nobody who'd miss me."

"So there wasn't anyone to question it."

"No."

Jake leaned back in his chair. "They had their bases covered. They dropped you at the mental hospital and went about their business. The question is, why not kill you outright?"

"They need the film," Sam said, shrugging. "With me dead, they'd never find it."

"So why didn't they torture it out of you? Sodium Pentothal would have been quicker if it had worked, but they had other options than locking you up in a hospital and drugging you."

"Torture?" The word conjured all sorts of unpleasant images that Sam didn't want to think about.

"Sure. They don't seem like they're above inflicting a little pain."

Sam began to shake. She gripped her glass tightly, trying to still the tremors shuddering through her body. "I never thought of that."

"Well, think about it the next time you decide to run off." Jake folded the articles and slid them into his back pocket. "By the way, who did you send the film to?"

"My father."

Jake stared at her. "I thought you said you didn't have any family."

"I haven't seen him in over twenty years. I might as well not have any family."

"So why in the hell did you send the film to him?"

Sam sighed. "I didn't even know where my father was until about a year ago. He left my mother and me when I was a kid and I never heard from him. I hired a private investigator to track him down. Turned out that he was living in Key West."

"So you decided to go visit him."

"Something like that. I got the Miami assignment and I thought I'd go see him." Sam shook her head. "Once I got to Miami I lost my nerve and changed my mind."

"Why?"

"It's been over twenty years. It's not likely we're going to bond now." Sam tried to laugh but emotion clogged her throat. For twenty years she'd wondered why her father didn't love her. Why he'd never called her or written her. Why he'd never even sent a birthday card.

"You must have thought differently when you hired someone to find him."

"Maybe. But once I got here, I didn't see the point. Then I got attacked by those men and I mailed the film to the first address that popped into my head." That had been easy enough, considering how many times she'd written letters to her father in the six months before going to Miami. Of course, she'd torn up all but the last letter.

"Did your father know you were coming?"

"I sent a letter to him the day I left Atlanta."

"But nobody knew he was alive?"

Sam shook her head. "He's not listed on anything but my birth certificate."

"So that means the men who are after you don't know he exists yet." Jake sat upright, disturbing Fletcher from his nap. The big dog looked up, then flopped back onto his side.

"Is that good?"

Jake nodded, a determined gleam in his eye. "It means we have an ally. And he's got the film. But they've had over a month to find out about you and it's only a matter of time before they track down your father."

Sam held up her hands. "Whoa. I don't know about the ally part. Didn't you hear me? My father hasn't wanted anything to do with me for the past twenty years."

"Fine. But he's still got the film."

"Right. And I still have people looking for me."

Jake stood. "Then I guess we'd better get going. Unless you're ready to give up."

"I've had a change of heart. I'm going to see this thing through." Sam pushed her chair in and took the last sip of her lemonade. "Or die trying."

"Thatta girl. Come on, Fletch," Jake called as he led the way back through the restaurant.

"What did you mean about me being their nightmare?" Sam asked when they were out on the street again.

"Just that you're the one person who can bring them to their knees." They stopped at the corner and waited for the light to change.

"Funny, I don't feel like it."

"But you are. Now all we have to do is make their worst nightmare come true."

"And we do that with the film?" They crossed Flagler Street, which was bustling at this hour with tourists and teenagers on spring break.

"Right. Once we figure out who it is we're dealing with, the battle is half won."

"And what's the other half?" she asked. They were almost at the library. Sam walked a little faster, anxious to be on their way. And away from Miami.

Jake didn't answer her until they reached the van. He unlocked her door and opened it. Fletcher squeezed into the back seat. "The other half is going to be convincing the police, the feds and whoever else it takes that we're telling the truth." He pushed the lock and slammed the door when she climbed in.

Sam buckled her seat belt as Jake stepped into the driver's seat. "How are we going to convince them?"

Jake started the engine. "I don't know. We'll figure it out after we know who's after us."

"You don't really have a plan, do you?"

Jake shot her a hard look tempered with a halfhearted smile as they pulled out into the congested traffic. "Planning is highly overrated."

"Yeah? What about living?"

"Very funny." He drove through the clogged streets of downtown Miami and into what looked like an older section of the city.

"Where are we going?"

"I want to check out my place."

Every muscle in Sam's body tensed. "Do you think that's smart?"

"I'm not going in. I just want to see if they've been here." He turned onto a shady, tree-lined street. There were brick and stucco town houses on both sides. "Damn."

Sam looked around. "What?"

"They're still here."

She was missing something. "How can you tell?"

Jake never slowed down. They got to the end of the street and he made a right turn. "Two unmarked cars across the street. They were hoping I'd come back."

Sam looked over her shoulder. "Do you think they saw us?"

"Probably not. They're looking for my SUV. Just the same, let's get out of here."

"Fine by me. The farther I get from Miami, the better I'll feel."

"Glad to hear it," Jake said. "But I do know one thing."

"Yeah? What?" Sam asked, staring out the window as the streets of Miami rolled by.

"Kissing you was definitely more fun than shaking you would have been. And you know what else?"

Sam shook her head, feeling her cheeks grow warm. What had she been thinking? Her conscience told her that where Jake was concerned, she didn't seem to do much thinking at all.

"If you do anything so stupid as try to run off without me again, I may not stop at just kissing you."

"Is that a threat?" she asked hoarsely, her mouth suddenly going dry despite the faint, lingering taste of lemonade. She wanted to believe it was just another side effect of the tranquillizers.

Jake's voice thrummed with emotion. "Oh, no, sweetheart. It's a promise." He sent her a sideways glance before returning his eyes to the road. "One I wouldn't mind keeping."

Chapter 7

The air conditioner died an hour outside Miami. Jake glanced at the clock and cursed his lousy luck.

Sam was trying to keep cool by fanning herself with a map she'd found in the glove box. Once in a while a breeze would waft to Jake's side of the van, bringing a moment of tepid relief from the hot stillness. Sam shifted in her seat, mumbling under her breath. Jake was thankful he couldn't hear her, because she didn't sound too happy.

"Stop fidgeting. You're making me crazy," he said, his fingers skipping over the radio buttons as he tried to get a station to come in clear. Nothing but static. "To hell with it." He switched off the radio and swiped at the sweat that beaded his forehead.

"Sorry to bother you," she said, not sounding sorry at all. "Maybe you haven't noticed but it's hot in here." Fletcher whined in agreement.

"There's nothing I can do about it now."

"Thanks for nothing," she snapped.

He knew she was still going through withdrawal and he

shouldn't listen to her. But the heat was bothering him, too. "I'm sorry I can't provide you with the luxurious accommodations you're used to."

"You have no idea what I'm used to."

"That's right. So why don't you stop complaining and let me drive?"

"You started it."

She was right about that. He'd started it back there in Miami. Kissing her hadn't been on his agenda, but when it got right down to it, he hadn't minded one bit. In fact, given half a chance, he'd probably do it again.

She was right about something else, too, he mused. He didn't have a plan. Not much of one, anyway. He was winging this one by the seat of his pants—pants that felt glued to his skin by a layer of perspiration. He shifted uncomfortably in his seat. Thinking about kissing Sam again was the last thing he needed on his mind.

"I started it," he said. "And I'm finishing it. Just make do. We'll be in Key West in about three hours." He glanced at the dashboard clock. They'd have to spend the night in Key West because there was no way he was going to make the return trip today.

"Three hours with no air," Sam grumbled, shifting in her seat again.

"Sorry."

"I'll bet you are."

Out of the corner of his eye Jake watched Sam's fingers undo a button on her shirt. When her fingers didn't hesitate to undo a second button, he swallowed hard. A horn honked behind them and Jake noticed he'd let up on the gas. He refocused his attention on the road, determined not to look Sam's way.

"I've got to get out of these clothes," Sam said. "I'm dying." She unfastened her seat belt.

"Where do you think you're going?" Jake glanced over as she

turned toward him, and he caught a glimpse of pale skin disappearing into tempting shadows beneath her shirt.

"To change."

Jake watched her in the rearview mirror as she lurched toward the back of the van. She leaned over into the cargo bin to get her bag and then turned, meeting his eyes in the mirror.

"Sorry, no peep shows today. Keep your eyes on the road. You, too, Fletcher."

If it hadn't been so damn hot already, Jake probably would have blushed. Instead, he angled the rearview mirror up. "Whatever you say, boss." Fletcher's tags jingled. Lucky dog, he could probably get away with a quick look.

It was quiet, as if she expected him to turn around and look. Then Jake heard the distinct sound of a zipper. He gripped the steering wheel tighter, focusing on a point in the distance.

Sam moved up into his field of vision after a moment and he nearly lost control of the van again. She was wearing some kind of T-shirt—a red one with no sleeves and a low neckline.

"You can fix that now," she said, climbing back into her seat and fastening the seat belt.

"What?"

"The mirror." She gestured at the rearview mirror. "You can adjust it now."

"Oh. Right," Jake said, tearing his eyes away from the full slope of her breasts to tilt the mirror. The T-shirt came down to her thighs, he noticed. And that wasn't all he noticed.

"Are you wearing anything under that?" he asked, determined to keep his eyes on the road.

"Of course I am."

He thought twice about asking her what.

Sam leaned forward and fumbled with the radio dial. The neck of her T-shirt dipped impossibly low and Jake sighed. It was going to be a long drive. She tuned in to a Latin station and settled back in her chair. The rhythmic music conjured up images of fire and passion; of sensual, fluid motion; skin against skin; pure heat....

"Salsa."

"Huh?" Jake said, his face as hot as the time his mother had caught him with a nudie magazine.

"I think this is what they call salsa music. I like it."

Sam sat back in her seat and Jake noticed the telltale sway of her breasts beneath the shirt. God help him, she wasn't wearing a bra. No bra and just that flimsy little T-shirt. He groaned.

She was silent for a heartbeat and he thought, prayed, that it would last. He was walking a thin edge of control, here. How she did it to him he couldn't begin to figure out. But one thing was certain: the lady got him hot.

"Jake?"

"Will you be quiet for ten minutes? And sit still." He kept his eyes on the long stretch of highway ahead of him, refusing to look at her. Now, if he could only figure out a way to stop thinking about her.

"I'll sit still if you'll talk to me instead of snapping my head off every time I say something."

"Fine."

"There you go again."

Instead of answering her and opening a whole other can of worms, he changed tactics. "Sorry. The heat is getting to me, too." He just wouldn't tell her it was the heat she radiated and not the Florida sun that caused his problems. "What do you want to talk about?" He braced himself for the worst.

"Tell me about your family."

"Why?" Of all the things she could have said, that one was a surprise.

"I don't know. It just sounds like you've got a nice family."

Jake shrugged, feeling some of the tension ease out of his shoulders. "I guess. There are a couple we don't invite to the reunions, but on the whole they're an okay bunch."

"Even you," she said.

"If you say so."

"I say so. So there's you, Mac, Brian and Annie?"

"That's us. The Four Musketeers." Jake grinned at the nickname their mother had given them when they were kids. For siblings, they'd been pretty close.

"What about your parents?"

"My mom died two years ago," Jake said. He adjusted the visor as the afternoon sun glinted off the hood of the van. "Dad was killed when I was fourteen. He was a cop."

"I'm sorry." Sam's voice was hushed. "Is that why you became a cop?"

"Not really. I intended to be a psychologist." He smiled in response to Sam's snort. No doubt she was trying to imagine him in a suit sitting across a desk from a patient. He had to admit, it was difficult.

"So how'd you end up being a detective?"

"A double major in psychology and criminal justice. A friend of my dad's recruited me right out of grad school. I was sick of sitting in a classroom so it sounded like a good deal for a year or two."

Sam played with the radio dial as the Latin music turned to static and found an oldies station. He glanced over at her, into eyes that were as green as the Caribbean in this light. Again Jake felt the sensual pull toward her that he'd felt back in Miami. What was it about this woman that turned his insides upside down?

"But you stayed," she said, nodding.

"Something like that. Before I knew it, I was on the fast track."

"What happened?"

It was a reasonable question. But it still left a raw spot on his ego to answer it. "I was suspended."

He glanced over at her and saw her eyes widen. "Why?"

"Long story. Basically, I screwed up and got my partner killed." He heard Sam's gasp and it reverberated through the hollow space inside him. "I was cleared of any wrongdoing, but

I didn't see the point in staying on." There was more to it than
that, but he didn't elaborate. He flashed her a grin. "Now I'm
living the easy life," he said, assuming a smooth Jamaican drawl.
"No worries."

"Right. Except me and this nightmare I've dragged you into."

"Yeah, well, I was starting to enjoy life a little too much, I
guess. Time to shake things up a bit, huh?"

"I could live without it," Sam answered.

"A hotshot photographer like you? I'd figure you for the high-
profile dangerous life."

Sam shook her head. "Not anymore. Give me a quiet beach
and a book and I'm happy."

"Tell me about the Pulitzer. That's a pretty big deal."

"I don't want to talk about that." Her words were sharp with
pain and anger.

"All right," Jake said gently. "Tell me about your life."

He could almost feel Sam pull away. "That's not a great topic,
either." She sighed and looked out the window.

The sun shone brilliantly on the ocean. The only thing separating them from the water was a narrow strip of sand and asphalt.
Viewed from the sticky heat of the van, the ocean was a temptation. Jake looked at the soft curve of Sam's cheek, at her pale
lashes against pale skin. Temptation. He turned his eyes back to
the road, resisting the ocean and Sam. For now.

"Tell me anyway," he said.

She sighed. "My father left us when I was six. He was in the
navy. My mother had never worked a day in her life so we spent
the next ten years moving from state to state, living with various
relatives while she tried to earn a living for us." Her hand came
up to her face and he wondered if she was crying.

"No brothers or sisters?"

"No, just me and Mom. She died the year I left for college."

"I'm sorry."

Sam shrugged and pushed her hair back off her neck. "She did
the best she could."

"What made you want to find your father?"

He could feel her hesitation. "I'm not sure. I guess I wanted to know if he had another family, if he thought about us. If I had any siblings."

"What do you think you'll say to him when you see him?" It wasn't an idle question. Jake could empathize with Sam, but the last thing they needed right now was a family squabble. They had to get the film and deal with that.

"I don't know. I'll probably ask him why he left. Why he never called or wrote." Her voice got raspy and Jake could hear her fight for control. "Why he didn't love me enough to stay."

"I didn't mean to upset you," he said, uncomfortable with her pain.

"Not your fault." She swiped at her face with the back of her hand. "I'm still feeling a little raw from the drugs. It makes me emotional." It was an excuse and they both knew it, but Jake kept quiet.

"Anyway, the important thing is the film, right?"

He nodded. "Right."

"And maybe getting the air conditioner fixed before we go back to Miami?" she asked hopefully.

"Sorry. No can do. We don't have that kind of time."

"And you're the one making the decisions."

"That's right," he said.

"Tell me, is that a macho thing or a cop thing?"

"Neither. It's just practical."

"I stand corrected. It's a control thing."

He slid a glance her way. "What are you talking about?"

"Never mind," she replied, turning toward the window.

"Oh, please tell me you're not one of those."

"One of what?"

"Those 'Never mind' women. If you've got something to say, say it."

She turned and he could feel her glaring at him. "Okay. You're the most irritating, infuriating, obnoxious, contradictory—"

"I think I get your point," he said, rolling his eyes. "Try to remember this isn't a vacation and we're not supposed to be having fun."

"Well, that's a relief because I'm sure as hell not having any. And believe me, if I had any other choice, I'd hop out here—"

"Sam, will you shut up for a minute?" Jake glanced in the rearview mirror again.

"See what I mean? Contradictory. You said if I had something to say I should say it. So I say it and you tell me to shut up."

"I have something to say, too, if you'll be quiet long enough for me to say it."

"What is it now?"

One more look in the mirror confirmed what he already knew. "We're being followed."

"Are you sure?" Sam felt a cold shiver race up her spine.

"I'm sure. I've switched lanes, adjusted my speed, but they're still back there. Close enough that they can see me, but far enough away that they're hoping I won't notice them."

Sam wrapped her arms around herself, thankful that it was daylight. Her imagination already played havoc with her nerves without the benefit of darkness. She shivered. Suddenly it didn't feel so hot inside the van anymore. "What can they do out here with other cars around?"

"Not much," he said. "But they know we're here and soon enough they'll know where we're going."

"So what do we do?"

He shot her a dark look. "We get to Key West in one piece without letting them know we know they're back there."

"Then what?"

"Then we find out who they are and why they're following us."

"How do you propose we do that?" Sam asked, irritated by his oversimplification of things.

He grinned at her and she saw a dangerous gleam in his eyes. "We'll figure that out when we get there."

"Great," she muttered. She gripped the arms of her chair, wondering what the second obituary would say. Would they even bother with a second one? Tense silence wrapped around them as the numbers on the mile markers dwindled. Sam looked out the side mirror and saw the sedan, still two cars behind them. She felt trapped and helpless, cooped up in a hot van with a dog that was beginning to smell and a man who both intrigued and infuriated her. She dug her nails into her palms and bit her tongue to keep from screaming.

At the mile marker for Big Pine Key, Jake jerked the wheel and the van went careening off the highway. Sam slammed into the passenger door and gasped as the wind was knocked out of her. She clung to the door for dear life as they flew down the off-ramp at breakneck speed.

"What the hell are you doing?"

"Change of plans," Jake said, his face set in grim lines.

Sam looked at the speedometer and gasped. They weren't slowing down. She gripped her seat, grateful for the safety belt that secured her as they blew through a red light.

Scenery blurred as the van picked up speed. She caught a glimpse of a shopping center and the entrance of a subdivision as the van barreled down what looked like the main street of Big Pine Key.

"Have we lost them?"

"That's not what I want." Jake glanced in the rearview mirror and Sam felt the van slowing.

"Are you crazy?"

"No crazier than you. I've got a plan."

Before Sam could respond, Jake whipped the van down a narrow dirt road lined with pine trees. The van kicked up dust and sand as they bounced along the uneven road. Sam's stomach flip-flopped sickly as they hit a deep rut. Fletcher's tags jingled as he dropped to the floorboards and nudged up between Sam and Jake.

"Listen, Sam," Jake said. "Grab my duffel bag in back. Quick. They're not that far behind us."

Sam clawed open her seat belt as the van raced down the narrow road. She nudged Fletcher aside with her foot and stumbled to the back of the van. Leaning over the rear seat, she grasped the duffel bag. She swayed, the heavy bag throwing her off-balance as she made her way back to Jake.

"Now what, boss?"

"Give it to me." Jake kept his eyes on the road as she handed him the bag. Feeling down into the side pocket of the bag, he pulled out a gun.

Sam's pulse trip-hammered in her veins and she swallowed hard. This was what he hadn't wanted her to see back at Annie's house. "What are you planning to do—have a shoot-out with them?"

"Not if I can help it," he answered. He leaned forward, tucking the gun into the waistband of his jeans. "Hang on."

Sam barely had time to register the warning before the van went careening onto an even narrower side road. Jake slammed on the brakes and shifted into neutral.

"Now what?" she asked. This didn't look like much of a plan to her.

Jake was already climbing out of the van. "Get over here in the driver's seat. If things don't go the way I want, get the hell out of here."

"What are you going to do, Jake?"

He had the audacity to grin at her. "You'll see." His smile faded. "Don't do anything stupid, all right? Just sit tight, keep your head down and if you hear shots, throw this thing into reverse and get the hell out of here."

"All right." Sam slipped behind the steering wheel. "Hey!" she called as Jake started to head into the densely wooded forest.

He looked over his shoulder, dappled sunlight playing across his face. "What?"

"Don't get yourself killed."

"Promise."

Sam watched Jake disappear into the woods, blending into the shadows. Suddenly, she felt very much alone. She heard the hum of the sedan's engine and scooted down in her seat. Fletcher whined beside her and she patted his head. "Hang on, big fella. Jake is going to get us out of this—I hope."

She saw the sedan in the side mirror as it slowly moved into her field of vision. It turned down the side road and stopped behind the van. Sam counted the minutes silently, her heart hammering in her chest. There was no sign of Jake, at least not from here.

Finally, the slam of a car door broke the silence. She sank lower in the seat and pulled Fletcher with her. The crunch of dry twigs outside the window was her only warning. "All right, out of the van!"

A gun pointed in the window, never wavering from her head. The man holding the gun had the cold-eyed expression of a killer. Sam didn't move. Fletcher growled. Where the hell was Jake?

"Freeze! Police!"

Jake's voice ripped through the stillness and Sam jerked into action, lunging for the passenger door. She heard the sounds of a scuffle outside the van. The vehicle shook as someone slammed against it. She reached for the door handle. She hesitated only long enough to remember Jake's warning.

The two men didn't even notice her. They squared off, circling each other, guns drawn. The other man was of a heavier build than Jake, but Jake moved with feline grace, watching every motion he made.

Jake glanced at her. "I told you to stay in the van," he growled.

"I thought you might need some help."

"Put it down, Cavanaugh. It's over," the man said, perspiring heavily in the Florida humidity.

"Not a chance. Who are you and who sent you?"

"I'm not authorized to tell you anything," the man said. "Now put the gun down."

Every instinct in Sam told her to run while she could. But she couldn't leave Jake like this. "What do you want with us?" she demanded.

"Tell him to put the gun down and we'll talk."

"Why should I trust you?" Sam asked.

In the split second it took for the man to look at her, Jake lunged forward and brought his arm down hard on his opponent's gun hand. Sam bit back a scream as the weapon skittered across the ground. The two men struggled roughly but silently until the sound of Jake's gun being cocked froze the man in his place.

"Look, why don't I just go ahead and kill you now? I'm being framed for murders I didn't commit, so what's one more?" Jake said, pointing his gun at the man's chest.

"You don't want to do that, Cavanaugh."

"Well, since you know my name, why don't you give me yours?"

"John Manning."

"Well, that's a start," Jake said, stepping around behind the man. He poked Manning in the back with the gun. "Who do you work for? You're carrying a gun, so maybe you intend to assassinate us."

Manning shook his head. "I was just sent to follow you."

"Sam, check his wallet. Let's see what Johnny is carrying."

Reluctantly, Sam moved forward. Jake was starting to scare her. She didn't really think he could just kill this guy, but looking into his eyes, she began to doubt herself. Sam extracted Manning's wallet from his pants pocket and retreated to the van. Fletcher hung his head out the window and nuzzled her neck.

"Well?" Jake asked as she thumbed through Manning's wallet.

Sam's heart skipped a beat. "He works for the government, Jake." She held up the official-looking government ID for Jake to see.

"What agency?" Jake asked.

"It just says United States Government."

"Who do you work for?" He prodded Manning with the gun.

"That's classified information," Manning answered, every muscle in his body taut.

"Funny, I would have thought you'd be more cooperative," Jake said, pushing Manning to his knees and holding the gun to his head. "Does it say anything else, Sam?"

She flipped the ID over. "No."

"It's classified," Manning repeated stoically, but his calm facade began to crack. "I was supposed to follow you. That's it."

"Then what?"

"Then I was supposed to call headquarters. They would have sent backup."

"To kill us." Jake's jaw clenched on the words.

"No. My boss gave me very clear orders. You're to be detained only."

"Who, Manning? Who's your boss?"

Manning swallowed hard. "Classified."

Sam could see the coiled tension in Jake's body and she held her breath. "Come on, Jake," she said quietly. "He's not going to tell us anything."

"I can't tell you who I work for," Manning said. "But we're not the only ones who want you. Come with me and we'll straighten it out."

The gun came up again. "Somebody else is after us?"

Manning nodded.

Jake prodded him gently with the weapon. "Who?"

"We're trying to protect you."

Jake's harsh laugh startled a flock of crows into flight. "Try again. You don't help people by killing them."

"All I know is that there are some hired guns after you."

"Is it the same goons who killed the people at the diner?"

"That's what I was told."

"A cop was killed at the diner," Jake ground out between

clenched teeth. "Did they tell you that, Manning? Did they tell you the man had a wife and two kids?"

Manning blinked, his bravado deflating under Jake's fury. "Yeah, they told me. That's why I'm following you. To make sure they don't get to you next."

"Who are your protecting us from?"

Manning shook his head. "I don't know."

"Don't know or won't tell?"

"Don't know. They only tell me what I need to know."

"Great. I'm talking to a mushroom," Jake said, raking his hand through his hair. "All right, Manning. You've been a little co-operative so I guess I can't just kill you."

Sam relaxed. "Can we go now?"

"In a minute. Get the keys out of the sedan."

Sam retrieved the keys from the sedan and returned to where Jake and Manning stood. As soon as Sam passed the keys to Jake, he sent them flying. Sam watched the sunlight glint on the metal as they arced through the air, disappearing into the woods.

"What are you going to do with me?" Manning asked, his gaze shifting from Jake to Sam.

"Not a thing. We're going to leave you right here. But let me show you something." Jake took Manning by the arm and dragged him to the side of the road. "See that?"

Sam moved closer to see what Jake was pointing at. All she saw was a fairly large hole in the ground.

Manning nodded and Jake explained. "That's a sinkhole. There's a whole labyrinth of them under Big Pine. I'd stay away from them if I were you."

"Why?" Manning asked, obviously curious despite his predic-ament.

"Gators love 'em. They move around down there and if some-body, like you, should happen to fall into one, well, let's just say they'll never know what happened to you back at headquarters."

Sam backtracked several steps, wondering if Jake was telling the truth. Maybe he was just trying to scare Manning. Manning didn't look half as intimidated as she thought he should be.

Jake pulled him back to the road and led him to his car. "All right, Manning, it's time for us to go. You just sit tight in the car until we're gone. Then you can head back in the direction you came. Shouldn't take you more than half an hour."

Manning turned toward the car and Jake opened the door. Before Manning could get in, Jake raised the gun. For one terrifying moment, Sam thought he was going to shoot the man. Instead, he brought the butt of the gun down hard on the back of Manning's head. He crumpled to the ground and Jake eased him into the car, closing the door behind him.

"What did you do that for?" Sam asked.

Jake shrugged. "Insurance. I want more than half an hour's lead time on this guy."

"Oh."

"Come on, let's get out of here," Jake said, tucking his gun back into his jeans while he bent to retrieve Manning's. Fletcher whined from the van. "Right after a doggy pit-stop."

Chapter 8

"I thought you were going to kill him." The words were a murmur, almost as if she spoke to herself.

Jake kept his eyes on the road. She'd hardly said a thing since they'd gotten back on the highway. He knew he'd scared her back there. He'd seen it in her eyes. Fear. She was afraid of him. It tugged at his conscience and hit a little too close to home.

"I wasn't going to kill him," he said. "I had to find out what he knew."

"Will he be all right?"

There went his conscience again. "If he sticks to the main path, he'll be fine."

"Were you telling the truth? About the sinkhole, I mean." Sam's voice was still a quiet monotone. He wondered if she were in shock over his behavior or still recovering from the drugs. "Yeah, Big Pine is full of them. Gators love to make their dens there."

"But he'll be all right?" She repeated it like a mantra.

"He'll be fine, Sam," he replied, exasperation in his voice.

She had a way of making him feel bad when he knew he hadn't done anything wrong. "Why are you all fired up to protect the bad guys?"

He could feel her gaze on his face. It made him uncomfortable, like she could see right through him. He didn't like that. Didn't want her to know more than what he felt like telling.

"I don't want anyone to get hurt," she whispered.

Jake adjusted his speed and switched lanes, passing a silver-colored motor home. "He could have killed us, Sam. Even if someone else is after us, I don't know who Manning works for. Besides, there was no chance I was going to kill him."

"Why?"

Jake didn't answer her at first. He was angry, but not at Sam. He'd screwed up back there with Manning. He'd gotten so spooked by having a gun in his hand again, he'd forgotten one crucial thing—getting the phone number of Manning's boss. They still didn't know who they were up against, and it was his fault.

"I can't do it anymore."

"Do what?"

He wished he'd never said anything to begin with. "I can't deal with guns anymore."

"But you were a cop."

"'Were' being the operative word. I hate even touching a gun anymore."

He could feel her eyes watching him. "You could have fooled me, back there."

"I'm a good actor. I did what I had to do. But when it comes right down to it, I couldn't have killed him any more than you could have." He glanced at her, seeing the concern in her face and hating how helpless he felt. "Probably less."

"What really happened, Jake?" Her gentle voice did little to soothe the ache of his conscience.

"I left the force because I lost my nerve and I didn't want to be stuck behind a desk." He nearly choked on the words.

She didn't speak and for that he was grateful. He didn't want to relive his mistakes, or the pain they had caused. His hesitation had been what had killed Charlie. And he'd be damned if he'd ever put himself in that position again. He was nobody's hero.

Key West was an explosion of activity. In other words, it was a typical day.

"What's going on?" Sam asked.

Jake pointed to the banner draped across the road between two telephone poles. "It's the Conch Festival."

"What's that?"

He reminded himself that she wasn't a Florida native. "Key West had a problem years ago with drug blockades to the mainland. It slowed traffic and annoyed the tourists. The island seceded from the union in protest and proclaimed itself the Conch Republic."

"You're joking."

"Well, it was really just another excuse for a party." He recalled the wilder days of the island nation. Key West shone now, but he missed the old days, the rough-around-the-edges, gritty Key West. Now it was just another glittering gem on the Florida tourist trail. He sighed.

"Well, it certainly looks like a party."

Two women, clad in bikinis and body paint, crossed in front of the van at a red light. They waved at Jake and Sam.

"Wait until it gets dark," Jake said. "The clothing rules get a little more relaxed."

"And you complained about my outfit," Sam grumbled.

"Yeah, well, that's different." Jake didn't need to be reminded of her outfit, and a sidelong glance set his pulse racing. If she put on a bikini, he'd have a heart attack.

"Now what?"

Sam's question brought him back to the road. The light was green. "Now we find your father."

Sam repeated her father's address from memory and Jake navigated the narrow streets lined with cars and pink rental mopeds.

They pulled up in front of a small bungalow, neat by Key West standards. It was freshly painted a bright canary yellow. The gravel driveway was empty.

Jake parked by the curb and shut off the engine. "Well, are you ready?" he asked when Sam showed no signs of getting out.

"I don't know."

He heard her fear and her indecision in those three words. "You can wait here if you want," he offered. If he were seeing his father for the first time in over twenty years, he'd be a little nervous, too. Under these circumstances, he couldn't blame her for wanting to bolt.

"No, I'll go."

Her decision made, Sam swung into action. She fumbled with the door for a minute, then seemed to steady herself. Standing outside the van, she eyed the house like it was a morgue.

"Doesn't look like anyone's home," she said.

Jake followed her to the front door. She hadn't been lying. She was wearing shorts under her T-shirt—black, skintight, hip-hugging shorts that made her legs look a mile long. He swallowed hard. She did crazy things to his pulse. But he'd have her out of his life and out of his system soon enough. He didn't need the complications she caused, no matter how nicely wrapped those complications were.

Her knuckles were poised to knock when her hand fell to the side. "Looks like we're too late."

"What's the matter?" he asked.

Sam gestured to the doorknob. "He's gone."

Sure enough, hanging from a string was a sign that read, Gone Fishing.

"You've got to be kidding," Jake said.

"Naw, Sammy Martin is no kidder," came a lilting female voice from behind them.

Jake and Sam turned to see a dark-skinned woman in a floral-print bikini top and a long yellow skirt. She looked to be in her mid-forties and her waist-length braids were tied with brightly colored bits of ribbon and beads. They clicked as she shook her head and smiled.

"Sammy's out on the boat. He's got a load of tourists fishing for marlin."

"Are you his neighbor?" Jake glanced past the woman. No car. But in Key West you didn't necessarily need a car.

She winked and shook her head again, the braids clicking merrily. "No, I'm Amalinaú Martin."

Sam had stood silently throughout the exchange and Jake almost jumped out of his skin when she spoke.

"Martin?"

Jake asked the question Sam couldn't. "Are you some relation of Sam Martin's?"

"Oh, yes." The woman's smile widened. "I'm Sammy's wife."

Sam nearly choked. "His wife?"

The woman's chocolate-colored eyes went hard. She propped her fists on her hips and stared at Sam. "Yes. What business do you have here?"

Jake jumped in. "We need to see Mr. Martin. It's urgent."

"Well, now, I already told you. Sammy is out."

Her father had remarried. She should have expected that, but it still rattled her. The woman was the complete opposite of her mother. Dark and full figured, plain but somehow exotic.

Sam tried to gather her scattered thoughts and forced a smile for the woman's benefit. "When will he be back?"

"Tomorrow." The woman's tone was curt. "Do you know Sammy?"

Sam exchanged glances with Jake. The concern she saw in his eyes helped calm her frayed nerves. She took a deep breath but before she could speak, the woman's eyes widened as she studied Sam's face.

"You're Sammy's daughter."

It was more a statement than a question, but Sam nodded anyway. "How did you know?"

The woman's hand floated in the air, not quite touching Sam. "Here," she said, gesturing at Sam's cheek. "And here." Her fingertips hovered above Sam's lips. "You look so much like him."

Sam felt tears prick her eyes. She looked like her father. She had only the vaguest childhood recollections of him. All she could remember was a tall man, but at the age of six, everyone seemed tall. She remembered his laugh—hearty, full of life. That was how she remembered her father. A blond man with a big laugh.

The woman's own eyes seemed moist as she dropped her hand to her side. "Why are you here now? Why, after so long?"

Sam wanted to scream. Why? She wanted to ask her own questions. The tears sparkled along her lashes now; she could see them reflected through the sunlight. "I need his help."

The woman nodded, her dark eyes shuttered. "Ah. Well, he won't be back until tomorrow." She started past them toward the house and Jake put his hand on her arm.

"Sam didn't know where her father was until recently," he said. Sam wondered why he was defending her, why his voice sounded so fiercely protective.

"Well, now she knows." The woman turned to look at Sam. "Come back tomorrow, Samantha. Sammy will want to see you."

The door closed before Sam could answer. Then she remembered. "The film!"

Jake shook his head, his hand firmly on her elbow. "Tomorrow, Sam. You have to see your father anyway." He glanced at the darkening sky. "Tomorrow is soon enough."

Sam let Jake lead her back to the van. Fletcher licked at her ear as she climbed in. Tomorrow. She had to wait another day to see the father she hardly remembered.

Jake put the van into gear and maneuvered out of the narrow driveway. He looked over at her and she couldn't read the expression in his eyes.

"I'm sorry, Sam."

"Don't." She waved her hand in the air, turning her face to the window. "Don't be nice to me or I will cry." Tears flooded her eyes and her throat felt painfully tight.

"All right," Jake said. "Do you want me to yell at you a little bit? Maybe tell you what a pain in the ass you are?"

Sam managed a smile. "No, but don't worry. I'm sure you'll get your chance."

Jake steered out into the busy main road, which was cluttered with cars and tourists. "You're probably right."

Sam pushed thoughts of her father to the back of her mind. There was still so much to deal with. "So now what do we do?"

"We kill time until tomorrow. Hopefully your father will get back early."

"And how do we go about killing time?" Sam asked as laughter drifted in the window.

"Aw, sweetheart," Jake drawled. "You're in Key West. There's no better place to kill time." He frowned at the bumper-to-bumper traffic. "Problem is, with the Conch Festival going on, I don't know if we're going to find a place to stay."

"No. Don't say it."

Jake nodded. "Yep. We might have to sleep in the van tonight."

Sam groaned.

As luck would have it, they were able to find a hotel that not only had a vacancy but also accepted cash. It was an added boon that they could park the van in the yard behind the inn, out of sight. The aging hippie behind the counter leered at Sam and stroked his long greasy ponytail as Jake paid the outrageously high rate.

"Had to kick out a bunch of teenyboppers last night," the hippie rasped around the cigar clenched between his teeth. His enormous potbelly was barely contained by a faded Deadhead T-shirt. "They were tearing up the place. Smoking, drinking. Wild kids." He shook his head.

Jake took the room key. "We'll try to keep it down."

The hotel manager nodded, giving Jake a man-to-man wink that made Sam's skin crawl. "Ain't got yourself one of those moaners, huh?"

A hot retort burned on Sam's lips but Jake clamped his fingers around her wrist.

"Come on, honey." He practically dragged her out of the stuffy, smoky office. He opened the van for Fletcher and the dog bounded out, his tail wagging hard. "Let's check out the room. I'll get our stuff later."

The Flying Dolphin Inn was actually a renovated three-story house. The island-style Victorian boasted the famed gingerbread trim that Sam had seen in more than one travel spread. Unfortunately, the hotel was in the kind of disrepair that articles would refer to as the "before" shot.

"Why didn't you let me smack him?" she complained, rubbing her wrist as she followed him up the three flights of rickety stairs to the third-floor landing.

"Because we need the room."

Jake's key fit the lock to the only room on the third floor. The door creaked open to the smell of beer and sea salt. Fletcher pushed past them, clearly delighted at having a new place to explore.

A double bed and an ugly, squat dresser crowded the small space. A large ceramic vase with hideous fake hibiscus blooms sat on the dresser. Bright green-and-pink tropical-print fabric covered the bed and windows, clashing with the thickly padded aqua-colored chair wedged into one corner. Sam could see the bathroom through a narrow doorway. She hoped it was clean.

"This isn't so bad," Jake said, cranking the decrepit air conditioner up to full blast. He sat on the edge of the bed and the mattress sagged under his weight.

Sam rolled her eyes. "That's my line. Compared to my last

accommodations, this is heaven." She crossed to the window and pulled the cord on the curtains, revealing a sliding-glass door and a tiny balcony. The view took her breath away. "My, that's gorgeous."

From three floors up, they had a spectacular view of the beach and ocean. Azure waves capped with white foam brought a sense of tranquillity to the dingy little room. The ocean's roar acted as backup for the screeching gulls and the sounds of traffic. Sam started when Jake touched her shoulder.

"I never get tired of the view," he murmured near her ear. For one heart-stopping moment, she wondered if he was talking about the ocean or her. Then she almost laughed. He sure as hell wasn't talking about her.

Sam moved away from the glass door, flipped on the bathroom light, and saw clean white porcelain. She sighed and said a silent prayer to the patron saint of housekeepers. The bathtub looked big enough for two.

"Must be the honeymoon suite," she mumbled.

"Don't be getting any ideas." Jake shook his finger at her. "You heard the man. No wild behavior."

A tap at the door wiped the smiles off both their faces. Jake's hand reflexively patted his waist where the gun had been. He'd tucked it back in the duffel bag when they'd gotten to the hotel.

"Damn!" he swore softly and Fletcher's low woof echoed him.

"Now what?" Sam asked, wondering how many bones she'd break, jumping out a third-story window.

"Answer the door."

Jake stood beside the door, tension in every muscle, as Sam called, "Who's there?"

A muffled voice replied, "Maid service."

Jake nodded for Sam to open the door. "Slowly," he mouthed.

Cracking the door, Sam looked out. Sure enough, a young woman stood there with a stack of towels in her arms. "For tomorrow," she said, handing the towels over when Sam showed no signs of moving away from the door. "You might want to go to the beach. It's supposed to be a beautiful day."

"Thanks." Sam grabbed the towels and closed the door on the woman's surprised expression. She made a face at Jake. "It was the maid. Imagine that."

Jake locked the door, but the flimsy hardware didn't look like it would be much protection. Sam wondered if Fletcher had any hidden guard-dog talents he'd yet to reveal.

"Can't be too careful," Jake said.

"Right. Now we have towels, we have a room and we have nowhere to be until tomorrow morning. Now what?"

He gave her the once-over before answering. She must look like a refugee. "I'd suggest a shower and some clean clothes."

"Maybe you've forgotten. All I have is a couple of shirts and the jeans I was wearing earlier." She shook her head. "I am not putting those jeans back on."

Jake's blue eyes darkened like a sky before a thunderstorm. "Then I guess I'll have to buy you something to wear." His voice was deep and throaty. A quivering awareness traveled up Sam's spine.

"You don't have to," she protested.

"You can't walk around here naked," he growled. He stepped over to the dresser and pulled open drawers until he came up with a pen and a pad of paper with the inn's name printed across it. He handed it to her. "Write down what size you wear. Shoe size, too."

"Jake, really."

"Just do it."

Sam hesitated for a moment. Now was not the time for feminine vanity. She hurriedly scribbled her clothing and shoe sizes and handed it back to him. She felt warmth creep into her cheeks when he glanced at the paper and his eyebrows shot up.

"You look smaller," was all he said.

"Thanks," she muttered.

Jake left with Fletcher on his heels. "I'll be back soon," he said over his shoulder. "Try not to get into trouble."

Chapter 9

Key West was alive. Jake loved everything about the town, from the sunburned tourists picking out seashell souvenirs that weren't even from this continent, much less Key West, to the strange assortment of street vendors hawking their wares.

Fletcher kept pace beside him, his tail in constant motion. Over the past couple of years, Jake hadn't gotten out much, preferring solitude to crowds. But Fletcher seemed to be having a ball on their little adventure.

"Having fun, Fletch?" Jake murmured to the excited mutt. Jake knew how he felt. After being cooped up in the van for hours, it felt good to stretch his legs. His knee ached a little, the scar tissue pulling taut with every step.

He found his way back to Sam's father's house easily. The house stood still and quiet, and he hoped Amalinaú Martin was still around. Rapping twice on the door, he waited.

"You're back?" the woman asked, eyeing him suspiciously through a narrow crack in the door. "I told you Sammy won't be home until tomorrow."

Jake nodded, pulling Fletcher back as he lunged in friendly curiosity. "I know. I thought you could help me."

The door opened a crack wider. "What can I do for you?"

Jake looked behind him, scanning the street. He expected Sam to show up at any moment. He turned back to Amalinaú and forced a smile. "Samantha mailed a package to her father about a month or so ago."

She nodded. "Right after the letter telling Sammy she was coming. Then she didn't come." Her voice hardened. "Sammy was so hurt when she didn't show up."

"Yes, well, Samantha got into some trouble. She couldn't come."

Amalinaú's dark eyes went wide. "Trouble? With the police?"

"Something like that. But it was a misunderstanding."

The suspicion in her eyes didn't fade. "And who are you?"

Jake hesitated. Just who the hell was he to Sam? "I'm a friend." As an afterthought, he added, "A cop."

Her face cleared a little. "So what do you want?"

"I need the package Samantha sent. It has something that will help her take care of this problem."

She nodded. "I remember the package. Sammy didn't say what it was." She opened the door wider. "Come in."

Fletcher pulled at his leash, anxious to explore all the new smells the dim interior offered. Jake shrugged apologetically. "Maybe we should stay out here."

Amalinaú stooped to pet Fletcher. "It's all right. Rover will love him."

Jake followed her into the house, right behind Fletcher. The small bungalow was decorated in bright shades of yellow and green. White wicker furniture filled the narrow living room. Fletcher moved about as much as his leash would allow, sniffing every surface.

Amalinaú smiled at the dog before turning a more serious expression on Jake. "Come with me. I'll see if I can find the package."

She disappeared into another room that, from the looks of it, was an office. Jake and Fletcher followed her. The space was dominated by a large pine desk, overloaded with papers and books. Shelves lined three of the walls, crammed with everything from an ancient-looking set of encyclopedias to a recent copy of the latest thriller. But it was the fourth wall that caught Jake's attention.

Pictures were hung so closely together that they looked like wallpaper. Most of them were black-and-white but an occasional color photo stood out. Some looked like newspaper clippings, others were glossies.

Jake moved closer to examine the pictures while Amalinaú rifled through the papers on the desk. The photographs were as varied as Sammy Martin's reading material. Many were candid shots of people. In one, two young Asian girls played next to a river. In another, a teenage boy smoked a cigarette and stared defiantly at the camera. Still another showed three young men toting guns, one of them with blood streaming from a shoulder wound.

"Those are Samantha's pictures," Amalinaú said softly.

"Her father collects them?"

She nodded. "Every one. Sometimes he writes the magazines or the newspapers and gets a copy of the original. Sometimes he just cuts them out. He's had to take down a lot." She laughed, her voice sounding more youthful than her years. "We don't have enough room for all of them."

Jake looked back at the wall, his eyes riveted to one particular black-and-white photo. In it, a young woman stared at the camera. The picture was an extreme close-up—just her face. Her eyes were haunted, deeply shadowed. She had dark hair, curving around her features like a frame. Her cheeks were hollow, gaunt to the point of starvation.

The lines around her eyes and mouth spoke of sadness—the kind that didn't go away; the kind of grief someone that beautiful shouldn't know anything about.

"That's the Pulitzer," Amalinaú said.

"What?" he asked, unable to take his eyes off the girl's face. Her eyes would haunt his dreams.

"Samantha won the Pulitzer for that one." Amalinaú touched the photo gently. "Sammy was so proud of her. But then..." Her words trailed off as she shrugged.

"Then what?" He had a vague recollection of seeing the picture in the paper but his memory didn't serve him well. No wonder, after the drinking binges he'd indulged in back then.

Amalinaú's smile was tinged with sadness. "It's hard to be the eyes of the world when the world doesn't want to see."

He wanted to ask her what she meant, but she held out a manila envelope. He took it and noticed that it had been opened. He looked inside and saw a roll of professional color film wrapped in a folded piece of paper. He pulled out the note and read Sam's small, neat handwriting.

Please keep this for me. It's important.

Samantha

"You will help Samantha, won't you?" Amalinaú's dark eyes, full of wisdom, stared up him.

Jake nodded and tried not to feel guilty for going behind Sam's back. He reminded himself that he hardly knew her. And even if he didn't think she was capable of murder, he had no reason to trust her. His only reason for being here was to clear himself. "I'll do my best."

"Make sure Samantha comes back tomorrow. It will break Sammy's heart to know she was here and didn't come to see him."

"We'll be back," Jake promised. Something bumped against his leg and he looked down. "What the hell is that?"

A large greenish-brown reptile nudged him again, its long tongue snaking out to taste Jake's jeans. Fletcher edged away from the beast, letting out a low whine. The fat lizard waddled toward Fletcher, its sharp claws rasping against the tile floor.

Amalinaú smiled and leaned down to pet the creature. "This is Rover."

Sure enough, around his neck was a bright yellow collar with a tag that said Rover. Jake took a guess. "Monitor lizard?"

She nodded. "And a wonderful pet."

Used to the unpredictable ways of alligators, Jake wasn't so sure. But this guy seemed docile enough. "Why'd he push me?"

She shrugged. "He's just like a dog. Loves to be scratched." She demonstrated by rubbing her fingertips down Rover's snout. "He's Sammy's best buddy."

Jake shook his head. "Some pet." He tugged at Fletcher's leash, and the frightened dog followed him to the door. "C'mon Fletcher." To Amalinaú he said, "Thanks. You've been a big help."

She put her hand on his arm before he left. "Don't forget. Tomorrow."

"We'll be here. When will Mr. Martin be back?"

"Around nine, I should think. He will be so happy to see Samantha."

Jake wanted to ask why he hadn't bothered to "see" her for the past twenty years, but figured it was better to stay out of it. He'd already gotten more involved in Sam's life than he needed to be. It was hard to believe, considering he'd only known her for a day. He chalked it up to the situation. He wasn't going to get any closer than he had to.

He walked down the street, the film tucked safely in his pocket, mulling over the most recent events. Now that he had the film, he could find out who was after them. But that couldn't begin to answer all his questions. Not by a long shot.

Party revelers were already coming out of the woodwork and the sun hadn't even begun to go down. Jake moved through the crowds, the smell of conch fritters and beer filling the air. He ducked into one of the many quickie photo labs and dropped the film off, only to be told he'd have to wait until the next morning to pick it up because they were so busy.

Convinced that nothing was going to get done until tomorrow, Jake slipped back out into the street. "Let's go, Fletch. We have to buy some clothes."

The thought of Sam back at the inn, practically naked, made Jake's mouth go dry. For the first time in a long time, he wanted a drink. Badly.

Sam took a long, cool shower, standing under the spray until she felt the tension ebbing away. Grateful for the little bottles of shampoo and conditioner the hotel provided, she scrubbed her hair until it squeaked. After being cooped up in the van, it felt nice to be clean again.

She stepped out of the shower and towel-dried her hair, wishing for a blow dryer. It would take hours to air-dry her thick hair.

Sam wrapped herself in another fluffy towel and returned to the bedroom. She wished Jake had thought to bring up the bags before leaving. She'd have to sit around in a damp towel until he got back. The thought of being half naked when he returned did terrible things to her senses.

A shiver glided over her skin at the memory of their kiss back in Miami. A flush spread through her, undermining the cold shower. She suddenly felt very warm.

Sitting on the edge of the bed, she turned on the television. She flipped through the channels until she found the evening news and sat through the local and state news. When the sportscaster came on, she sighed in relief. They hadn't made the headlines here—yet.

Sam felt the first real hunger pang she'd felt in weeks. It felt good to be hungry; normal, even. She realized the drugs were working their way out of her system. The dizzy spells and light-headedness still plagued her, but the hallucinations hadn't come back. She was beginning to feel more like her old self.

Sam stared at the television screen, hardly aware of the weather report or the dapper weatherman promising sunny days ahead. She was somewhere else, in a time before all the madness had started.

She rubbed at her hair with the towel. The damp tendrils trailing down her back made her shiver. How had this happened to her? She'd left New York because she was tired of the danger, the pressure, the constant demands. Somehow, this wasn't what she'd had in mind.

A rap on the door startled her out of her dark thoughts. Cautiously, she crossed to the door. "Who is it?"

"Jake."

She opened the door and was nearly flattened by Fletcher. "Hey, get off me!" She pushed at the exuberant dog with one hand, keeping a tight grip on her towel with the other.

With his hands full of luggage, Jake had Fletcher's leash looped around his wrist. He dropped the bags and pulled Fletcher back so he could unsnap his leash. "He missed you." His expression was unreadable as he took in her too-short towel and damp hair. "That the best you could do?"

"What did you expect? For me to make an outfit out of the curtains?" she snapped, yanking the plastic boutique bag from the pile of luggage. "I assume this is for me?"

A long, slow smile crossed his face. "All yours," he drawled.

Sam peeked inside the bag and frowned. "Are you sure there's an outfit in here? Looks like you left part of it back at the store."

"Try it on," he urged. "The store closes in twenty minutes, so if it's too small I can exchange it."

Too small. He couldn't have said too big. Sam stomped off to the bathroom without a backward glance and slammed the door. She dumped the contents of the bag on the bathroom floor. He'd bought her some kind of sundress, it looked like. She picked it up and marveled at the softness of the deep green material. It would never fit, though. It looked barely large enough to clothe a Barbie doll.

Sam shook her head. What had he been thinking? The only

other thing in the bag was a pair of tan leather sandals. Those, at least, looked like they would fit.

"Well? Does it fit?" Jake's impatient voice drifted through the door.

"I don't think so." She frowned at her reflection in the mirror. She wasn't about to tell him that it was too small. "I think it's a little too big."

Jake rattled the doorknob. "Let me see."

"Will you wait a second?" Exasperated, Sam knew he wasn't going to leave her alone until she showed him the dress. Or told him the truth—that the damn thing was meant for Kate Moss, not her.

"Let me see," he said again.

She let the soggy towel fall to the floor, her skin prickling with goose flesh. Funny, it didn't feel cold in here. Reluctantly she pulled the dress over her head, hoping the garment wouldn't burst at the seams. But she was surprised when it slid down her body and swirled around her hips. Looking into the mirror again, she caught her breath.

Instead of making her look pasty, the deep green color complemented her pale skin tone. The spaghetti straps caressed her shoulders, while the dipping neckline hinted at her ample attributes in a way she never could have imagined. The dress was a little snug across the bust, but not uncomfortably so, and the waist seemed to fit her perfectly. The hem was mid-thigh—the same length as the towel she'd been wearing, but much more flattering. She had to admit, she looked good. Damn good.

"Well?" It sounded like Jake was leaning against the bathroom door.

"Ready or not," she muttered under her breath. She opened the door and stepped out into the room.

Jake didn't say anything. He didn't even blink. He just stared.

"What do you think?" she asked him, taking a tremendous amount of pleasure from his stricken expression.

Jake still didn't speak, but the look in his eyes told her enough.

She stepped back into the bathroom to get the sandals. "Thanks," she murmured, brushing past him on the way to the bed.

He caught her by the arm and pulled her around, staring into her eyes. "You look great," he said hoarsely.

"I could use a little makeup." He was making her self-conscious, staring at her like that.

"You don't need it."

She felt the warmth in her cheeks spiraling downward. "It's a little young for me." She tugged at the low neckline, suddenly wishing she'd never put the dress on at all.

He pulled her hand away from her chest and gave her a long look that sent a shiver down her back even as his gaze trailed over her body. "It's perfect for you. You're perfect."

His eyes came up to her face. When they focused on her mouth, she knew he was thinking about the kiss. Suddenly the temperature in the room shot up. He dropped her hand and stepped back, his jaw tightening with some emotion she couldn't begin to decipher.

Sam sat on the edge of the bed and concentrated on figuring out how to put the sandals on. They were the softest leather she'd ever felt, with long laces that wrapped around her ankles and calves. She got them on and wrapped the laces, tying them securely. It hardly felt like she had shoes on at all. They were gorgeous and comfortable, but hardly appropriate under the circumstances. These sandals were made for leisurely strolls on the beach, not for running from bad guys.

She looked up and met Jake's intense gaze. Her words froze in her throat as his eyes burned into her. Ducking her head, she said, "Thanks for the clothes. But this is a little fancier than I expected."

"Well, it's better than what you were wearing," he answered gruffly. He turned his attention to his own bag, pulling out a pair of faded jeans and a white oxford-cloth shirt.

Sam stared as he undid the button of his jeans. Her pulse fluttered erratically as she watched his masculine hands at his waistband. For a fleeting moment she wondered if he intended to strip in front of her, but then he crossed to the bathroom and closed the door firmly without another word.

Something was on Jake's mind. And she wondered if it was her.

Fifteen minutes later, he came out of the steamy bathroom, his shirt unbuttoned. She could see the muscles of his flat stomach bunch under her gaze. He exuded a masculine strength that would have made her toes curl if she'd been the kind of woman to fall for that whole macho thing. As it was, she had to remind herself to breathe. He ran a hand through his damp hair and then buttoned his shirt and tucked it into his jeans.

"Are we going somewhere?" she asked finally, uncomfortable with the silence.

"I figured you might be hungry."

Her stomach growled in answer. "Good guess."

"Then let's go." He opened the door for her and she stepped around him, more than a little conscious of his eyes on her.

"What about Fletcher?"

At hearing his name, the dog pricked up his ears. He sat by the bed, wagging his tale earnestly.

Jake shook his head. "Sorry, buddy. Adults' night out."

As if understanding, Fletcher stretched out by the bed and flopped over on his side.

"He'll be fine," Jake said. "Besides, I don't want any of our friends to be waiting for us when we come back."

Sam turned wide eyes on him. "Do you think they know we're here?"

He locked the door and pocketed the key. "I don't know. But Fletcher will keep them away if they show up."

Sam inclined her head. "Are you sure? He doesn't seem so tough to me."

With his hand firmly on her elbow, Jake guided her down the stairs. "Trust me. When the chips are down, Fletcher knows what to do."

Chapter 10

"Where are we going?" Sam asked as she fell into step beside Jake. They headed down the street, joining the crowds of people spilling out onto the sidewalk from various stores and cafés.

"You'll see."

Jake's arm draped casually around her shoulders. Her skin warmed under his touch, sending her senses reeling. At her questioning look, he said simply, "I don't want you to get lost."

Sam started to argue, but the comfortable pressure of his arm kept her quiet. They followed the stream of people down the narrow street. Everyone seemed to be headed in the same direction.

"Where is everyone going?"

Jake's arm tightened around her. "To watch the sunset."

"But—"

"Shh. You'll see."

They joined a huge crowd in what looked like a parking lot by the ocean. The sun was dipping low in the sky, casting long shadows across the water. Tourists jockeyed for position at the water's edge and Jake led Sam to a small dock. The sound of bagpipes filtered through the air as a brawny-looking man in a kilt strolled by.

A woman on a bike offered cookies for sale, while a man with a large snake wrapped around him enthralled a small group of people by swallowing a sword.

"What is this?" Sam asked, taking in the various other attractions, including a magic show and a man with at least a dozen cats.

"Mallory Square's nightly sunset," Jake said, grinning.

"You mean they do this every night?" Sam watched another magician at the end of the dock pull a rabbit out of a battered top hat.

"Every night like clockwork."

"But why?"

He winked. "It's a celebration, Sam. Don't ask why."

She felt warmth pool low in her belly when his arm slipped from her shoulders to her waist. A group of tourists walked by and a swaggering teenager bumped into Sam, causing her to lean heavily against Jake before regaining her balance. She pulled away, mumbling, "Sorry."

His arm tightened around her as he drew her closer. "It's all right," he murmured against her hair. She looked up at him, but his attention was on the setting sun.

Sam had to admit he was doing some strange things to her senses. She would have liked to blame it on the drugs, but she knew better. Of course, she didn't have to admit it to him. Sneaking a glance at him from under her lashes, she traced the angular planes of his face with her eyes. She'd gotten to know his features almost as well as she knew her own.

"What are you thinking?"

He'd caught her watching him and she blushed, thankful for the deepening shadows. "Just how strange it is to be so comfortable with you."

His expression was unreadable. "This whole thing is strange, Sam."

"Yeah." For one precious moment she'd almost forgotten what had brought them here. She forced a smile. "Thanks for reminding me."

A cheer went up from the crowd and she turned her gaze to the ocean. The sun lit the water like fire as it disappeared from the horizon. She felt Jake's breath on her cheek a moment before his hand came up to cradle her chin. She looked up into those brooding eyes, losing herself in them. Seconds later, his lips descended on hers.

She melted against him as the kiss deepened into a soul-searing embrace. It reminded her of the sun and ocean coming together. The world fell away and it was just the two of them, standing on the dock, locked on to each other.

"Let's forget about everything for tonight," he murmured against her lips.

This whole thing was insane. Jake knew it and he didn't care. He liked the way Sam felt in his arms. He liked the way she pulled him close, wrapping her arms around him and pressing her gorgeous curves against him. She had him hot and hard and he didn't care. Crazy or not, he wanted her.

She pulled back from him and he could read the desire in her emerald eyes. And the confusion. "What was that all about?" Her breathless voice and pink, inviting lips did nothing to quell his lust.

"Tradition," he answered, taking a step away from her. It was partly true, but tradition had nothing to do with the way he'd kissed her.

"Oh." She turned away from him to watch the sun's final moments. "Tradition," she repeated.

As the crowd dispersed, Jake took her hand and headed away from Mallory Square into the heart of Key West. "Hope you like seafood,'' he said, trying to keep his mind off the woman beside him. It proved to be an impossible task.

He'd never expected the dress to look so good or to fit so well. It hugged every part of her, giving his imagination a healthy taste of what lay beneath.

He knew better than this. He knew better than to get involved with Sam. She was trouble. Correction: she was a hell of a woman, and under different circumstances... But it didn't make sense to dwell on what might have been. Trouble seemed to follow Sam—and him, as long as he was with her. The sooner he got away from her, the better.

''That's fine,'' she replied, her mind clearly elsewhere.

They walked to Haley's, an open-air café on a busy corner. The restaurant was already packed. Jake elbowed his way through the crowd, holding Sam's hand tightly in his. He claimed a table by the street just as the band began to play. While Sam watched the band, he watched her.

He could hardly believe that this was the same woman he'd rescued from the glades only yesterday. She looked calm, self-possessed. She absorbed the activity around them with the sharp awareness only a photographer could have. He was glad to see that she seemed to have recovered from the worst effects of the drugs. But he knew it would be days before she felt like her old self. By then she would be long gone from his life if everything worked out the way it was supposed to. For some reason he didn't want to analyze, that thought left a bad taste in his mouth.

The band launched into a lively rock tune that vibrated the floor and made talking impossible. A young, harried-looking waitress came over and leaned close to Jake. ''What do you want?'' she yelled.

Jake leaned close to Sam. ''You want me to order for you?''

Sam waved her hand and nodded, her concentration focused on the music. Jake placed their order and the waitress pressed through the crush of people to the bar. Turning back to Sam, Jake saw the glazed look in her eyes and his stomach clenched into a knot.

"Sam? You all right?" His hand reached out to steady her as she swayed toward him.

She gave him an apologetic smile. "Sorry. Just feeling a little dizzy."

He rested his arm along the back of her chair. He was close enough to kiss her if he wanted to. And he did want to, but knew it was wiser to keep his distance. "It'll get better," he said. "You just need to get some food in you."

She nodded. The haunted look in her eyes reminded him of the photograph on the wall at the Martins'. He wanted to ask her about it but figured she'd clam up like before. He wasn't going to ruin tonight by telling her he'd gone back to her father's house. He'd meant what he said at Mallory Square. He wanted to forget about everything for tonight.

The waitress brought back their drinks and Sam's eyes went wide as she placed a mug of beer in front of Jake. Sipping her soda, she eyed him suspiciously.

"Two-drink minimum," he said, shrugging. He turned to the table next to them and offered the beer. A beefy guy in a loud shirt grinned and took it.

"I didn't say anything," she countered.

"But you would have if I'd turned up the mug."

She tilted her head toward him, her expression serious but green eyes twinkling with mischief. "Nope. I would have up-ended that mug on your head and given you hell."

He grinned. "That's the kind of hell I could get used to."

The waitress returned with another beer and two plates heaped with fried shrimp and calamari. Jake passed off the second beer and ordered a soda for himself. The waitress winked at him. "Good for you."

The band took a break and he and Sam were able to talk at a comfortable level. She bit into a shrimp and rolled her eyes heavenward. "This is delicious."

"The best on the island." Jake dug into his own food. Funny how the food always tasted better down here. He felt like he'd come home.

Echoing his thoughts, Sam said, "It's almost easy to forget the trouble I'm in."

Jake reached over and ran his fingertips across her lips. "Stop. We're not going to talk about any of that tonight. Tonight is festival time. Enjoy it." He didn't have to add the words *while it lasts*—he could see it in her eyes.

The band started playing again, doing a lively rendition of an old tune. Sam's eyes lit up. Tables were moved out of the way as couples got up to dance. Sam watched them and Jake could detect a note of wistful longing in her eyes. He didn't even realize what he was going to say until he heard the words coming out of his mouth.

"Want to dance?"

Whatever his misgivings, Jake was rewarded with a faint smile. At Sam's hesitant nod, he led her out onto the makeshift dance floor. He didn't know what he'd been thinking. He wasn't much of a dancer. He didn't even like to dance. But after fifteen seconds on the dance floor with Sam, it didn't seem to matter.

She moved like a Florida panther, smooth and lithe. She wasn't one of those willowy, blond model-types—all pointy angles. Sam had the most luscious curves he'd ever seen. Her hips swayed to the beat and her hair swirled in a golden swath around her bare shoulders. Jake was mesmerized and moved without thinking, following her motions with something close to awe. Sam's head was tossed back, her eyes closed, and for a moment he would have sworn she was in the throes of passion.

The song ended—not that Jake noticed—and the band moved right into a slow, sensuous ballad. It was as if they'd been watching Sam dance, too. She ducked her head self-consciously and headed back to their table. But Jake reached out for her wrist and pulled her back onto the dance floor and into his arms. She melted against him, fitting perfectly. He knew he was hard, could feel the rigid length pressing against his jeans. But there weren't any recriminations in Sam's eyes as she looked up at him. Only awareness.

"You're an incredible dancer," he murmured in her ear as her arms came up to drape around his neck. He liked that she smelled of soap and woman, instead of perfume.

Her smile was slow, languid, fitting the mood of the song. "Thanks."

For a moment, the shadows disappeared and he felt himself grow harder because her smile was for him. Because of him. She was slightly out of breath and he wondered if it was from the dancing or from the growing sexual tension between them. They swayed to the steady beat, barely moving on the crowded dance floor. At some point, he lost the ability to know where he stopped and she started. It was as if they were making love fully clothed. He groaned.

"Something wrong?"

She pressed against him subtly and he had no doubt that she knew exactly what was wrong with him. He brushed a stray piece of hair back from her cheek and looked into her eyes. He could drown in those eyes.

"Nothing you can't cure," he said. His brain must have gone on vacation for him to say something so sappy.

But she only smiled. "I'll have to see what I can do about that." She tucked her head against his chest and swayed her hips in a way that left no doubt about her intentions.

"What's that?" Sam asked as Jake led her out of the restaurant and back into the street.

The driving beat of reggae music got louder as they merged with the growing crowd. She didn't know what she'd been thinking at the restaurant. Something about Jake made her feel reckless, and a little wild. She'd lost all inhibitions while they danced, feeling free for the first time since leaving Sunlight and Serenity. He didn't help matters much. He watched her with eyes that seemed to see everything, know everything. He wanted her. She'd felt his arousal as they'd slow-danced and had felt her body respond in kind. Their attraction to each other didn't make any sense. It was irrational, illogical. Dangerous.

Jake started across the street, past a tattoo parlor and an occult bookstore. "Parade," he answered, close to her ear. His arm wrapped tightly around her waist and she enjoyed the strength of him, the feeling of being protected.

"It's been years since I've seen a parade."

"I promise you've never seen anything like this."

Before she could ask him what he meant, the procession came into view, led by a ragtag band of musicians. The parade was a bizarre scene, complete with floats and costumes.

The float in the lead was a giant silver cylinder, with glitter and metal reflecting the bright white lights that decorated the length of it. A utility truck masqueraded as the base for the creation, while diaphanous material shaped into wings swept out into the street on both sides. At first, Sam thought it was an alien, or perhaps some nightmarish angel.

"It's a mosquito," Jake said in response to her puzzled look.

Sam laughed, finally recognizing the creation. The float motored past as a group of men, dressed in coconut-shell bras and grass skirts, danced by, playing "I Feel Pretty" on kazoos.

After that, Sam lost track of things. There was something surreal and almost frightening about the parade. She shivered, feeling suddenly claustrophobic. Jake took her hand and pulled her onto a side street, away from the crowd that pressed in on them from every side.

"Are you ready to go back?" he asked.

She looked up at him in the shadows, his expression lost in the darkness. "If you are."

A smile quirked at the corner of his mouth and he nodded. "I think I've had enough fun for one night."

They were standing close—only inches apart—and Sam could feel the heat of his body. Tension crackled between them, so sharp and clear it was almost tangible. He started to lower his head and she held her breath, waiting. But then something caught his attention over her shoulder and he jerked back.

"What? What is it?"

He looked past her. "I thought I saw—" He shook his head and gave her a halfhearted smile. "Never mind. It's nothing."

She knew it was something, but didn't press it. The moment was over and when he took her hand again it was only so they wouldn't get separated as they rejoined the crowd.

"Let's go home," he said.

Home. She wondered when she'd know what that word meant.

It had to be the beer. Sure, he didn't drink any of it, but maybe he absorbed it through osmosis. Yeah, that had to be it. As Jake and Sam walked back to the inn, he wondered what in the hell had gotten into him. He was thinking more about taking Sam to bed than the trouble they were in. She mesmerized him with her laughter, paralyzed him with the look in her eyes and aroused him with her earthy beauty.

It was bad enough that he'd gotten dragged into her life, her problems, but suddenly he wanted to know what she would feel like in bed. It wasn't a good thing. Nothing good could possibly come out of a relationship with her. Hell, relationships had never been his strong point, anyway.

"It's beautiful," she said, as they strolled past the beach.

It was beautiful. The moon reflected off the dark ocean waves and the sand shimmered before them like an oasis. Jake could almost forget why they were here. Almost.

Instinctively, he cast a look over his shoulder. They were safe for now. But for how long? His gut told him that this moment of reprieve was the calm before the storm.

He could have sworn he'd seen the same sedan tonight that had been at the diner. Could they have been tracked down that quickly? He knew now that the goons at the diner and Manning's organization weren't connected, but that didn't make him feel any better. Twice as many people after them meant twice as many chances of getting caught. And getting killed.

As if sensing his tension, Sam moved a little closer to him. Their hands came together of their own accord and Jake enjoyed the feel of her fingers entwined with his. It was nice to have Sam on his arm as they strolled down the quiet, moonlit street. It felt...right.

"What's the matter, Jake?"

She was forever asking him what was wrong, what he was thinking. It drove him mad, but then again, it was kind of nice. "Just figuring out what we're going to do tomorrow." He hadn't told her about the film. He knew she would be angry with him for going back to her father's house without her. And right now, he didn't want her mad at him.

She stopped on the sidewalk, her hair shimmering like spun gold. She looked up at him and flashed him a wistful smile. "We're not supposed to think about anything tonight. Remember?"

His arms came around her, settling on her hips as he pulled her closer. "But there's a problem. I can't stop thinking about you." He bent his head, tasting her lips.

She molded her body to his, every curve fitting so tightly against him he didn't think he'd be able to breathe. Her tongue touched his, tentative at first, then inviting as he deepened the kiss. Her fingertips trailed down his back, then up again, scratching lightly at his shirt. He groaned into her mouth as she shifted closer, the thin material of her dress reminding him how little she was wearing.

She pulled back, her heavy-lidded eyes speaking volumes. "I think we should go back to the room." Her voice was husky and oh, so sexy.

Wordlessly, he took her hand as they walked. This was a mistake, his mind warned. His body didn't seem to care, reacting to just the scent of her on his clothes. They hardly spoke as they reached the hotel and climbed the stairs, his eyes on her well-rounded backside as she led the way.

His rational mind warred with his emotions. Sam was still withdrawing from the drugs. Her mood swings were to be expected. But what was his excuse for being so damn irrational? Lust. That was all it was. All it could be.

His passion had cooled only slightly by the time they got back to the room. But Jake had forgotten something. As soon as he fit the key in the door and opened it for her, he remembered. Fletcher. The dog shook himself awake, his tail thumping on the floor as he greeted them with a long howl. The sensual spell was broken with one slurp from the excited mutt.

"Sorry, big guy. Didn't mean to forget you." He gave Sam an apologetic shrug. "I have to take him for a walk and get his dog food out of the van."

Sam avoided his gaze. "That's all right. I'm getting a little sleepy. I think I'll just get ready for bed." She turned her back on him and started rummaging through her bag.

"I'll be back in a little while." Jake closed the door behind him and cursed his rotten luck.

Fletcher let out a low woof of agreement and pulled him downstairs and out to the street.

Chapter 11

Sam didn't want to take the dress off. She liked the way the soft fabric glided across her skin like silk. And she liked the way she looked in it—feminine and almost sexy. Most of all, she liked the way Jake had looked at her. She sighed and sat down on the end of the bed, wondering just what would have happened if Fletcher hadn't been there. If her feelings hadn't been in such a turmoil, she would have laughed.

One thing was for sure, she wanted Jake like she'd never wanted any other man. And it scared her. They hardly knew each other and yet she could imagine making love with him. She shivered. She knew what he meant about active imaginations.

The door swung open with a noisy bang and Fletcher bounded into the room. She started, not realizing how long she'd been sitting there. Jake followed, his expression unfathomable in the dim gloom. He set the box he was carrying on the floor, fishing out a large bowl and a bag of crunchy dog food.

"C'mon, Fletcher. I thought you were hungry," he said to the dog who was sniffing Sam's legs.

It irked Sam that after the hot and heavy kiss they'd shared, Jake could just pretend that she wasn't even there. Fletcher abandoned Sam in favor of the dog bowl, chewing noisily. She glanced up at Jake, who stood leaning casually against the wall, watching her with an intense gaze.

"What?" she asked, unnerved by his steady appraisal.

His eyebrows shot up and he shrugged. "Nothing."

"Fine." Sam stood with a determination she didn't feel. She grabbed the shirt she intended to sleep in from the end of the bed, keeping her gaze safely averted. If she looked at him she'd fall apart.

He held out a shopping bag. "Here. I meant to give this to you earlier. It's some clothes for tomorrow."

"Thanks."

When she didn't take the bag from him, he put it on the dresser. "You okay?"

She ignored his question and the intensity in his voice. "I'm going to change and go to bed." It was later than she'd realized; too late to be playing games with Jake.

"Wait," he said, his voice low and husky, but nonetheless compelling.

"What?"

"You're beautiful."

They stood a room's length apart, separated by a large, hungry dog, but Sam felt his eyes on her like a caress. "Thanks for the dress. And for tonight."

"It's not over, Sam."

She didn't ask what he meant. She didn't need to. The burning in his eyes answered her questions as he sidestepped Fletcher and crossed the room. He stood in front of her, hands at his sides. His well-formed lips compressed into a thin line as he contemplated her.

"It's not over," he repeated, his voice rough with emotion.

His arms came up and around her. She could feel the heat of him, radiating through the thin material of her dress and warming her skin to a feverish pitch. She shivered as he ran his hands down her shoulders, pulling her hips against him. She stared into his face, not ready to give in to the emotions that flooded her senses.

"What is this, Jake? What are we doing?"

"Let me show you."

His lips came down on hers, warm and demanding, as he picked up where they had left off on the street. He kissed her until she went weak in the knees, unable to think of anything except this man. He trailed kisses down her neck and across her collarbone, bringing a whimper to her throat as she shivered with delicious anticipation.

His hands roamed her back, sliding effortlessly over the silken material, scorching her skin beneath. He cupped her bottom in his hands, pulling her up against his hardened shaft. She moaned aloud then, wanting what he offered, needing what only he could give her.

"I've been wanting to strip this dress off you all night."

Sam's breath caught in her throat as his mouth descended over her nipple through the fabric of the dress. It hardened under his gentle tugging.

"Then do it, Jake."

He groaned.

Surging up against her, every inch of his muscular body caressed her. His callused fingertips stroked her shoulders gently, sliding the straps of her dress down her arms. She shivered with awareness. The material clung to her curves and a gentle tug from Jake left her naked from the waist up. His gaze glided across her breasts and she felt her nipples tighten in anticipation.

"God, you're beautiful." He knelt before her, cupping her breasts in the palms of his hands, squeezing them, stroking them until she groaned.

"Jake!"

"Yes, darlin'," he drawled, his lips and tongue bringing her nipples to sensitive hardness.

"You're making me crazy," she gasped. Her hands descended to his shoulders, kneading the warm muscles beneath his shirt.

He looked up at her, his eyes cloudy with his passion. "Not half as crazy as you're making me."

Her dress clung to her hips and Jake's hands slid beneath the silky fabric to caress them. He hooked her panties with his thumbs and skimmed them down her thighs. She trembled under his touch, quivering not from withdrawal from the drugs, but from the heady effect he had on her senses.

He got to his feet, pulling her dress over her head in one swift motion that left her naked to his gaze. A soft moan caught in the back of her throat at the look in his eyes. He wanted her.

"You are so incredible," he murmured, pulling her into his arms again, burying his face in her hair.

The rough fabric of his jeans did wild things to the tender skin of her thighs. She pressed closer, needing his touch. "Make love to me, Jake," she whispered against his shoulder, afraid he would say no. Afraid he would say yes.

"I thought you'd never ask." He scooped her up in his arms.

"Jake, put me down. I'm too heavy."

He grinned that devastating, all-male grin of his. "Trust me, this time I don't mind carrying you at all."

He went to the bed and gently laid her across it. She watched him in breathless anticipation as he shed his shirt. His broad chest rippled with muscles as he undid the first button on his jeans.

His gaze caressed every inch of her, seeming to drink her in. The bed sagged under his weight as he sat beside her. He took her in his arms again and rained kisses down on her face and neck. His hands teased her breasts until they felt full and heavy. Then his fingers slid lower, finding the slick entrance of her, ready for him. She moaned.

"You want me," he said, and it was true. She clung to him as his fingers dipped inside, bringing forth wetness and warmth.

"Jake!" Her hands went to the waistband of his jeans. "I want you naked."

He chuckled, but it was an erotic sound that inflamed her. "Impatient, aren't you?" But he obliged, standing again and shedding his jeans and briefs.

His arousal was apparent, straining upward. She moaned again, her imagination vividly anticipating what he would do. She held out her arms to him and sighed when he joined her again, flesh against flesh. They were both breathing hard and she could feel his heartbeat accelerate under her touch. She let her hands trail down his waist, marveling at the muscular strength of him. Wrapping her fingers around him, she stroked him until he groaned against her hair and rolled her over onto her back.

"Not so fast," he growled. "I want to take this nice and slow."

She arched her hips, so ready for him. "Jake," she breathed against his lips.

Poised above her, his velvet-soft tip so close to touching her wetness, he looked into her eyes. His features lost their intensity and his voice was quiet and somber when he spoke. "I haven't been with anyone in a while. A really long while."

Realizing what he was saying, she smiled. "Me neither."

"I don't like danger in bed," he said, planting a gentle kiss on the tip of her nose.

She was practically writhing with her need, wanting him inside her. "Neither do I."

His eyes regained that hooded, lust-filled look. "Good." He prodded her slick entrance. "You're so wet."

She quivered from the erotic words. "For you." She raised her hips slightly, taking just the tip of him inside her. "Now, Jake. Now."

He complied, sliding deep within her, filling her. He was big, but she was more than ready for him and her body opened to accommodate his size. He stilled for a moment, staring into her eyes. They were joined in the most intimate way possible and she felt time stand still. Her pulse raced as she shifted her hips ever so slightly, bringing a groan to his lips.

"I want to make it last," he said, slowly thrusting into her.

She moved against him, moaning into his shoulder as he made love to her. Her hands trailed down his back to his muscular buttocks as she pulled him deeper into her. Her nails raked his shoulders as he thrust more urgently, building up the tempo of their lovemaking.

Moonlight filtered through the curtains, casting shadows across the planes of Jake's face. But she didn't need to see him to know what he was thinking and feeling. He shifted slightly, until his erection rubbed the point of her desire. He pressed his lips to her neck, nipping lightly, making her moan. He ran his tongue around the shell of her ear, his breath heavy and hot. Sam's body wrapped around him, pulling him deeper, enveloping his hardness. She felt her passion building as he coaxed her to the height of erotic awareness.

Gasping, Sam clung to him as she was swept into the darkness. Reality ceased to exist; the world was only Jake inside her, driving her over the edge into oblivion. Moments later, she felt him go rigid above her, groaning her name as he thrust deeply one last time.

He eased over onto his side, bringing her with him. They were both breathing harshly, and she was still caught up in the throes of her pleasure when he chuckled.

"What?" she asked, hearing the tremor in her voice.

He pulled her closer and his fingers were gentle against her cheek, his voice deep and drowsy. "That dress was the best investment I ever made."

He twined his fingers in her hair, reveling in the softness of the silken strands. The curves of her warm, pliant body fit perfectly to the hard angles of his. "You're a hell of a woman, Samantha Martin."

She let out a breathy sigh that went straight to his groin as she turned in the circle of his arms. Her breasts pressed tightly against his chest and he took immense pleasure in the languid, satisfied expression on her face. "I'll take that as a compliment."

"It is."

She tucked her head against his shoulder, her fingers tracing idle patterns in his chest hair until he shivered. "I don't normally do this."

"This?" He chuckled, feeling sleep tug at him. Not yet, not just yet. "There's nothing normal about any of this."

She sighed again, pressing the sweetest, gentlest kiss on his jaw. "I know. So much for playing it safe."

"Is that what you were doing, Sam? Playing it safe?"

She nodded, her hair brushing across his shoulder. "I thought so."

"Why?" He wanted to know. He knew so little about her past and nothing about her future.

"It hurts too much, otherwise. You can't get involved, can't care."

He didn't think she was talking about him, judging by the raw tone of her voice. "What do you mean?" He didn't expect her to answer, but she did.

"I was in Central America, doing a photo layout on the resort port cities. I met all the dignitaries, got to dress up and act civilized. I was tired of living in huts, drinking God-only-knows-what, taking showers once in a blue moon."

He forced a lighthearted tone. "Sounds like the way you looked when I found you."

"Yeah, well, it was my job. I covered all the things no one else wanted to. Third World civil wars, disasters, disease breakouts, endangered African animals. We called it the Peace Corps beat."

"It must have gotten old after a while."

"I liked it. It was tough, demanding. Lonely. But I was good at it. Still, I snapped at the chance to be pampered and sleep in a real bed. Then everything came crashing down around my ears."

"What?" He tensed, bracing for her words although he didn't know what to expect.

"My editor called, wanted me to hike to some remote mountainous region to cover a famine. It was a day's trip and I wasn't very excited about the prospect." She laughed bitterly. "It wasn't like I hadn't covered that kind of thing a dozen times before."

Jake had seen the aftermath of famine spread out across the daily news. He couldn't imagine what it must be like to face it in person. "It must have been difficult."

"Not at first." Her voice was dead, empty. "If you've seen one famine, you've seen them all."

"Sam," he whispered hoarsely, wincing at the harsh tone of her voice. His heart lurched at the thought of Sam caught up in that sort of tragedy. Suddenly it was more than a headline, more than a story.

"I did what I was there for. Half the village had already been wiped out. Disease follows famine, of course. Most of the elderly and the very young were already gone." She took a deep breath. "They were the lucky ones."

"Tell me what happened."

"I was supposed to be there for a couple of days. But my guide got sick and I was stuck there for nearly a week. We'd brought supplies, food and fresh water."

"But not enough for a week," he guessed.

"Right. We rationed it, eating in our tent so we wouldn't have to look at them—" Sam's voice broke on the last word. "I wanted to share what we had, but Benji, my guide, said there wouldn't be enough."

"There was nothing you could do," he soothed, knowing how empty the words were in the face of her agony.

"No. There wasn't. All I could do was take pictures. By the fifth day, I was feeling light-headed because I'd been giving most of my food to Benji." Her hand was clammy against his chest as her fingers curled into a fist. "He felt better and we decided to leave the next day. I intended to talk to their government, get them some emergency relief."

Jake could imagine what that had garnered her. "What happened?"

"That evening, a young woman came to me. She begged me to go with her."

The hair stood up on the back of his neck. "Did you?"

She nodded against his chest. "She took me to her house. She had two young children—a boy and a girl. She wanted me to take them when we left the village."

"Why?"

"They were sick." Sam's voice was thick with tears. "They'd eaten some spoiled food. She thought I could get help for them. She looked so frail herself, I don't know how she had the energy to walk."

"Wasn't there a doctor in the village?"

She shook her head. "He'd died. I wanted to take the children with me but Benji said they'd never make it. I didn't want to believe it, but he was right. They were dying."

Jake could feel moisture against his chest and realized she was crying.

"I stayed with her the rest of the night and held her hand. The children were so sick and she was terrified. I didn't know what to do." Sam's voice trailed off in the darkness. "By morning, the children were dead."

Jake had to swallow past the knot in his throat. "And the mother?"

"She was inconsolable." Sam turned her head into his shoulder and he held her tighter, trying to cushion her from the pain. "When we left the next morning, she stood apart from the others, watching me. I went to her and she hugged me like I'd done something."

"You did. You stayed with her."

Sam's hands moved restlessly against his chest. "It wasn't enough. I don't know why, but I took her picture as we were leaving." She sighed quietly. "I wanted to capture her strength in that picture."

It all clicked together in Jake's mind. "That was the Pulitzer."

She nodded against him. "Instead of helping her, I took her picture and won a prize."

"What else could you have done?"

Her voice broke, a dry sob escaping. "I don't know. I tried to go to the government. They didn't want to listen. I was asked to leave the country." She swiped at her eyes with the back of her hand. "I tried to find out what had happened to the village, but no one would give me any information."

Jake didn't know what to say to her. He'd seen enough people die to know that helpless feeling, that sense of unbearable loss. He'd felt it when Charlie was killed. He'd felt it at the diner.

"When I got back to the States, my editor wanted the pictures. I handed over the film. Two days later, they were plastered all over the wire." She shuddered in his arms.

"It was your job."

She sobbed quietly, wrapped up in her own grief. "I wanted to be a photographer, not witness misery and be helpless to do anything about it."

She rolled away from him, her back pale in the moonlight. His fingers caressed the nape of her neck. She looked so vulnerable. So alone. He was lost.

"Sam, Sam," he groaned, curling around her, trying to protect her from the demons that assailed her from within.

"I didn't want the Pulitzer. I tried to turn it down. I was taking new assignments, being careful not to get too involved, not to care too much. Then they had to go and reward me." She spat the words out, anger and pain oozing from her.

"I've seen the photograph," he murmured against her hair. "It's haunting. Incredible."

"Incredible? It was horrific. The prize money would have fed that village for a year. I gave the money to charity, hoping it would do some good." She sighed, her body going limp against his. "I didn't want the money. I never wanted what it represented."

"That picture you took reminds us all how fragile we are, Sam. You captured the essence of human existence."

"She was in so much pain. I couldn't forget her face, no matter how much I tried," Sam whispered, her body rigid as her own thoughts took her to a place she didn't want to go. "I watched her through the lens, thinking I was protected from her pain, numb to it." Sam twisted in his arms and he could see the tears shimmering on her lashes.

"Why did you leave New York?" He knew the answer, but also knew she had to say it.

"When the announcement I'd won came, it was like I was back there, with her. I couldn't live with myself for profiting from her pain. When the job in Atlanta came up, I took it. 'Safe, easy, nobody dies'—so much for that theory."

He pulled her close, feeling her tremble with emotion. She felt so good against him; but he couldn't think about pleasure, only about pain. Her pain.

It struck him that he wasn't so different from her. "When my partner died, I felt like that. I didn't want to be responsible for anyone. I didn't want to have anyone's life—or death—hanging over my head." He took a deep, shuddering breath. "We all have demons, Sam. You were just trying to conquer yours."

Her eyes closed and she sighed deeply. Jake could almost feel the tension unraveling in her as her body relaxed against him. "I know. I'd done pretty well, too. Until all this started happening to me. Until you."

"You'll get through this," he murmured, pressing a kiss to her cheek.

She nuzzled against him and he let out a groan as her arm went around his neck and she pulled his mouth down to hers. "I know. Thanks to you."

The kiss seared him with a white-hot jolt of arousal. "Any time," he whispered, delving into the satiny depths of her mouth, tasting her, tasting the salty tears. He couldn't get enough. Part of him—the self-preserving side—didn't want to be responsible for her happiness. But on a purer level, he wanted to erase her pain, make her forget. If only for tonight.

Jake pulled her over on top of him, so that she was straddling him. Her eyes still had that faraway, sad look, but her smile was pure sin. "How about now?"

Desire rumbled up through him, making him even harder than he already was. "Sure, sweetheart," he drawled. His hands spanned the softness of her hips, pulling her closer. He nudged the hot, wet center of her with his erection, drowning in her gasp of raw pleasure.

"Jake!"

His hands moved to her breasts, teasing her nipples into hard pebbles of arousal. "I promised you tonight," he said, filling her. "And tonight isn't over yet."

"I hope it never is," she murmured against his mouth.

Chapter 12

Sam woke up with a start, her heart pounding. Morning light was just beginning to creep into the room. The television in the corner was on, the eerie glow and sound of static reminding her where she was. Jake had turned the television on after they'd made love again, embarrassed by his need for noise. She remembered his confession about not wanting to be responsible for anyone and she wondered what demons still tormented him.

She could feel his warmth surrounding her like a cocoon. Sleeping with him felt right. Actually, when she thought about it, being with Jake was the only part of her life that seemed to make sense.

She was lying on her side, with Jake's arm draped over her, his fingers grazing her breast. She felt satiated, replete. And thirsty. She slipped out from under Jake's arm and slid to the edge of the bed. Sitting up, she jumped when her feet touched something warm and furry.

Fletcher let out a low woof and she petted his head. He really was a good dog, even if he wasn't the best watchdog. Edging

past him, she turned the air conditioner down, shivering in the
cool blast. As she carefully crossed to the bathroom, the sound
of Jake's even breathing let her know she hadn't woken him.
Funny, she'd expected him to be a light sleeper.

In the glare of the bathroom light, she washed her face. She
ran her tongue over her teeth and grimaced at her reflection in
the mirror. She'd kill for a toothbrush, but hadn't remembered to
tell Jake to buy one. She went back into the bedroom and opened
the bag he'd brought her. Two pairs of panties, a hot-pink Florida
T-shirt, a matching pair of shorts, and a pair of canvas sneakers.
No toothbrush or toothpaste, though. She could settle for the fin-
ger-brush trick until tomorrow if Jake had remembered to bring
toothpaste.

She went to the corner where he'd stacked their bags. She
hesitated for a moment, remembering how upset Jake had been
when he'd caught her with his duffel bag. He'd probably figured
she'd shoot him. How had they gotten from that total lack of trust
to last night? She smiled in the semidarkness, hauling the bag up
onto the dresser.

It was amazing how much had happened to her. Sunlight and
Serenity now seemed like a dim nightmare. But she couldn't for
one minute let herself forget that there were still people after
her—people who would do anything to keep her quiet. At least
she felt better, healthier. She was starting to feel like she had
some control over things now. Some say in what happened to her.

The zipper on the bag was impossibly loud in the quiet room.
Fletcher's head came up again, his tags jingling noisily. Sam cast
a glance in Jake's direction, but he slept on. A movement in the
darkness caught her eye and she froze. The doorknob was slowly
turning—so slowly she almost hadn't noticed it in the dimness.

Fletcher had seen it, too. He growled, low and quiet in his
throat. Sam quickly crossed to the bed and crouched beside it,
giving Jake a firm shake.

"What?"

She laid her fingers across his mouth. "Shh. Someone's trying to break in."

He was instantly alert, swinging his legs over the edge of the bed and pulling his jeans on. "Get dressed," he said softly as he went to the dresser and pulled out his gun.

Sam slipped back into her dress, her heart pounding in her chest, but her hands quick and steady. Jake motioned for her to stand beside him behind the door. Fletcher got to his feet, fur bristling.

"Fletcher, here," Jake commanded, his voice the barest whisper. But it was enough for the big dog, who moved to stand beside his master. "Stay back, Sam."

The words were barely out of his mouth when the door opened. Sam froze against the wall as a man about Jake's height but more heavily muscled moved into the room, gun extended. It didn't appear that anyone was with him. There was enough light for the man to see that the bed was empty. Apparently sensing a trap, he swung around just as Jake raised his weapon.

Jake's voice was deadly quiet. "Don't move."

The man's expression quickly changed from frozen surprise to cold calculation. He held up his hands, the gun dangling loosely from his fingers. "Don't shoot."

"Drop it."

The weapon thudded softly to the carpet.

Jake gestured toward the bed. "Get over there." To Sam he said, "Look in the box I brought up earlier. There's a roll of duct tape. Get it."

Sam skirted the bed, where the man sat at Jake's command. She found the heavy roll of duct tape. She knew they had to tie this guy up or he'd be after them again, but she didn't have any desire to get close to him.

"Wrap him up good, Sam."

She took a breath and approached the man. His eyes glittered in his hard-featured face but he didn't speak as she quickly bound his hands behind his back. She was sure the tape would hold, but she didn't want to take any chances and bound his feet, as well.

"Where's your partner?" Jake asked, never taking his eyes off their captive.

The man shrugged as best he could with his hands behind him. "I'm alone."

"Like hell. Next you'll tell me you weren't the one at the diner."

The man grinned with self-satisfaction. "Sure, that was me. Nice piece of work, I thought."

Jake's look was one of pure fury. "You killed a cop. Do you think you're just going to get away with it?"

"I already have."

"Why did you have to kill him? It was me you wanted," Sam said. She couldn't begin to understand the kind of predatory behavior that would allow one man to kill another in cold blood.

"He recognized us. 'No loose ends, no witnesses.' That's what I was told."

"By whom?" Jake asked.

"You'll find out soon enough."

Jake swore softly. "Slap a piece of tape over his mouth, too, Sam. I'm tired of listening to him."

Sam peeled off another length of tape and bit it in two with her teeth. She pasted it over the man's mouth, ignoring his last words before he was silenced: "You're going to die."

"Let's get the hell out of here," Jake said.

Sam couldn't have agreed more. She went quickly to the dresser, scooping up her clothes. Jake was patting down the guy on the bed and came up with another gun tucked inside his jacket.

Sam found her sneakers behind the door and slipped into them. There was no time to waste with the pretty sandals Jake had bought. Something—maybe the creak of the door or Fletcher's low woof—made her look up. A second man came into the room, so focused on Jake that he failed to see her.

Instinct took over and she grabbed for the only thing within arm's reach. The ceramic vase shattered on the back of the intruder's head and he crumpled to the floor, with plastic hibiscus fluttering around him. Fletcher stood over him, sniffing and growling. Jake whirled around, looking from the unconscious man to Sam.

"Nice going," he said with a grin. "Of course, you know we're going to be charged for that."

"It was worth it."

"Let's get this one tied up, too."

Jake tucked his gun in his waistband and together they got the second intruder over to the bed. They quickly bound him and then taped the two men back to back. Jake wrapped a length of tape around both men's ankles and secured it to a leg of the bed. Even if they managed to get up, they couldn't go anywhere.

"That should hold them."

Sam wasn't so sure. The one who had told her she was going to die watched her with a cold fury that made her shiver. "Let's get out of here," she whispered, turning away and gathering the rest of their stuff.

"Good idea." He pocketed the men's wallets and put their guns in his bag.

As a final measure, Jake put the Do Not Disturb sign on the door as they left the room. "That will buy us some time."

Sam nodded as he closed the door and locked it. She hoped Jake was right.

While Jake was inside the rental agency trading Annie's van for a compact car for the day, Sam changed clothes in the rear of the van. Even though Jake didn't want to drive back to Miami, he thought it would be better not to make it any easier for their friends back at The Flying Dolphin to find them. Sam couldn't agree more. As soon as they picked up the film and saw her father, she wanted to get out of town. The farther, the better.

Fletcher had staked out his space in the back seat and seemed content to settle down for a morning nap as they pulled out of the parking lot. It was barely eight o'clock.

A few minutes later Jake parallel-parked the car in front of a row of shops. He shut off the engine and turned to her. He cleared his throat, avoiding her eyes. "Look, there's something I didn't tell you."

Her skin prickled with unease. Keeping her voice calm, she asked, "What?"

"Yesterday, when I was out buying your clothes, I went back to your father's house to get the film and dropped it off to be processed, Sam."

Anger replaced her unease. "You told me it could wait."

"I wanted to be sure we had the film. Anything could happen. Manning was sure to get to a phone eventually." Jake looked out the windshield. "And I still haven't figured out how those two goons found us."

"So you went behind my back."

"It wasn't like that," he said. "I didn't want to take any chances."

She shook her head. "You didn't trust me."

"This has nothing to do with trust, Sam."

"Doesn't it?"

"No, it doesn't."

She didn't like the look in his eyes. It reminded her too much of the men back at the hotel—cold. He wanted to call the shots even though it was her life. "Look, maybe it's best if we split up here. They're looking for two of us. Maybe we'd both have a better chance alone."

A vein throbbed in his neck and she had the ridiculous urge to press her lips to it. "You have no money, you don't know who's after you. Where will you go?"

She shrugged. "I'll get the film and figure it out from there."

"Alone?"

That did it. "I was alone when all this started. I don't need you, Jake."

He gave her a cocky grin. "That's not what you were telling me last night." His eyes raked over her, setting her skin on fire.

"Forget about last night. It didn't mean anything."

His smile faltered. "Really? Is that what you think, Sam?"

"What I think is that last night I was regaining my freedom," she said quietly, not quite able to meet his gaze. "I did what I wanted with who I wanted. It didn't mean anything beyond that." Even as she said the words, her mind screamed that she was a liar. Jake had become an important part of her life in a short span of time. But she refused to admit that she was terrified to go on without him.

His face hardened into a cold mask. "Liberated lady, huh? You wanted to get laid, so you got laid."

She forced herself to keep from wincing at his harsh words. Instead, she nodded. "Exactly."

"Glad I could oblige. But we're in this together. My life is on the line, too—because of you. Once I'm cleared, I'll get out of your life. Until then, you're stuck with me."

She tried not to show her relief. She wasn't on her own. But she couldn't shake the guilt about what might happen to him just because he was with her. "Fine, Jake." She turned her head away. "Let's just get the pictures and go."

He started to say something. His jaw worked over the words, but then he shrugged. "Right."

He slammed the car door and walked into the photo shop while Sam waited. This was it. Those pictures were the key to everything. She had the irrational fear that there wouldn't be anything on them—that somehow, whoever was behind this had once again gotten the upper hand and destroyed the images. What if the only piece of evidence she had was gone?

Jake returned just when she had started to work herself into a paranoid panic. He got behind the wheel and held out the package of photos. "Here."

"Did you look at them?" she asked, her heart pounding. What if there wasn't anything in those pictures to help her?

"Not yet. I thought you'd want to."

It was a peace offering and she took it with a tentative smile. "Thanks."

Thumbing through the prints she had a strange, disconnected feeling. She recognized the pictures but it had been weeks since she'd taken them. She flipped through the images of Miami Beach and various architectural sites until she came to the telephoto-shots of the courthouse.

"Here's the courthouse," she said, stacking the prints on her knee. She'd taken pictures of the building from several angles and there were people in most of the shots. But the last few were the ones she knew were important. "These are the ones."

Eight photos showed the side and back of the courthouse. Two sedans were parked in the alley. Several men in dark suits were descending the back stairs. In the forefront of the last picture, she could see the shoulder of the security guard who had ordered her to leave.

She studied the images carefully, her eyes going from one figure to the next. All but one of the men were strangers to her. The last stirred some memory, but she couldn't pin down his name.

"Let me see." Jake took the photos from her and studied them. His grim expression told her more than his words could. "This doesn't make any sense, Sam."

"What do you mean? Do you recognize those men?"

Before he could answer her, a car door slammed behind them. Jake looked into the rearview mirror and cursed. His jaw tightened into a hard line. "Police."

The cop gave them a friendly smile as he walked into view. "Morning, folks."

Sam forced a smile, feeling her pulse accelerate erratically. "Morning, officer."

Jake nodded casually, his jaw clenched so tightly a vein throbbed. "Good morning."

"I have to ask you to move along. This space is ten-minute parking only."

Sam could see Jake's shoulder muscles relaxing against the seat. "Sorry about that. Just trying to decide what to do this morning."

"I understand." The cop nodded, his friendly smile firmly in place. "You might want to check out the south-side beach. I hear they're filming a spy movie over there. Might be good for a little excitement."

"Thanks for the suggestion." Jake started the car and nodded to the cop. "Have a good one."

The officer stepped back and Jake pulled out into the street. "Do you think he suspected anything?" Sam asked.

"If he did, he would have detained us."

"Do you know who is in the pictures, Jake?"

Instead of answering, he said, "Tell me again when you took these pictures."

"I told you. Five weeks ago. Why?" She didn't like the way he was avoiding her question.

"Is there any way you can prove that?"

"My editor can vouch for the fact that I was in Miami in February. I had a plane ticket, but I don't know what they did with my stuff—"

He shook his head, cutting her off. "No. I mean can you prove that you took those pictures when you say you did?"

She didn't understand what he wanted. "I don't know. Probably not. Why is that so important?"

"Because one of those men in the pictures is dead."

Shaking her head, Sam asked, "What does that have to do with me?"

"He's been dead for a while now."

She didn't want to ask but she had to. "How long, Jake?"

"Over a year."

Sam's eyes went wide as she stared at him. "That's impossible."

Jake didn't like this feeling. When he'd first looked at the pictures he had wondered if the drugs had altered Sam's perception of time. Next he'd wondered what kind of scam she was pulling. If he hadn't seen the false newspaper report of her death, he wouldn't have trusted her at all. Now he knew that these days, the impossible was more than likely possible.

"It's not only possible, Sam, it's probable. It's another setup. They faked your death, and they faked his death, too. The question is why?"

"Who is he, Jake?"

"The burly guy in the pinstripes is Carlos Montegna." He glanced over at her and when she didn't show any signs of recognition, he went on. "He was probably the most vicious of the Central American crime bosses."

"I thought he looked familiar. I know I've seen his picture before."

"His face was plastered in every police precinct from Florida to Canada. You name it, he was into it. Drugs, guns, mercenaries. His tight little band was invincible and deadly. I never ran into him, but every cop from rookie on up knew his reputation."

"What happened to him?" Sam's voice sounded faint.

"Big sting operation out of Tampa. His goons were wise to the coasties along Miami, so they were doing roundabout flights up the west side of the state." Jake recalled the details of Montegna's bust vividly even though he hadn't been on the force anymore. "But someone tipped the feds off and Montegna's plane was intercepted."

"And they supposedly killed him?"

Jake shook his head. "Montegna gave up peacefully enough. The word was that he'd cut a deal. Next thing I heard, he'd committed suicide in his cell."

Sam nodded slowly. "But they faked his death as part of the deal."

"That's what I'm thinking."

They were almost to Sam's father's house, but she didn't seem to notice. Every cop instinct in Jake's body screamed that they needed to get the hell out of Dodge. But he'd promised Amalinaú Martin they'd return. It hit him with sickening clarity that they might be putting the Martins in danger by being here. For once in his life, Jake wished he had a plan.

"Do you recognize any of the other men?" Sam asked.

The question pulled him out of his thoughts and he gave Sam a tight smile. He shook his head, negotiating the crowded streets. The last thing they needed was for him to run down a tourist. "I would have expected to see a familiar face or two there, but I don't recognize any of them. That's what has me worried."

"Why?"

"Because of what Manning said. Whoever he works for is after you. I think some of the men in your pictures are part of whatever government organization Manning works for. This is their dirty little secret."

Jake pulled up in front of the Martins' house and killed the engine. "And I'd bet my last dollar that those two at the hotel are Montegna's boys."

"Montegna is who Manning was talking about when he said someone else is after us."

"Right. But I don't like not knowing who Manning works for." It had been nagging at him since the confrontation on Big Pine Key. He had to know who Manning worked for in order to know where to start.

Jake watched Sam stare at her father's house. She tucked a loose strand of hair behind her ear, a nervous gesture that spoke volumes. She shouldn't be meeting her father like this. Jake wanted to fix her problems just as surely as he'd wanted to make love to her last night. But he knew better than to think he could help her. He'd failed too many people to take that chance again.

"We can't stay long, Sam," he said quietly.

She nodded, reaching for the door. "I know. I just want to see him. Okay?" The hopeful, pleading tone of her voice would be his undoing.

"There will be plenty of time to see him once this is over." His words sounded false to his own ears.

"I know."

"Do you want me to wait here?"

Sam shook her head. "No. I'd like you there." She flashed him one of those rare smiles that he couldn't get enough of. "I could use the moral support." With that, she climbed out of the car, looking at her father's house with something close to terror on her face.

They walked to the front door, Fletcher in the lead. Something—maybe it was his training or maybe it was the increasing evidence that their chances of surviving this ordeal were slim—made Jake glance back over his shoulder—just in time to see a black, windowless van turn the corner in their direction. Under normal circumstances, Jake wouldn't have thought twice about it. This wasn't normal.

Jake grabbed Sam's elbow as she raised her hand to knock on the door, but it was too late. Her knuckles grazed the door and it swung inward. She whipped her head around and saw the van. At her expression of fear, Jake knew she understood what it meant.

"It's a trap," he said.

Chapter 13

Clutching at Jake's arm, Sam braced herself for gunshots. But they never came. The door swung open and instead of armed killers, Amalinaú greeted them.

"Good morning. I'm so glad you came back." Stooping, she rubbed Fletcher's ears. In turn, the dog wagged his tail harder. "He sure is a friendly dog, isn't he?"

Sam nodded, her pulse pounding so hard she couldn't speak. The van traveled past them, never slowing nor showing signs of stopping. Still expecting gunfire, Sam grabbed Amalinaú's arm and pulled her into the house. Jake and Fletcher crowded in right behind them.

Through a crack in the door, Jake pointed to the retreating vehicle and asked Amalinaú, "Have you ever seen that van before?"

Squinting after the van, she nodded. "Sure. Don't know who it belongs to, but I've seen it around." She turned her curious gaze back to them. "Is this about the trouble you're in?"

Sam threw a startled look at Jake, who nodded. "I told Amalinaú the film would help straighten out the legal mess."

Sam caught his unspoken warning. He obviously hadn't told Amalinaú the extent of the trouble they were in. With the threat of danger over for the moment, Sam's heart began pounding for a different reason. She offered Amalinaú a hesitant smile. "Is my—my father home yet?"

The word "father" tripped over twenty years of abandonment and pain. Sam felt her cheeks grow warm as Amalinaú's penetrating eyes looked into her soul. Seemingly satisfied with what she saw, Amalinaú nodded.

"Sammy's out back tendin' his garden." She gestured toward the rear of the house, then added more gently, "He will be happy to see you, Samantha."

Sam nodded again, feeling Jake's hand on her elbow steering her into the cool interior. "Thank you," she said faintly, to no one in particular.

Once inside the living room, Jake offered her an encouraging smile. "Why don't you go talk to your father. Fletcher and I will hang out with Rover."

"'Rover'?" At her question, a large, lumbering lizard wandered into the room. Sam took an unconscious step back, her recent run-in with a gator still fresh in her mind.

"Family pet," Jake said.

"He won't hurt you," Amalinaú added.

The large reptile made its way across the floor, the sound of his sharp nails rasping on the tile. He stopped next to Fletcher, who cautiously smelled the foreigner, his tale quivering slightly. Sam decided that even if the lizard was harmless, she'd just as soon not take any chances.

"I guess I'll go out back," she murmured, heading for the sliding-glass door that led to a narrow yard beyond.

"Take your time," Jake called, even though they both knew time wasn't something they had much of.

Sam nodded silently. She felt as if the thin control she had over her life was tilting precariously off-balance. She still didn't know where she stood with Jake and she had no idea what to expect from her newfound father. Taking a deep breath, she opened the door, determined to put at least one aspect of her life in order.

The yard was bursting with color. Fragrant gardenias and colorful hibiscus bushes lined a chain-link fence that bordered the small yard. Off to the right, Sam spotted what Amalinaú had called the "garden." Raised two-by-fours bordered a small plot filled with greenery.

On the far side of the garden, a man dug in the dirt with a trowel. Sam could see that his short blond hair was thinning on top, he had a small bald spot pink from the sun. The man looked up and the trowel dropped to the dirt with a thud. He stared at her, his facial features familiar, but faded.

Her father.

"Samantha," he mouthed, although she wasn't sure if she heard him or not.

"Hello." Her voice sounded like it was coming from a million miles away—or twenty years.

"Oh, Samantha." He made no move toward her, though she could tell he wanted to. She didn't approach him, didn't know how.

He looked down at the forgotten trowel in the overturned soil, then back at her. "There's no real dirt on the island. Have to buy it by the truckload." He shrugged, his tanned face breaking into a tentative smile.

She didn't know what to say. "Oh."

"Amy said you were coming."

Sam realized he was talking about Amalinaú. His wife. "Yes. We were here yesterday, but you were gone." She hadn't meant the words to sound accusatory, but she could tell by the way he flinched that that was how they sounded.

"It's the tail end of tourist season," he said. "I had another boatload for today, but canceled when I heard you were coming."

His voice pleaded for something—understanding? Sam's hands alternately clenched and unclenched at her sides, her throat constricting painfully. "Well, I wanted to come last month..." The

words trailed off. How could she begin to explain everything that
had happened to her? He was a virtual stranger, yet she felt a
need to explain. "I couldn't come."

He nodded, his eyes that pale blue she remembered so well.
Crow's feet wrinkled his face—"smile lines," her mother had
called them. It bothered Sam that her father might have had a lot
to smile about over the past twenty years.

"Why?" she asked, her voice refusing to finish her thought.

Somehow, he knew what she'd asked. His shoulders drooped
and she was suddenly struck by how very old he looked. She'd
been just a child when he'd left. Hot tears pricked her eyes. He
had missed so much.

"Why did you leave?" she asked, tempering her voice with a
compassion she was only beginning to feel.

"Your mother and I thought it would be best."

It was too simple, too pat. She knew it didn't begin to explain
things. "But, why?"

He sighed, a gusty sound that ripped through her. "She left
me, Sam. She didn't want me in her life anymore. Or yours."

"No. That's not true!" She hadn't come here for him to crit-
icize her mother.

He nodded, pain etched on his face. "You don't remember,
Sam. I wasn't home much when your mother and I were together.
She wanted stability, a full-time husband—something I couldn't
give her as long as I was in the navy. When she'd had enough,
she left and took you with her."

A vague memory came to her: her father leaving for yet another
sea tour; her mother crying. She hadn't understood then and she
still didn't understand. Her mother wouldn't have kept her from
her father just because he was gone a lot.

"I don't believe you. You didn't care about her or me. You
didn't even come to the funeral." That last was meant to hurt,
and it must have succeeded because he doubled over as if she'd
hit him in the stomach.

"Your mother? She's dead?"

She nodded, realizing he hadn't known. "Ten years ago. I would have let you know, but I didn't know how to reach you."

His face had paled noticeably under his tan. "I lost track of you. You kept moving."

That much was true. They'd moved half a dozen times over the years. Sam had always wondered if her mother wasn't looking for something; some meaning to an otherwise-lonely life. "You should have stayed." It was all she could think of, all she could say.

The sun was hot, and nearly blinding. Sam squinted as much from the brightness as from the need to keep from crying.

Her father shook his head, sadness etched in every line on his face. He walked around the garden toward her, invading the carefully constructed wall she'd put up. He held out his hands and she noticed they were covered in dirt. He came to a stop inches from her, his hands extended like that, not touching her, but too close for her to feel safe.

"I wish to God I hadn't left, Sam," he said quietly.

The dam burst then and she found herself folded in her father's embrace. "No, no, no," she said, over and over, not even knowing what she was protesting.

"Shh." He stroked her hair and memories came flooding back—memories of bedtime and a father who could always get the tangles out without hurting. How she wished he could take away her pain now!

She pulled back, embarrassed by her emotional display. She didn't want this; she didn't want to let him affect her like this. He couldn't hurt her anymore if she didn't let him. "I'm sorry. It— It's been a rough week." That was an understatement, but he obligingly let her go, stepping back.

"I'm sorry, Sam. I never meant to hurt you." It was clichéd, trite. But she wanted to believe him. In her heart of hearts, she needed to believe him.

Jake sat on the couch next to Amalinaú making small talk, glancing occasionally out the sliding-glass door. He had a side view of Sam and he could tell by her face that it wasn't going well.

"Pictures help?"

He realized Amalinaú had asked him a question. He gave her an apologetic look. "Sorry. I didn't catch what you said."

She smiled and tilted her head toward the pair outside. "Don't worry. She'll be all right."

Jake nodded. He certainly hoped so. Problem was, this meeting with her father was a minor event compared to the hot water she was in. His mind kept turning over the facts. The photos she had were only a tiny piece of a much larger puzzle. Until he figured out the rest of it, the pictures were next to worthless.

Fletcher and Rover were doing a strange tango back and forth across the floor. Each time Rover's forked tongue snaked out toward the curious dog, Fletcher took a step backward.

"They like each other," Amalinaú said.

Jake nodded. "They just don't trust each other yet."

"Trust takes time."

Her brown eyes watched him too closely. He didn't like it one bit. And he wondered if all this talk of trust had some other meaning.

The glass door slid open and Sam came in, followed by her father. Her eyes were red-rimmed, tearstains streaking her cheeks. They stared at each other for a long moment and he wanted to say something to ease the pain in her eyes. "You okay?"

"Yes." She gave him a halfhearted smile before looking past him to Amalinaú.

"Could I use your bathroom?"

Amalinaú stood and went to Sam's side, wrapping her arm around Sam's shoulders. "Of course. And I think you could use a cup of herbal tea."

The two women left the room, leaving Jake to face Sam's father. He felt like he was on trial—or worse, meeting his girlfriend's parents for the first time. Only Sam wouldn't appreciate him calling her his "girlfriend."

He stood and stretched his hand out to the older man, resisting the urge to wipe his palms on his jeans first. "I'm Jake Cavanaugh, Mr. Martin."

"Call me Sammy," he said, gripping Jake's hand.

"Sammy," Jake agreed. He glanced over his shoulder toward the other end of the house. "Did you two— Did you work everything out?"

Sammy's gaze trailed past Jake. "I don't know. I don't think I can fix twenty years of loss in twenty minutes."

Jake tended to agree, but never having dealt with this type situation, he decided to keep his mouth shut. "It meant a lot to her, seeing you."

Sammy nodded, meeting Jake's gaze. "Maybe you'd like to tell me what kind of trouble she's in."

At a loss, Jake shrugged. "It's...complicated. I'd explain it to you, but I don't have all the answers myself."

Sammy nodded slowly, faded blond hair dipping over his forehead. "All right. Then maybe you can answer another question for me."

"I can try."

"Who are you to Samantha?"

Jake would have preferred to tell him the whole sordid story, what little he knew, rather than attempt an answer to that loaded question. "We're friends," he offered, hoping that would be the end of it.

"Good friends?"

Jake sighed. "You could say that."

"Well, now, I'd rather hear you say it, Jake. Amy tells me you're a cop and Samantha's in some kind of trouble. So I'm asking you how long you've known my daughter and where your interests lie." Sammy Martin was a lot like his daughter—tenacious as a bulldog and determined as all get-out.

"I haven't known your daughter long," Jake said. "But I can

promise you that her welfare and well-being are my top priorities.''

That much, at least, was true. It startled him to realize just how much he cared about Sam. She wasn't just another victim anymore, and he wasn't quite sure when things had changed. Certainly, before last night.

Making love to Sam had been heaven on earth, but it hadn't made him care for her. He'd cared about her before they'd ever gotten into bed. He didn't want to have these feelings about her, didn't want to let her too close, but there it was. She'd gotten under his skin, and he wasn't so sure he minded.

Sammy Martin smiled then—a relaxed, easygoing smile that reminded Jake of Sam's childhood description. It saddened him that these two had lost so much. ''Well, you take good care of her. She's my daughter.''

Jake wanted to ask him where he'd been for all those years; why he hadn't taken care of his daughter himself. But just then, the two women came back into the room. Sam cradled a teacup in her hands and he was relieved to see that she looked better. The redness had faded from around her eyes, and her face had been washed clean. She looked both vulnerable and strong at the same time.

''Everything all right?'' Amalinaú asked, her eyes shifting between the two men. Jake imagined they looked like they were in a standoff and he stepped back from Sammy.

''Everything's fine, Amy. You feeling better, Sam?''

At her father's question, Sam's eyes flew to his face. She nodded, then glanced at Jake. ''I need— We need to go soon. Right, Jake?''

Her voice still sounded raw and Jake ached to hold her. But he knew she wouldn't welcome him. Not after this morning. It was better this way. He needed to keep his distance. ''Right.''

''So soon?'' Amalinaú and Sammy exchanged glances and Jake could feel the tension in the room. He was suddenly very thankful for his close-knit family.

Sam surprised Jake by answering. "We have to get that film to the authorities."

Seeing the pained expression on Sammy Martin's face, Jake added, "But as soon as it's taken care of, we will be back."

He hadn't meant to say "we." He'd meant to say Sam would be back. Dammit, he was getting himself in deeper than he wanted to be, making promises he couldn't keep. She didn't want anything to do with him anymore, he reminded himself. They would part company at the earliest possible moment and he would be happy about it.

Sam passed her cup to Amalinaú and slowly approached her father. Her voice was low but steady. "I don't know you. There was a time when I hated you."

At that, Sammy looked like he'd been punched. "I know."

"Please," Sam said, holding her hands up, "let me finish. I don't know what happened between you and Mom, but you shouldn't have left me. You shouldn't have just left me like that."

Her voice broke and she paused, regaining her composure. "I don't know if I can ever forgive you or if I can ever love you. But if you want, maybe I could come back sometime. We could get to know each other."

There were tears in Sammy's eyes. Hell, there were tears in Jake's eyes. He deliberately turned his attention to Fletcher, who had stretched out on the cool tile beside the lizard. They made an odd pair, those two. Then again, the same could be said for Sam and him.

He roused Fletcher and led him toward the front door, trying not to intrude any more than he already had on Sam's newfound family.

"Wait," Sammy called to him. "I'd like to speak to you privately."

Jake groaned inwardly, hoping Sam's father didn't intend to give him the birds-and-the-bees lecture. Graciously, Amalinaú crossed the room and took Fletcher's leash from him. "Why don't Samantha and I go outside?"

Sam followed without a word. The emotional impact of this meeting had taken its toll and she looked exhausted.

"I'll be out in a minute," Jake said.

After the women left, Sammy said, "Wait here for a second." At that, he disappeared into the cluttered office Amalinaú had shown him the day before. Jake heard him rummaging around and hoped it wouldn't take all day to find whatever it was he was hunting for.

Sammy returned, carrying a battered shoe box and an envelope. He crossed the room and handed both to Jake. The box was heavy. At Jake's puzzled expression, he explained, "This is for Samantha. She's not ready yet, but when she is, would you give it to her?"

Jake looked down at the box. A piece of paper was taped to the top bearing the faded name Samantha Ann Martin. "What is it?"

"Letters. Her mother always sent them back. Or moved. I lost track of them for good when Samantha was about eighteen. When I got her letter a few weeks ago, I wrote this one."

Jake sighed. He didn't want to be the one responsible for handing this piece of news over to Sam. "She should hear this from you."

Sammy shook his head. "She doesn't want to listen. I don't know when she'll be ready. You know her. You care about her— you said so yourself. All you have to do is give her the letters." He tapped the lid of the box. "The answers she needs are in here."

He didn't like it, but Jake figured he could do that much for the man. His estimation of Sammy Martin went up a few notches. He hadn't abandoned his daughter, after all. He wondered how Sam would take that information. He was curious as hell to know what had happened between the Martins, but it wasn't his place to ask.

He glanced at the door as he tucked the envelope in his back pocket. "All right. I just hope I know when she's ready to hear about this."

"You'll know when the time is right. You'll say the right thing."

Jake wanted to laugh at the man's misplaced trust. But he wasn't about to tell Sammy Martin that. Instead, he nodded. "I'll do my best."

He just hoped to hell that when the time came he knew what that was.

Sam was uncomfortable with Amalinaú. It had nothing to do with the woman herself. In fact, she'd been more than kind. She'd let Sam cry on her shoulder in the kitchen, venting years' worth of pain and anger. She'd made her tea and offered her only friendship.

No, the problem she had with Amalinaú had more to do with her relationship with her father. This was her stepmother. She didn't know what to call her, how to think of her. She knew more about her father than Sam could ever hope to learn. Sam remembered the question that had been on her mind since childhood.

"Did you and my father— I mean, do I have any siblings?"

Amalinaú's laughter reminded Sam of her mother's wind chimes—quiet and musical. "Oh, sweet girl, I do wish. No, your father and I didn't meet until five years ago. We've been married for two. It took me that long to convince him I loved him."

She gave Sam a wistful smile. "By then, I was too old to be thinking about babies. But I always wanted a child." She leveled her gaze on Sam. "A daughter."

Uncomfortable under her scrutiny, Sam turned her gaze toward the front door. She couldn't imagine what in the world her father wanted to talk to Jake about. "Well, I just wondered."

"Your father was very lonely when I met him, Samantha. He missed you."

"Not enough to visit me. Not even enough to let me know that he was still alive. Not enough—'' Sam's voice broke and she put her fingers to her trembling lips, holding in the emotions.

"You don't know—'' Amalinaú started, her voice edged with anger. She took a deep breath and then began again. "Your father loves you very much."

Sam nodded, not knowing what to believe. She didn't know whether her father loved her or not. He seemed sorry for what he'd done, but that wasn't love. All those years of silence seemed pretty contrary to love.

"No, you don't know. Not yet. But give him a chance, Samantha," Amalinaú pleaded.

"I'll try." It was the best she could do. Judging by Amalinaú's smile, she figured it was enough.

The door opened and Jake came out, carrying a small box. Her father hesitated in the doorway, the expression on his face one of hope and fear. She knew that expression well, had seen it on a million orphans in half-a-dozen countries. She offered him a tentative smile and was rewarded with a beaming grin.

"You ready?" Jake asked.

Sam nodded. "Thank you," she said to Amalinaú, but her gaze included her father. "I hope I can come back soon."

Amalinaú surprised her with a tight hug. "You're always welcome here, Samantha," she whispered in Sam's ear.

Sam's father took a step toward her, his mouth struggling with words he couldn't seem to get out. "Take care of yourself," he managed finally.

Sam surprised herself by meeting her father halfway. "You, too," she said, hugging him close.

Jake was already in the car with Fletcher by the time she stepped away from her father and got in. "Goodbye," she said out the open passenger window.

Her father and Amalinaú waved as they pulled away from the curb and Sam was struck by how perfect they seemed together. How happy.

She turned her head to watch them until the car rounded a corner. As she caught one last glimpse of her father, she wondered if she would ever see him again.

Chapter 14

"You okay?"

Jake didn't like how quiet Sam had been since leaving her father's house. He kept waiting for her to ask about the box, even though he didn't know what he would tell her. He wanted to protect her from the truth, but then again, the truth was what she had come here for.

"I'm fine. Where are we going?"

"The airport."

"Why?"

"We need to get out of Key West and there's no way I'm driving back the way we came. They'll be looking for us."

"So we're going back to Miami?"

He shook his head. He'd considered that, but had realized Miami was a dead end. Literally. "Tallahassee."

"What's in Tallahassee?" Yeah, Sam was fine. Her questions were already driving him crazy.

"A friend. Someone I can trust, I think."

Her voice went up a notch. "'Think'? Are you kidding? Everybody and their brother is after us and you think you might be able to trust your friend?''

''Relax.'' Jake steered the car into the small Key West airport. He glanced at his watch. With any luck, Brian or Mac would be landing shortly. He just hoped to hell they hadn't messed with the schedule. ''It'll be all right, Sam.''

''Up until this morning, I might have believed you.'' Her words tore through him, but he didn't blame her. And he couldn't argue with that kind of logic, either.

''One of my brothers should be through here any minute,'' he said, hoping she'd drop the subject. ''Then we'll fly to Tallahassee. If nothing else, no one will know where to look for us.''

''What are you going to tell your brother?''

''Nothing.''

''What are you going to do, steal the plane?''

''Let me handle it, Sam.''

Jake parked in the side lot as close to the runway as he dared. They had to wait out here because he couldn't take a chance on going into the airport. Every employee and pilot who flew through here knew his face. One of them was bound to have seen the newspaper in the past two days.

In less than an hour, a Particular Harbor Tours plane came into view, its hot-pink-and-turquoise emblem a welcome sight. The twin-engine Cessna touched down smoothly and taxied toward them along the runway. It glided to a stop just beyond the car.

''Looks like Mac,'' Jake said, just to break the uncomfortable silence. ''Brian likes to bounce a little on the landing. Gives the passengers a thrill.''

Jake watched Mac and the handful of passengers exit the plane. Mac was older than Jake by three years, and his dark hair was beginning to take on a salt-and-pepper look. It reminded Jake that he wasn't getting any younger, either. And what did he have to show for his life? Not much, he decided.

''Now what?'' Sam asked.

Mac unloaded the last of the luggage and headed for the ter-

minal without even glancing in their direction. That was good.
The last thing Jake needed was a confrontation with his brother.
"The gas truck should be out to refuel in a few minutes. They're
pretty good about taking care of the charters fast."

"We're just going to take the plane?"

Jake's conscience twinged at that. Mac would be furious when
he found out the plane was missing. But there was no way Mac
would just let him go. He'd insist on coming along. And Jake
wasn't going to let his brother's good intentions get him killed.
"Yeah. I'll call Brian from Tallahassee and let him know where
the plane is."

Sam fidgeted in her seat. "I don't know, Jake...."

"What?"

Her brow creased as she frowned. "Stealing a plane? Won't
that just bring more trouble down on our heads?"

Jake stifled a groan. Sam's lack of faith was more aggravating
than Mac's big-brother routine. "It's not stealing. I'm part owner
of that plane."

"What about your brother? How's he going to get back?"

"He can go pick up Annie's van." He glanced at his watch.
"Mac will be home by five."

"I hope you know what you're doing."

"So do I."

By the time the fuel truck puttered out to the plane, Sam was
melting from the heat. Fletcher paced across the back seat of the
car, panting and drooling all over the place, and his incessant
whining was getting on her one last nerve. On the other hand,
Jake looked cool and collected, his hands tucked behind his head
as he watched the plane.

"Well?" Sam asked.

"Well, what?"

"How long is it going to take to refuel the plane?"

His slow grin only served to infuriate her. "Changing your

tune? I figured you'd rather drive to Tallahassee than steal a plane.''

''Maybe you haven't noticed, but it's got to be over a hundred degrees in this car.'' She jerked her head toward the back seat. ''And your dog is making a slobbering mess back there.'' Fletcher whined again.

''I'd better walk him before we go anywhere.'' Jake got out of the car and called to Fletcher. The dog bounded out after him and stood still while Jake clipped his leash on. Leaning in the window, Jake said, ''If you want, you can get out and stretch your legs. It's going to be a long flight.''

Fletcher whined and pulled Jake down the grassy slope beside the runway. Sam jumped out of the car, pulling her damp shirt away from her skin. A warm breeze stirred the air, making it feel ten degrees cooler.

Another plane taxied in and the deafening roar of the engine made her ears ring. She glanced over at the Particular Harbors plane and saw the fuel truck pulling away. Sam went around the side of the car to tell Jake they could leave, when something caught her eye.

A beige sedan had left the access road to the airport and was headed across the field toward the runway—toward them. It bounced along, picking up speed on the open ground.

''Jake! We've got trouble!''

Jake and Fletcher trotted up the incline, Jake's eyes on the car. ''Son of a bitch!'' he swore. ''I thought we'd have more time.''

''It looks like time's run out.''

Jake slapped Fletcher's leash into Sam's hand, he opened the car door and grabbed their bags. He shoved one of the duffel bags at Sam and she nearly dropped it.

''Hang on to Fletcher and let's go!'' Jake took off at a run for the plane and Sam did her best to keep up. The dog trotted beside her, tongue lolling out of his mouth.

Jake dropped the bags next to the plane. ''Dammit!''

''What?''

"I forgot something." He darted back toward the car and it was all Sam could do to keep Fletcher from jerking out of her grasp and following him.

"Leave it!" she yelled at Jake, but he ignored her.

Standing beside the plane, Sam watched the approaching sedan kick up dirt and tufts of grass. It was less than fifty yards away. Fear chilled her to the bone.

"Hurry, hurry," she muttered under her breath. Jake seemed to be moving in slow motion. He would never make it in time. They were sitting ducks waiting to be picked off.

With a painful grinding sound, the beige sedan came to an abrupt stop as it hit a ditch. The back tires spun and the engine roared, but the front end was firmly wedged into the soft dirt. Sam's stomach knotted painfully when she saw the doors open and two men jump out. It was the same men from The Flying Dolphin. And they both held guns.

"Come on!" she screamed to Jake. Fletcher whined beside her, dancing around her feet.

Jake was running full tilt toward the plane. He had the box from her father's house tucked under his arm like a football.

He shoved the box at her, then struggled with the door before wrenching it open. "Go, go, go!"

She tripped up the stairs of the plane, Fletcher on her heels and Jake behind him. She grabbed their bags from Jake as he scrambled up the steps and secured the door.

Pushing past her, he climbed into the front seat. "Sit down and buckle up," he ordered.

She strapped herself into the seat beside him as he started flipping switches. Sam peered out the side window and saw the two men running toward the plane. "For God's sake, hurry!"

The engine roared to life and Sam braced her arms on the seat as the plane started moving in reverse, then swiveled around. Fletcher hugged against her legs as the aircraft gradually picked up speed.

"Come on, baby," Jake muttered under his breath. "They're going to outrun us at this rate."

Sam looked out the window and down the side of the aircraft. The two men had to be within ten feet of the plane's tail. She kept waiting for them to fire.

Jake pushed the throttle. The engine whined. The plane was bucking along the runway at a fairly good clip now and the men were losing ground. Sam was thankful she hadn't eaten breakfast. It would have been on its way up, thanks to this roller-coaster ride.

"Here we go."

Jake's words were followed by a moment of weightlessness as the plane left the ground. She realized then that what had sounded like a misfire of the engine had actually been a gunshot. Another shot rang out over the steady hum of the engine. It connected with a metallic thud.

"Dammit! Where'd they hit us?" Jake asked, his eyes straight ahead on the wide-open sky.

"I don't know," Sam answered, twisting in her seat. "The wing, I think. I'm not sure."

The plane gained altitude and the sound of gunfire faded. The radio squawked to life. "Who the hell is that?" Mac's voice exploded over the open line.

Jake picked up the mike. "Hey, Mac, it's me."

"Jake? What the hell are you doing up there?"

"I'll explain later. I can't talk right now," Jake replied. "I left a rental. Annie's van is at the rental agency. Do me a favor and get it back home."

"I know what's going on, Jake. Get your ass back here so we can work it out."

"Can't do it, Mac." He hesitated. "You can pick the plane up in Tally. I'd appreciate it if you'd keep that to yourself." Jake reached over and switched the radio off. He leveled the plane out, then made a half turn to the north.

Sam cast a quick glance at Jake. She could see his shoulders relax a bit as he handled the controls with practiced ease. She wished she felt half as calm as he looked.

Jake glanced over at her. "Everything okay?"

Sam nodded slowly, never taking her eyes off the endless sky in front of them. "I'll be just fine as soon as I'm back on the ground."

"Don't tell me you're afraid of flying." Jake's voice was incredulous.

"I'm not afraid of flying," she said, talking through gritted teeth as the plane climbed in the sky. "I'm afraid of crashing."

"Come on." Jake settled back in his seat, looking for all the world like he was sitting in his living room. "You must have flown a million times."

Sam tore her eyes away from the sky. "Yeah. But I never sat up front."

"Well, we'll be in Tallahassee in a few hours," he said. "If this tailwind holds. Right now we need all the luck we can get."

She didn't like the sound of that. "Why?"

He looked over at her, hesitating as if he were debating what to say. "We'll be flying on fumes by the time we get to Tallahassee."

Sam groaned.

"Hey, it's not that bad. We're flying over water most of the way. That makes for a smoother flight. We'll be fine. The tailwind just helps things out a little."

Sam just shook her head and looked out the window. "I would have insisted we drive if you'd told me that back there."

"Trust me, Sam."

"It looks like I don't have a choice." The steady hum of the engine underscored the thumping of her heart. "Who's in Tallahassee?" Sam noticed that if she avoided looking out the window she didn't feel nearly as shaky.

"A friend of mine. Sherry Johnson. At least I hope she still considers me a friend."

"Great," Sam muttered under her breath. That wasn't exactly

what she'd hoped to hear. If Jake was hanging all their hopes on some ex-flame with a grudge, Sam might as well jump out of the plane now. Why wait for it to crash?

Jake glanced over at her. "Hungry?"

Sam nodded. "Sure." Anything to take her mind off crashing.

"If I know Mac, he's got a cooler of goodies stashed back in the cargo hold." Jake unstrapped himself and stood, crouching over to keep from bumping his head.

"Uh—Jake—" Sam stuttered, her eyes going from the yoke to the sky, then up at Jake.

"Relax. Autopilot." He paused, looking down at her. He squeezed her shoulder reassuringly. "You'll be all right. I'm not going to let anything happen to you."

"Promise?" She didn't know what made her ask such a stupid question.

He squatted beside her, a hint of a smile playing on his lips. He leaned close to her—so close she could feel the warmth of his breath against her face. He looked like he was going to kiss her and her heart careened wildly in her chest at the thought.

Instead of kissing her, he whispered, "Promise."

Sam heard him disappear into the back of the plane, but she didn't dare turn around.

Autopilot. Planes flew on autopilot all the time. That was all right. Her fingernails dug into her palms but she hardly noticed the pain. "Hurry up, please," she said, her throat constricting on the words.

"Hang on," came Jake's muffled reply from somewhere near the back of the plane.

She heard a thud and risked a glance over her shoulder. Jake was hauling a medium-size picnic cooler up the aisle. Nudging Fletcher out of the way, he wedged the cooler next to Sam. He settled back into his seat and she let out a gusty breath. At least he was sitting down. She still wished he'd put his hands back on the controls.

Jake popped the lid off the cooler and rummaged around in the ice. He passed her a canned soda and a blueberry muffin wrapped in plastic wrap. "It's not the most well-balanced meal, but it'll have to do."

Sam uncurled her fists and took the offering. "Thanks." She examined the muffin before taking a bite. "This is good. I expected beef jerky and stale peanuts."

Jake fished out another soda and two more muffins, feeding one to Fletcher. The dog wolfed down the bite-size pieces and sniffed Jake's hands for more. "Mac likes to bake."

Sam devoured the rest of her muffin and forced a grin. She felt ten times better with some food in her stomach. She'd feel a hundred times better when her feet were back on the ground. "Glad one of you Cavanaughs has some practical use."

"Mac says it relaxes him. His ex hated cooking. It made her crazy that he was always banging around in the kitchen." Jake finished the rest of his muffin and fed Fletcher an ice cube from the cooler. "I keep telling him most women appreciate that sort of thing."

"Is that the voice of experience?"

Jake's playful smile faded. He darted a glance at Sam, his face expressionless. He slid the lid of the cooler into place before turning back to the controls.

"I wouldn't know. None of the Cavanaugh boys have been lucky in love. My ex said I was gone so much she hardly remembered my name," he muttered.

"How long were you married?"

"Six years."

She could tell by the way he kept his attention on the sky that he didn't want to talk about it. But she persisted, wanting to know about him, wanting to understand what made this man tick. "Kids?"

"No. I wanted some, but Margo said—" He bit back whatever he was going to say. "Well, it wouldn't do to have a cop for a father, would it?"

"I'm sorry." It was the only response she could think of.

He shrugged. "Don't be. Margo decided she was tired of competing with my job for my attention. It worked out for the best."

"Did it?" He didn't answer and she studied his profile. "My father said my mother threw him out."

He glanced over at her. "Why?"

"Because he was never home."

A wry smile twisted Jake's mouth. "Sounds familiar."

"I don't know if I believe him."

Jake sighed. "Sam, I can't tell you what to do. But I lost my father when I was a kid and if someone gave me a chance to spend time with him again, I'd jump at it."

"Are you saying I should just forget everything that happened?"

"I'm saying, give the man a chance. It won't hurt you. And you might be glad you did."

Sam sighed and rested her head against the back of her seat. White fluffy clouds hung in a perfect, brilliant blue sky. It really was quite beautiful as long as she didn't think about crashing. Or about the guys back at the airport with guns.

The hot sun glinting off the tinted glass was giving her a headache. She closed her eyes and tried to relax. But she couldn't help wondering if she'd ever be able to figure out Jake Cavanaugh.

Sam woke up disoriented, with a crick in her neck. Reaching up to rub the sore spot, she winced. "How much longer until we land?" Her throat felt like gravel.

"Hey, sleepyhead. We're almost there." Jake glanced at her. "You okay?"

She nodded and rested her head against the seat, feeling the plane begin its descent. "As good as can be expected."

"Hang in there. You'll be on the ground in a few minutes."

Sam trusted his flying skills, but she wasn't so sure about his plan. She suspected he was grasping at straws. Knowing that she'd taken pictures of some supposedly-deceased Central American crime boss didn't answer the question of who was after her and why they would go to such lengths to keep her quiet.

The radio squawked to life when Jake turned it on. He made contact with the air tower and requested clearance to land.

Minutes later, the runway loomed as the plane began its approach. Sam closed her eyes but that didn't stop her stomach from climbing into her throat. Her heart hammered in her chest as the plane touched down.

As the plane rolled to a stop, she cracked her eyes open. They'd landed in one piece.

Jake looked over and gave her a grim smile. "This is it. It's over."

The finality of his words made her shiver. Nodding at him, she unfastened her seat belt. Beside her, wedged in next to the cooler, Fletcher came to life. He stretched his gangly limbs and yawned, the sound trailing off into a howl. She knew how he felt.

They gathered their bags and Sam reached for the box Jake had been carrying. Jake's hand got there first. She met his gaze over the seat. "I can carry it."

"That's all right. I've got it."

She arched an eyebrow. "You going to tell me what's in there?"

"Later."

She shrugged. "Fine. Keep your secrets."

"Sam—" he started.

"Forget it, Jake. It's no big deal." She pulled her hand back and waited for him to get the door open.

"I need to call Sherry and ask her to pick us up," Jake said as they headed across the tarmac.

Sam nodded and hoped that Jake wasn't making a mistake in trusting this woman. "I desperately need a bathroom," she told him.

"Hang on." When they got to the main building, Jake pointed to a pay phone by the main door. "I'll be right there. Don't go running off."

She didn't bother to respond.

Chapter 15

Relief washed over Jake when Sherry picked up on the second ring. "Sher? It's Jake."

"Jake? Who died?"

Startled, he said, "What?"

Her relaxed laugh filled his ear. "I figure that's the only reason you'd be calling me."

He could feel a slow flush creeping up the back of his neck. She was right. And he wouldn't be calling her now if he didn't need to. "Sorry about that, Sherry. I just thought— Well, I guess I thought—"

"You thought I wouldn't want to hear from you," she interrupted.

He nodded to himself. "Yeah."

"Jake Cavanaugh, you're the most stubborn, pigheaded man I've ever known next to Charlie."

At the mention of his partner, Jake swallowed the lump in his throat. He didn't deserve her kindness. But he'd take it. "Look, Sherry, I need to ask you a favor."

"Well, now, I guess hell must have frozen over. Ask away, sugar."

"It's complicated. I'd rather explain it in person." What an understatement. "I'm at the airport. I hate to put you out, but—"

"Give me twenty minutes, Jake. I have to pick up Emily at school."

Jake glanced over as the automatic doors slid open and Sam came out. "Well, I'm not alone. I have a friend with me." At a tug of the leash in his hand, Jake added, "And Fletcher."

"It'll be a regular party." Sherry chuckled, then her voice got husky. "Emily's missed you, Jake. Nearly as much as she misses her daddy."

"I'm sorry, Sher. You know I love that kid like she was my own." Jake caught the surprised expression on Sam's face out of the corner of his eye and could only imagine what she was thinking.

"Then don't be such a stranger from now on."

"I'll work on it," he promised.

He hung up the phone and turned to Sam. "She'll be here in a few minutes."

He gestured toward one of the plastic benches that lined the wall beside the row of pay phones. "Come on, Sam, pull up a seat."

She sat down, her eyes on anything but him. He sat down next to her, noticing the way she turned away from him. "You're being awfully quiet."

She shrugged, staring out at the parking lot. "What do you want me to say? I don't want your friend involved in my problems any more than I wanted to drag you into them. Things just keep snowballing out of control."

"Hey, it's not that bad."

"Stop it, Jake. I know the score as well as you do." She jerked her head around to look at him, her hair coming loose and swinging around her face. "We barely made it out of Key West alive."

He nodded. "I know." Unable to resist the soft look on her

face, he cupped her chin in his hand, forcing her to look at him. His heart trip-hammered in his chest at the vulnerability in her eyes. Why couldn't he have stayed out of her life? Why did she make him feel so damn protective? "But we made it. We made it, dammit. And we're going to keep on making it."

Her eyes shone with tears, but she blinked them back and pulled away from him. "I'm glad you're convinced. But what do we do now?"

He hadn't wanted to say anything until he was sure Sherry could help them. Hell, he still wasn't sure she could do anything for them. Or would want to. But he owed Sam some kind of explanation.

"My friend Sherry Johnson is coming to pick us up. She was more than a friend, really. She—"

Sam held up her hand. "I don't need the details of your love life."

"'Love life'?"

"I'd just as soon not know about your girlfriends."

Jake shook his head before it dawned on him. Sam thought he was romantically involved with Sherry. His heart thudded dully in his chest. The idea that Sam might be jealous appealed to him in a way he couldn't explain.

"Sherry was the wife of my partner. After Charlie died—" He swallowed hard before going on. "After Charlie died, I didn't see her much. She moved up here last year."

"Oh." The expression on Sam's face was priceless and confirmed Jake's suspicions. She'd been jealous.

"Sherry works for the governor's office. I thought she might be able to help."

"How?"

"I don't know, really. But she might know who we can go to, who we can trust. We need someone outside the local police on our side."

"You think this is some big conspiracy?"

He hesitated before nodding. It sounded paranoid as hell, but after everything they'd been through in the past couple of days, he didn't know what else to think. "Could be. There're too many loose ends we just don't have answers for."

The sliding doors opened and a group of laughing teenagers— probably college students, judging by the Florida State T-shirts— came out. Jake watched them walk toward the parking lot and felt very old all of a sudden. He dragged a hand through his hair, his shoulders slumping.

"I've got a few connections on the force," he said. "But so does Montegna. I need to talk to someone I can trust and find out what the hell agency Manning is working for. But I haven't run out of ideas yet."

Sam offered him a rueful smile. "I'll start worrying when you do."

"We'll figure something out," he said, wondering whom he was trying to convince. "For the moment, we have the upper hand."

She turned to him, her eyes wide and clear. "Knowledge is power."

"Right." He squeezed her shoulder, drawing strength from her. "We know something most of the world doesn't. Carlos Montegna is alive. Now all we have to do is figure out how to use that knowledge to our benefit."

"Before it's too late."

What she said was true, so he didn't bother to deny it. They'd been lucky to stay one step ahead of the game this far. It wouldn't take long for Montegna's men, or whatever shadow agency Manning worked for, to track them.

A white Toyota pulled up at the curb and Jake jumped to his feet. "It's Sherry."

The passenger door opened and a young girl scrambled out, leaving the door wide-open. The lump in Jake's throat threatened to undo him.

"Uncle Jake!" she screamed before launching herself at him, a tangle of gangly limbs and red-blond hair.

He laughed, staggering under the friendly assault. "Whoa! You can't be Emily." Fletcher barked excitedly and joined the fray, his leash tangling around them.

The energetic young girl in his arms hardly resembled the thin, hollow-looking child he'd known two years ago. Disease had ravaged her, aging her. But now she looked like a healthy kid, with her father's eyes. Jake's heart swelled to think that she'd beaten it. Charlie would have been proud.

Over Emily's shoulder, Jake saw Sherry get out of the car, her red curls bouncing. "Let the man breathe, Em," she said to Emily.

"It's all right," Jake said quickly. "It's been a while. You've grown up, kiddo."

Emily flashed a thousand-watt smile at him. "I'm almost thirteen."

"And I'm not getting any younger waiting for my hug." Sherry playfully nudged Emily aside and gave Jake the once-over. "You look tired."

Jake looked at Sam, recognizing the uncomfortable expression on her face. He'd felt the same way back at her father's house. "We've had a rough couple of days."

"Well, hug me anyway, big guy. Then you can introduce us."

When Sherry stepped back, Jake make the introductions. "Sherry Johnson, this is my friend Samantha Martin." One of Sam's eyebrows rose imperceptibly at the word "friend."

"Hi, Samantha," Sherry said, offering Sam her hand. "In case you're wondering, the little tornado is my daughter, Emily."

"Mo-om," Emily said, dragging the word out in that interminable way of adolescents. "Don't embarrass me!"

Jake scanned the parking lot. He knew they were safe for the moment but had no way of predicting how long that would last. Montegna's men had a peculiar way of showing up wherever they were. And he wasn't going to put Sherry and Emily in danger. His conscience reminded him that he might have already, just having them come here.

"Something wrong, Jake?" Sherry asked, her smile fading. "You look like you've seen a ghost."

Glancing at Sam, Jake picked up their bags and started for the car. "I'll tell you later."

"Sorry about the mess," Sherry said as she let them into her house.

Sam followed Jake into the two-story town house, at once charmed by Sherry's friendliness and uncomfortable with it. The woman seemed to readily accept her, while Sam couldn't reconcile her feelings one way or the other. She was thankful for Sherry's help but didn't want to be the cause of any more deaths.

The short drive from the airport had been filled with Emily's chatter and Fletcher's occasional barking at passing cars. Sam had been glad not to have to make conversation—or worse, explain her story all over again or her brief association with Jake.

It shouldn't matter who she was to Jake. All that mattered was whether Sherry Johnson could help them. But that knowledge didn't stop her heart from plummeting to her feet when Jake had called her his "friend." Sam reminded herself that she had no claim to Jake. She wasn't even sure she wanted one.

"You can put your bags down in here." Sherry gestured toward a room off the living room.

Jake followed Sherry into the room while Sam stood awkwardly in the living room. Emily had disappeared upstairs with Fletcher and she could hear the girl's squeals and what sounded like a fleet of soldiers tramping across the floor.

"If you're going to play like that, take it outside!" Sherry hollered.

Moments later, the girl and the dog bounded down the stairs. "Can I take him for a walk?" she asked as Jake and Sherry came out of the bedroom.

Jake nodded. "But I'd better go with you. He'll drag you down the street."

The two of them headed toward the back of the house, with

Fletcher following, his tail wagging. A door slammed. Sherry smiled at Sam. "Don't mind her. I lock her in the basement after dinner."

"She's terrific," she said sincerely.

"We've got a mother-daughter softball game tonight, so we'll be eating dinner in an hour or so," Sherry said. "You can take a nap if you like. You look like you could use one just as badly as Jake."

Sam found herself nodding. "Thanks."

"Do you want to give me a hand making the bed?"

"Sure."

The bed was a convertible sofa in a makeshift office. Books were piled on every surface, including the couch. Most were law-books, but Sam saw a couple of Emily's school textbooks in the mix.

Sherry cleared the sofa and stacked the books on a table already piled high. She apologized with a smile. "I'd let you have my room but I think Emily's music would keep you up all night." She grinned at Sam. "This way, the only thing that'll bother you will be Jake's snoring."

"Believe me, I'm grateful for any bed." Sam took the corner of the sheet and tucked it under the thin mattress. "Thank you. For everything."

"I haven't done anything yet. Jake hasn't told me how I can help you."

Sam sat on the edge of the bed, worrying her lip between her teeth. "I'd better let him fill in the details. It's a long story."

"Do you want to come out to the kitchen and keep me company while I make dinner?"

"I'd like that."

Sam followed her to the other end of the house. The kitchen was narrow, with a small dining area at one end that led to a tiny screened-in porch. Beyond that was a fenced-in yard. Sherry gestured toward the table. "Sit down. Can I get you something to drink?"

Sam nodded. "That would be great."

Sherry rummaged through the refrigerator. "I have soda and tea." She pulled out a milk container and shook it, wrinkling her nose in disgust. "I also have chunky milk."

"Tea would be wonderful," Sam said with a smile.

Sherry nodded and took a glass from the cabinet over the stove. "How long have you known Jake?"

Sam hedged, not sure how much she should tell her. "Not very long, though it feels like forever."

Sherry nodded again, her long red curls bouncing against her shoulders. "I haven't seen Jake in a couple of years. His choice. But I'm glad he's here now."

"He told me he was partners with your husband. I'm sorry about what happened."

The corner of Sherry's mouth tipped upward as she handed Sam the glass. "Thank you. Charlie was a wonderful husband, but his passion was police work. I like to think he died happy, doing what he loved to do."

"It must have been hard on you," Sam said. "And Emily."

Sherry returned to the refrigerator. Assorted vegetables were piled on the counter. "It was. But Emily kept me busy. If she hadn't been so sick I might have had a spare minute to feel sorry for myself."

"She was sick?"

"Acute lymphoblastic leukemia."

Sherry had her back to her so Sam couldn't see her expression. But she could hear the stark terror in every word. "That must have been awful."

"It was." Sherry took a knife to a head of lettuce, attacking it as if it were her child's disease. "The worst of it was the uncertainty. When Em needed a bone-marrow transplant I thought I was going to lose her."

No matter what Sam might have lived through, she couldn't imagine the helpless fear of losing a child. Or the grief of losing a husband. "I'm sorry."

Sherry looked up from her cutting and gave her a brilliant smile. "You know what they say. If it doesn't kill you, it makes you stronger." Her smile faded. "When Charlie died I knew I had to be strong for Em. I was all she had."

"Well, she's a beautiful girl. Is everything all right now?"

"She's been in remission for about eighteen months." Sherry added onions and green pepper slices to the large bowl in front of her. "She's a normal twelve-year-old now. Her goal in life is to make me crazy."

Sam laughed. "I remember those years. I don't know how you've handled all this on your own."

"I had to. I was one class short of finishing law school when Em got sick." Sherry put the salad bowl in the refrigerator and set a pot on the stove. "I was able to finish when she went into remission. After I passed the bar, I lucked out and got a job working for the state."

"How do you like it?"

"It's been good for me. Good for Em. Miami had too many memories. I wanted to start fresh." The can opener whirred as she opened cans and dumped them into the pot on the stove.

The front door banged open and Sam jumped.

"The troops are home," Sherry said as Jake and Emily came into the kitchen. "Where's Fletcher?"

Emily and Jake exchanged looks and Emily started giggling. "Fletcher got away from me."

"He found a mud puddle," Jake added, pointing to the muddy dog in the backyard. "He needs a bath."

"Well, you'd better hurry up. Dinner will be ready soon."

Jake inhaled, then winked at Sam. "What's for dinner?"

"My famous chili."

Emily groaned and clutched her stomach. "Can't we order pizza?"

Sherry's mock indignation made Sam laugh. She noticed Jake was having a hard time keeping a straight face, too. "Of course not. You will eat my chili and you will enjoy it."

"Come on, squirt. Let's wash the dog," Jake said, slinging his arm around Emily's shoulder.

"Make it quick," Sherry said. "Jake?"

He glanced back, looking more relaxed than Sam had seen him in the past couple of days. "Yeah?"

"It's good to have you here."

Sherry's words brought a bright flush to his cheeks. "It's good to be here, Sher. Thanks."

The door closed behind him and Sherry shook her head. "He's a heartbreaker, that one."

Sam didn't say anything, but she agreed.

"The last time I saw Jake was at Charlie's funeral. He's aged so much."

Sam glanced out the window at Emily and Jake. They were chasing Fletcher around the yard, the big dog evading their attempts to catch him. "Why didn't you see him?"

"About a month after Charlie's death, I heard Jake had resigned," Sherry said, stirring the chili. "I couldn't believe it. That boy loved police work almost as much as Charlie did."

Sam wiped droplets of water from her glass while she debated with herself. She had no right to intrude into Jake's life. No right at all. But somehow, in the space of a few short days, their lives had become intertwined. She cared about him. And his past was a part of him.

"He told me he lost his nerve," Sam said softly.

Sherry's smile turned into a sad, wistful look. "I don't believe that. I think he couldn't live with Charlie's death. He blames himself." Sherry nodded toward the window. "He's got a lot of guilt on his shoulders. But it's self-inflicted guilt. I know Jake. He wouldn't have done anything to put Charlie or himself in unnecessary danger."

Sam nodded. That fit with her image of Jake. "Did you tell him that?"

Sherry tapped the spoon on the edge of the pot before looking at Sam. "Many times. But he wouldn't listen. Then Emily went in for the marrow transplant and I just didn't have the energy to focus on Jake.'' She walked to the porch door and opened it. ''Hey, you two, dinner's almost ready!''

Emily yelled, ''Aw, Mo-om!''

''Five minutes,'' Sherry said, in a voice that brooked no argument. Turning to Sam, she smiled. ''I'd just as soon not talk about this in front of Emily. She looks tough, but she's still pretty fragile.''

''Of course.''

''But ask Jake about it. He needs to talk to someone who cares about him. Someone besides me.'' Sherry's expression was pained. ''And he needs to know that I don't blame him.''

''I'll try to talk to him sometime,'' Sam promised, ignoring the dull ache of her heart. She wished Jake would trust her enough to talk to her.

Sherry gave her a brilliant smile, all traces of sadness gone from her face. ''Thank you.''

''No,'' Sam said. ''Thank you for telling me.''

The back door banged open and Emily burst in, with a still-damp Fletcher right on her heels. Jake followed them, his wet shirt clinging to every muscle in his back. It took all Sam's willpower to look away from him before he caught her staring.

Sherry winked at Sam as Jake turned around. ''Don't thank me yet. You haven't tasted my cooking.''

Chapter 16

Something was going on between those two. Jake had sensed it from the moment he'd walked into the house. Sherry and Sam reminded him of his mom and Annie—sharing secrets and leaving the menfolk out of it.

"Let's eat. Then we'll talk," Sherry said as he took a seat.

Fletcher sat at attention beside him, his expression making it clear he was hoping for the leftovers. "After your little stunt, I think you should be outside hunting up your own dinner," Jake said brusquely.

Emily giggled and coaxed the dog over with a wave of a crouton. "He doesn't look like much of a hunter."

Dinner also served to remind Jake of his childhood. Emily kept things lively, regaling them with tales of seventh-grade woe. Jake had to smile. Oh, to be twelve again.

As Sam helped Emily clear the dishes, he turned to Sherry. "She's something special, Sher."

Sherry nodded, a wistful, faraway look in her eyes. "I know. I wish her father could see her now. I wish he knew how well she's doing."

Jake fought back his emotions for the second time that day. "Charlie knows."

"Would you like to see my room, Sam?" Emily asked after the table had been cleared.

Sam glanced at Jake and he nodded solemnly. "Go ahead. If you don't come back in an hour, we'll send out a search-and-rescue team."

In that way of preteens, Emily scorched him with a look. "Stop it, Uncle Jake!"

Sherry grinned. "Yeah, Jake, that's jumping the gun a bit. Give 'em at least two hours."

"C'mon, Emily," Sam said in mock indignation. "We don't have to listen to this."

Jake's emotions careened in an unfamiliar way as Sam favored him with a soft smile before following Emily. He chalked it up to lack of sleep. Sherry watched him with that knowing look of all mothers. He shrugged. "What?"

"I'm just wondering how much trouble you must be in to darken my doorstep after all this time." He could tell she was only half kidding.

Jake spread his hands over the tablecloth, feeling the smoothness of the pine table beneath it. The smoothness came from hours of sanding. Charlie had made the table and chairs, each curve and spindle, every painstaking detail a result of his own two hands. Now all Charlie's woodworking tools sat in Annie's garage, unused. Jake didn't have the heart to give them away.

Jake shook his head, the past settling around him like a tangible presence. Charlie should have been there to enjoy it. Charlie should never have died.

"I don't know what to say, Sherry. You're right, I wouldn't be here if it wasn't bad."

"How bad, Jake?"

Her soft voice echoed from the past. She'd said the same words to him in the emergency room of the hospital. Charlie had been stretched out in the next room, beyond help. Then, as now, Jake couldn't sweeten the truth.

"Pretty bad." He shook his head again, hating himself for dragging her into this. Whoever was chasing them had no compunction about killing innocent people. But like he'd told Sam, he didn't know where else to turn.

"Are you in trouble?"

"It's Sam, really. I got caught up in her mess."

Sherry's expression remained neutral. "She seems like a nice enough person. How long have you known her?"

Jake let out a bark of laughter. "A couple of days." When Sherry arched her brows in surprise, he added, "It's been a really long couple of days."

Sherry sighed. "Jake, honey, I'm not your mama and I'm not your wife. But are you sure you need to be getting yourself involved in Sam's problems?"

Anger flared for a moment but quickly faded. This was Sherry. Outside of family, she knew him better than anyone except Charlie. Margo had never really known him and she'd never let him forget it, either. It didn't surprise him just how few people he'd allowed into his life. What bothered him was why he wanted to add Sam to that short list.

"I'm in it as deep as she is now."

He left it at that, but it wasn't easy to rationalize his relationship with Sam even to himself. She had gotten to him in a way no one had before. This whole situation should have been strictly business. But where Sam was concerned, he had a hard time separating business from pleasure.

"That's my Jake. Loyal to the last." Sherry softened her voice. "Fine, sugar. You do what you have to do. And you know I'll do anything I can to help."

"I know you will." Jake cleared his throat, unable to meet her eyes. "The thing is, Sher, I don't know how safe you'll be if we hang around here."

"What do you mean?"

"People have already died because they got between us and who's after us," Jake told her, trying to give her the facts without scaring her. "I would never put you and Emily at risk, but you may be in danger just because we're here."

He should have said it differently. Tact had never been one of his strong suits.

Instead of flying off the handle, Sherry simply asked, "Should I send Em to stay with someone?"

Jake looked up then, not sure whether he should thank her or shake her. "And you accuse me of being loyal? You should probably run me out of town on a rail."

Her smile reminded him of happier times. "You've done far too much for this family for me to run you off without hearing you out first."

"It's a pretty far-fetched story," he warned.

"Save it for later, okay?" Sherry said as the sound of footsteps on the stairs signaled Sam and Emily's return.

Sherry ushered him and Sam into the living room while Emily went off to the garage to gather her softball gear. "My friend and her daughter usually pick us up, but I'll let Emily go on ahead so you can tell me what's going on," she said as soon as Emily was out of earshot.

"You don't have to do that," Sam protested.

"It's all right. We go early to watch the game before ours," Sherry said. Glancing at her watch, she added, "I'm yours until eight."

Outside, a horn honked. Emily came tearing into the room, her hot-pink T-shirt emblazoned with the name Amazons. She carried a well-worn softball glove and a bat. "Kelly and her mom are here," she said breathlessly.

"Honey, I need to talk to Jake and Sam for a bit," Sherry told her. "You go on without me. I'll catch up with you."

Emily's face clouded over and Jake felt like a jerk. Hadn't he done enough to them already? He was on the verge of telling

Sherry to go, when Emily smiled. "All right. But don't be late for the game."

"I won't," Sherry promised.

At the sound of the horn again, Emily went to the door, slinging the bat and glove over her shoulder. She glanced back at them before closing the door. Her serious features reminded Jake so much of Charlie. "You'll be here when I get back?"

Jake knew the words were for him, and his dose of guilt doubled. "Yeah, kiddo. I'll be here."

Emily nodded solemnly. "Love you, Mom."

"Love you, too." The door closed and Sherry smiled at him. "She's missed you."

"I know," Jake said gruffly, uncomfortable with the way Sam was looking at him. "I missed her, too."

Sherry left the room to get coffee and Jake eyed Sam suspiciously. "What's that look for?"

"What look?"

Jake didn't have a chance to argue the point. Sherry came back into the room carrying a tray of coffee mugs. "The two of you look like you could use this."

Sam nodded. Sipping the steaming contents of her mug, she smiled wearily. "More than you realize."

"Well, who's going to tell me what's going on? You've only got an hour."

Jake exchanged looks with Sam. "Why don't you explain how this started?"

Sam nodded and Jake could see her bracing herself. It wasn't an easy story for her to tell. He offered her an encouraging smile. "I'll pick it up from the time we met in the Everglades."

Sherry's eyes widened at that. "This sounds like it's going to be a doozer of a story."

"You don't know the half of it," Jake said.

Jake watched Sherry's expression shift from interest to amazement to horror. With the exception of a few questions to clarify points they made, she listened to their story in silence.

When Jake finished explaining what had brought them to Tallahassee, Sherry sat back in her chair. With a strangled laugh she said, "I wish I hadn't quit smoking. I could really use a cigarette right about now."

"I wouldn't have dumped this on your doorstep," Jake said, feeling both guilty and relieved to be sharing their story with someone else. "But I didn't know where else to turn."

Sam leaned forward on the couch, her eyes on Sherry. "I don't want to drag you into this, Sherry. If you can't help us—or don't want to—just say the word. We'll figure something out."

Jake's admiration for Sam grew. He knew as well as she did that they were out of options, but she was still willing to let Sherry off the hook.

Sherry shook her head. "It's a lot to digest at once. This is straight out of the movies."

"Tell me about it." Jake leaned back and sighed. He rubbed a hand over his face, feeling the stubble of beard. He had a sudden thought. "Are you hooked up to the Internet?"

Sherry grinned. "Are you kidding? Between work and Emily, I'm wired to the limit."

"What are you thinking, Jake?" Sam asked.

Jake headed for the office. "It's been a while, but I think I can find out who Manning works for."

Ten minutes later, the hum of Sherry's computer was the only sound in the room. Despite his expired police credentials, Jake was able to hack into the national database of motor vehicle records.

"Read out Manning's driver's license number," Jake told Sam, his fingers poised over the keys.

Sam read out the numbers. Fifteen minutes later, the database spat out five pages of information. "What did it give you?"

Jake scrolled through the documents. "Nothing too informative. But he was at Quantico. There's a bunch of government gibberish, but I don't see any mention of FBI or CIA.''

''Wait, what's that?'' Sherry asked, pointing to a notation toward the end of Manning's file.

'''BOCTA,''' Jake read. ''Never heard of it. How about you?'' Sherry shook her head.

''Could you cross-reference it?'' Sam asked.

Jake nodded slowly. ''Maybe. If I knew someone who could get me into the government's records.'' He looked at Sherry.

Sherry shook her head. ''That's illegal, you know.''

''I know.''

She sighed. ''All right, move over.''

It took Sherry even less time to access the federal government files because she had clearance. ''Here you go. BOCTA. Bureau of Organized Crime and Terrorist Activity.''

''Sounds like CIA to me,'' Jake said, leaning over Sherry's shoulder to read the brief bio. There wasn't much to go on.

''Maybe it's a branch of the CIA,'' Sam said.

''Maybe.'' Jake wondered just who was behind BOCTA and why it was such a secret. ''Could you print that up for me, Sherry?''

''Sure thing.''

''How does this help us?'' Sam asked.

''I don't know, but at least we know who Manning works for.''

Sherry pulled the pages from the printer, her brow drawing into a thoughtful frown. ''I might be able to help. I think I know someone you can talk to. Someone you could trust.''

''We're grateful for anything you can do,'' Sam said.

''Remember Joe Lafferty?''

Jake nodded. ''We worked together on the Smithson case.'' To Sam, he said, ''Joe's FBI. Not a close friend, but he was a good guy.''

''Still is,'' Sherry said. ''A straight arrow.''

Sherry glanced at her watch. ''First thing tomorrow, I'll call

Joe. He moved up here a few months ago to take over operations."

"Do you trust him, Sher?" Jake asked. "Under the circumstances—"

"I trust him. He was a real rock after Charlie...." Her words trailed off. "Anyway, I'd like to hear what Joe has to say about this mess. He should have some of the answers you need. And with any luck, he'll be able to help you."

"You don't know how much this means to me," Sam said.

"To us," Jake added.

Sherry brushed off their thanks with a wave of her hand. "Save it. When you get out of this nightmare, we'll talk." She looked pointedly at Jake. "And you will owe me. Big time, sugar."

Jake grinned. "You got it."

"I'd better get out of here or Emily is going to be on my case." She stood to go.

"Would you like us to come with you?" Sam asked.

Sherry looked from Sam to Jake and back again. "No, honey, you all stay here. Turn in early. You look like you both need it."

Jake nodded, feeling the slow drain of exhaustion settle over him. "Be careful."

Sherry winked at him. "I'm playing catcher for a bunch of adolescent girls. I have to be careful."

After they heard Sherry's car pull out of the driveway, Jake looked at Sam. She arched an eyebrow at him, the smoky look in her eyes making his blood boil.

"Well?" he asked finally.

She kept looking at him as if seeing him for the first time. It made him nervous. It made him uncomfortable. It made him want to take her in his arms and kiss her senseless. He was getting addicted to her sharp tongue and her soft eyes. What he needed, he decided, was one of those nicotine patches. Only this would be for women. Correction: not for women, just Sam. A Sam patch.

"Well, what?"

He rested his arms on his knees and laced his fingers. "What do you want to do?"

The corner of Sam's mouth tipped up in a tired smile. "You don't want to go to sleep?"

Two could play her cat-and-mouse game, Jake decided. "Only if you do."

"I took a nap on the plane," she reminded him.

"Right. So I guess you're not tired." He yawned. She might not be tired, but he sure as hell was. He stretched out on the couch and closed his eyes. "Maybe I'll just turn in for the night."

"Fine. You do that."

Jake cracked his eyes open and watched her take the mugs into the kitchen. He'd bet his plane that she put a little extra sway in her hips as she walked away. He shifted on the couch, painfully aware of what she was doing to him.

Sam returned, and slumped down in the chair. Then she stood. "I'm too restless to sleep. I think I'll go for a walk."

"Alone?"

"Sure, why not? I'll be all right."

"Wait a minute, Sam." He hadn't intended to say anything yet, but he wasn't sure how tomorrow would go. He pulled the crumpled envelope Sammy Martin had given him out of his back pocket. "You should read this."

She hesitated for only a moment before taking the envelope from him. "From my father?"

He nodded. "He thought I would know when to give it to you. Well, this seems as good a time as any."

"Thanks."

"Do you want me to leave?" he asked as she ripped open the envelope.

She shook her head, her eyes on the letter. "No, you're fine."

He tried to relax, but all his muscles were tightly coiled as he watched the play of emotions on her face. It couldn't be easy reading a letter from the father you hadn't known for most of your life.

Sammy had written a long letter and Sam took her time reading the small, neat handwriting. Jake watched as she went back and read it a second time, a small sigh escaping her lips as she folded the pages and put them back in the envelope.

Leaning back in her chair, she looked emotionally drained. He wanted to hold her, to soothe her. He wanted to protect her from the world. He was the last person on earth who should think he could take care of anyone, but he wanted to take care of Sam.

"So what did your father say?"

"That he was sorry, mostly."

"I think he is, Sam."

She nodded. "I know. I believe that now. He said he sent me other letters. A lot of them, apparently. That's what's in the box, right?"

He nodded. "Do you want me to get them?"

"No. Not now. It's enough to know they exist. My mother returned them, unopened. She let me think he didn't care about me."

"I'm sorry."

"It's all right. Now I know." Sam gave him a wan smile. "I probably should have known it before now. My mother had a lot of pain inside her, Jake. She didn't want him to be happy and she couldn't control that. But she could control me."

"What are you going to do now?"

"I'll go back and visit him. After we get this situation straightened out." She shook her head. "If we ever do."

"We will, Sam. I promise that."

"I hope so." She stood, worrying the letter between her fingers. "I think I'll take that walk now. I'm too wired to relax."

"I guess I'll just stay here and take a nap." He yawned again for emphasis. Beside him on the floor, Fletcher matched him yawn for yawn.

"You do that," she said, giving him that little half smile again. "You look like you need it."

The door closed and Jake bolted upright. "Fine. Go ahead

without me.'' He ran a hand through his hair as he debated whether or not to go after her.

''To hell with it.'' He sighed. He wasn't going to chase her like some puppy.

It took him less than sixty seconds to change his mind.

Chapter 17

Sam dashed the tears out of her eyes when she heard Jake's footfalls behind her. She smiled to herself. "Miss me?"

Falling into stride beside her, Jake shook his head. "I didn't want you to get lost."

"Right."

She liked that he had followed her. And she liked talking about her life with Jake. It felt right. He cared. Maybe for the wrong reasons, but still... She'd locked everyone out for so long, had been so afraid of getting hurt, that now her emotions were overflowing. She suspected it had been the same for him.

The tree-lined street was quiet at this hour. The setting sun cast long shadows across lawns and driveways. Sam and Jake walked in silence for a while, their hands brushing but not quite touching. Sam could almost let herself pretend that this was a normal day like any other.

They crossed the street and ambled down another avenue. The houses were all lined up in neat rows, with tidy lawns and carefully trimmed shrubs. An occasional bicycle left out on the sidewalk attested to the fact that it was a safe community. Sam could imagine potluck suppers and Sunday barbecues with smiling families. It was the kind of life she'd had too briefly as a child. She ached for it now.

An image of sharing a life with Jake taunted her, but she quickly dismissed it. The last thing she needed right now was fanciful daydreams about something that could never happen. They were strangers thrown together by circumstance.

Jake glanced at her. "What were you and Sherry talking about earlier?"

"She told me about Emily, what they've been through."

"They went to hell and back."

"But they survived." It gave Sam hope to see Sherry's strength. She had endured the worst that any woman—any parent—could imagine. She'd lost a husband and nearly lost her daughter. But she'd survived. Sam could only hope that she fared as well when this was all over.

A tree-shrouded park dominated a large corner lot of the neighborhood. Children's swings and seesaws dotted the grassy landscape, which was silent and empty now, its colors fading to grays and blues in the dwindling light.

Sam and Jake wandered through the park as darkness gathered around them. Their hands were still close, but not quite touching. Sam ached to reach out and make that small connection with him, to feel a part of his life if only for this moment. But she held back.

"Sherry's tough," Jake said finally. "She shouldn't have to be, but she is."

"I see how much you care about them," Sam said softly. "So why did you just drop out of their lives like that?"

"Sherry talks too much," Jake said, but there was no heat in his words. He sat down on a bench, his hands dangling between his knees. "I did it because if it hadn't been for me, Charlie wouldn't have died. They didn't need me around as a reminder of what they'd lost."

Here, at last, was the heart of the matter. Sam sat down carefully beside him, afraid of spooking him. "Why do you think that, Jake?"

"It was my fault."

"That's not what Sherry said."

"Sherry wasn't there." Jake didn't look at her and she sensed he had gone someplace else—back to the night Charlie had been killed. "I never should have turned my back on the girl. I broke the rules and Charlie died."

"Tell me what happened, Jake." Sam kept her voice low, afraid of breaking the spell. She could see the pain etched on his face. Two years had done nothing to cure the hurt he carried around inside him.

"Just another screwed-up teenager. A pretty blonde named Carla. The guy we were after was her boyfriend." Jake's jaw worked over the words, biting into each as if it were poison. "A small-time hood dealing drugs to kids."

A whippoorwill trilled overhead, its melancholy song a fitting tribute for Jake's anguish. When the bird's song trailed away into silence, Sam pressed Jake for more information. "What happened?"

"We cornered him in an alley. The bust went down without a hitch. We had the guy in cuffs, his girlfriend sobbing on the sidelines." Jake glanced at her. "She looked so helpless. We'd taken her in before—possession, prostitution. All of seventeen, and she'd lived a lifetime's worth."

Sam could only shake her head in sympathy. She'd seen the images before, through her camera lens. The epidemic wasn't drugs, it was apathy.

"I told Charlie to watch out for her. She was pretty pissed we'd busted her man. He was busy loading the boyfriend into the car and didn't hear me." Jake shook his head. "I was calling it in when I heard the shot."

"She shot Charlie?"

He nodded. "Pulled a gun out of her purse and fired like she'd been doing it all her life. For a second it didn't dawn on me where the shot had come from. I ran around the side of the car and saw the gun.''

Sam could feel the tension coming from him in waves, but she didn't push.

Lost in his memories, Jake drew a shaky breath. ''I froze. She fired again, nailing me in the leg.''

''Oh, my God,'' Sam breathed. She'd noticed the slight hitch in his walk but had never imagined he'd been shot. Last night they'd undressed in darkness. She had been too caught up in the moment to notice his injury.

Jake went on as if he hadn't heard her. ''I pulled my gun and warned her off. She was crying and cursing me. She fired again and I shot back. She died at the hospital.''

Sam gripped the bench seat until her fingers hurt, afraid Jake would pull away if she tried to touch him. ''It wasn't your fault.''

''You weren't there.'' He spat the words out between clenched teeth. ''If I hadn't screwed up—''

Finally Sam reached out, gently laying her hand on the clenched fist resting on his knee. ''It was an accident. A horrible mistake. But it wasn't your fault.'' She carefully enunciated each word, wanting so badly to make him see the truth that was so clear to her.

''I'm not going to argue about this,'' he said, pulling away from her. He stood, jamming his hands in the pockets of his jeans.

''Jake—''

''Don't, Sam,'' he pleaded. The pain in his voice embedded itself inside her, wrapping around her heart.

The muscles in Jake's broad back rippled under his shirt and Sam fought the urge to run her hands across his shoulder blades and ease some of the tension there. He wasn't ready to listen to her, wasn't ready to forgive himself. She sighed in helpless frustration and forced herself to change the subject.

''What happens tomorrow?''

She could see him shifting gears, moving out of the past and into the immediacy of the present. "I don't know." He kept his back to her, shaking his head. "I hope Sherry is right about Joe being able to help. I doubt he's dirty, but I don't know if he'll believe our story."

It seemed too much of a long shot to count on. Sam shivered, eyeing the deepening shadows around them. She'd been so caught up in Jake's emotions that she'd allowed herself to forget how much danger they were in. They'd gotten away this time. Next time they might not be so lucky.

"What if he doesn't?"

"I don't know." He shook his head, offering her a half smile that didn't quite reach his eyes. "I wish I did, Sam. But I don't know."

She searched frantically for some shred of hope. There had to be something they could do. "Maybe we could go public."

"A press conference in front of the governor's mansion, maybe?" Though he said the words sarcastically, Sam could see the wheels turning in Jake's mind.

"Sure. They wouldn't dare try to kill us then."

"No, but they could easily arrest us. I'm wanted for murder, remember?"

The small flicker of hope snuffed out. They couldn't win, no matter what they did. "Right."

"But it might work for you," Jake said. "They faked your death. We have proof of that. If you told your story with the evidence you've got, they couldn't touch you. Sherry could help you get the best attorney in the state."

She didn't like the way he was talking. It was as if he were distancing himself from her. "But what about you?"

He shrugged. "I can go underground for a while. It might blow over eventually."

Sam's breath caught in her throat. "No, Jake. You've been through hell for me. I'm not about to walk away now. We're in this together, remember?"

"You've been trying to get away from me since this started. I guess I've grown on you."

"You could say that." Her soft words were edged with pain. "Stay with me, Jake."

"Let's not worry about it until tomorrow," he said lightly. "We don't know what might happen."

Sam's senses screamed for her not to believe him. He turned to walk away and she caught him by the arm. He could have pulled away again, but he didn't. They stood there like that for several long moments before he turned around. She could tell by the firm set of his jaw that he'd already made up his mind.

"Promise me you're not going to leave me," she urged, her fingers wrapped so tightly around his wrist she could feel the steady beat of his pulse. She didn't care how desperate the words sounded, she only wanted to hear him say that they would stick together, no matter what.

"Don't, Sam," he said, his voice lowering in warning. He carefully pried her fingers from his arm and turned his back on her.

She watched him walk into the shadows, her hands clenched in tight fists at her sides. She was painfully aware of his nearly imperceptible limp. It made him seem all too human. All too fragile.

"Damn you, Jake Cavanaugh," she cried.

She was ripping his heart out but Jake didn't turn around. He couldn't. She made him too angry, made him feel too much. He didn't want to feel, he didn't want to admit his failure. He'd let too many people down in his life. He'd walk away from her before he'd do it again.

"Damn you," she said again and he could hear the tears in her voice.

He heard her footsteps behind him, felt her hand on his arm as she tried to stop him. She stepped in front of him, her eyes reflecting moonlight. They were angry eyes, but there was something else there, too—something that made his blood run hotter and quickened his pulse until it roared like the ocean in his ears.

"Don't walk away from me," she whispered before pressing the full length of her body against him.

Jake put his hands on her shoulders, intending to push her away. But it felt too right. He groaned low in his throat, his arms slipping down to her waist. He pulled her closer, knowing it was the last thing he should be doing, but not caring.

"Don't walk away," she said again, tilting her head up to him.

Her mouth was an enticement he couldn't refuse and Jake was long past trying. His lips meshed with hers in a hard, angry kiss. Instead of pulling away, she demanded more, her hands wrapping around his neck and pulling him closer.

Jake groaned again and dragged his mouth away from hers. He cupped her chin in his hand, his fingers trailing up her jaw and tangling in her hair. She was breathing hard. So was he, for that matter.

"We can't do this," he said, stepping away from her. He hoped that putting some distance between them would take the edge off his lust. It didn't.

"What are you afraid of, Jake?" she whispered in the darkness. When he didn't speak, she asked, "Are you afraid that maybe you won't be able to save the day this time? Are you afraid I'll leave you like your ex-wife? Are you afraid of letting me down?"

"What?"

She took a step closer, moonlight illuminating her uptilted face. It reminded him of the night he'd found her. She'd looked so helpless and vulnerable then—a lost angel in need of protection. She didn't look helpless now. She looked very much in control.

And very angry.

"You couldn't save Charlie, you couldn't save the girl. You couldn't salvage your marriage. You couldn't make everything all right for Sherry and Emily."

"Stop it, Sam."

She took another step closer, her chin edging up a notch as she ticked off his failings. "You don't have to save me, Jake. You don't have to be my knight or my hero. You don't have to be afraid."

Something inside him snapped—something dark and cold and hard. "I'm not afraid," he rasped, hanging on to his control by a thread.

"Liar."

She gasped when he swept her into his arms, but the sound barely registered in his fevered mind. Pressing her back against the tree, he slanted his lips down on hers, mindless of anything except the emotions she incited—the ache in his chest and the lust roaring in his veins.

She kissed him back after the first initial shock, her mouth open to his explorations, her body pliant under his hands. His thumbs circled her nipples through her thin T-shirt and she moaned softly against his mouth. He cupped her breasts fully, savoring their weight in his palms. Needing more, he slid his hands under her shirt, enjoying the way she responded to his touch on her naked skin.

"Jake," she breathed against his lips. She arched her back, pressing her breasts into his hands. Her nipples hardened into sweet, taut peaks and she moaned. "Jake."

Sam's hands circled his waist, drawing him closer. She rubbed against him with a sinuous, fluid motion that left him rock hard and panting. He tugged at the waistband of her shorts, needing to touch her all over.

When her shorts slipped down her legs, she froze against him. She looked up at him as if dazed by passion. "Here? Now?"

He couldn't answer, couldn't form the words to say that here and now was all they might have. He could only nod. He could think of no better time than here and now.

She stepped out of her shorts, her T-shirt still covering her to her hips. Reaching out, she pulled him to her, her hands working at the buttons on his shirt. She pushed the material back, planting warm, wet kisses on the skin she exposed.

He let her control the action, content with burying his face in her hair and trailing kisses down her neck. She turned her attention to his belt buckle. A moment later Jake heard the release of his zipper, felt her stroke the hot length of him. He groaned against her neck, shaking with his need to bury himself inside her.

He pushed her against the tree and she hooked her leg around his thigh. He pulled the hem of her shirt up to her waist, his hands molding over the lush curves of her body. The thin barrier of her panties was all that separated them. He stroked the damp cleft of her and was rewarded by her moan.

Impatient to feel her against him, he tugged at the wispy material until it tore. The sound aroused him beyond reason.

Sam palmed his arousal, driving him mad with her gentle touch. "You don't have to save me, Jake," she murmured against his chest, drawing him closer to the warm wetness at her core. "Just love me."

Sinking deep inside her, he did as she requested.

It didn't seem to matter that they were outside, in a public place. Sam didn't care that at any moment they could be caught. All she could focus on was the sensation of Jake moving against her, inside her. All that mattered to her was this moment, this man. She would say with her body what she couldn't say with words. She loved him. Heaven help her, but she loved him.

"Sam, oh, Sam," he groaned, moving deeper with every thrust.

She angled her hips up to meet him, drowning in the exquisite agony of desire. His large hands pulled her bottom up, pushing him deeper, bringing them closer. She felt the waves ripple through her, pooling in the center of her being. Swept away by her release, she bit into his shoulder to keep from crying out.

Jake gasped—whether from pain or passion, she didn't know. A moment later, he rasped out her name as he exploded within her.

In the aftermath of their lovemaking, he cradled her close. The hard, muscular planes of his chest were slick with moisture. She heard a rumbling coming from deep inside him and pulled back, startled. Looking up at him, she realized he was laughing.

''What's so funny?''

Without letting her go, he tugged her T-shirt down to cover her. ''This. Us,'' he said. Hunting in the dark, he retrieved her shorts and handed them to her. ''I think your panties were the only casualty.''

Stepping into her shorts while he supported her, Sam gave him a wry grin. ''You think that's funny?''

''No. What's funny is that after all that we've been through, it would serve us right to get arrested for indecent exposure.''

''It was your idea.''

''I didn't hear any complaints.''

His bantering was a front. She knew it and so did he. ''That wasn't your way of saying goodbye, was it?'' she asked softly.

His hands stilled on his shirt buttons and he lifted his eyes to meet hers. He started to say something, then shook his head as if changing his mind. ''What do you want, Sam?''

''I want us to stick together, no matter what happens. We'll see this thing through to the end. And then...'' Her words trailed off. She didn't know what would happen then.

''And then what?''

''Let's get through this first, all right?'' Suddenly she didn't want to think about the future. The thought of Jake walking away from her was too much to bear.

He didn't speak, and for that she was glad. She couldn't handle another argument tonight. Jake hadn't promised anything but she somehow knew he wouldn't leave her—for now. The future was too uncertain to predict.

Chapter 18

Sam awoke the next morning to a big, sloppy kiss. Startled, she looked up into soulful brown eyes. Fletcher.

"Oh, gross!" She scooted up the sofa bed, away from the drooling canine.

Jake came into the room, a towel draped around his hips. "What's the matter?"

"Your dog. He's slobbering all over me," she said, wiping her mouth with the back of her hand.

"He likes you."

Sam started to argue the point but was distracted by the fine masculine form Jake presented. He was too good-looking for his own good. Or hers. The damp towel clung to him, leaving nothing to her imagination.

It dawned on her that she'd never seen his body in the light. Last night they'd returned to Sherry's house and undressed in the darkness. They'd reached for each other almost in desperation, making love again—quietly, urgently. Then he had curled around her and promptly fallen asleep. But even in her exhaustion, sleep had eluded her. She'd sat up for hours, reading her father's letters and mourning the past.

"Something wrong?"

She blushed as he caught her staring. "Not a thing," she answered honestly. Nope, there wasn't anything wrong with him, she thought as she let her eyes trail down his body.

Her gaze stopped when she reached the scar on his left leg. Puckered pink flesh stood out in harsh relief. She almost winced, but managed to control her reaction when she realized he was watching her.

"It was a lot worse for Charlie," he said, turning his back on her.

Sam sighed and looked away, frustrated with him for being so stubborn, and angry at herself for loving him so much. She hadn't wanted to admit it, but it had been there in the shadows, taunting her with the promise of something she wasn't sure she could ever have.

"Better get a move on," Jake said, cocking his head to the side. "I think I hear Emily getting up. She'll hog all the hot water."

Sam climbed out of bed, acutely aware of Jake's nudity as he began dressing. She scooped up her clothes and scurried across the hall to the bathroom.

By the time she'd showered and dressed, everyone was in the kitchen. She paused in the doorway for a moment, surveying the scene. Sherry stood at the counter, nursing a cup of coffee, with a no-nonsense expression on her face.

"Come on, Mom. Let me stay home. Uncle Jake's here," Emily pleaded.

"I said no."

Jake backed Sherry up. "She's right, Em. I'll be here when you get home from school."

"Promise?"

Jake nodded solemnly. "Promise."

Emily grudgingly gave in. "Oh, all right." Gathering her back-

pack and the lunch bag from the counter, she headed for the door.
"Bye, Sam."

"Bye, Emily. Have fun at school."

The girl sighed and rolled her eyes dramatically. "I'll try."

"She's making up for lost time since her illness," Sherry said
as the door slammed.

"She's just acting her age," Jake said mildly. "She'll grow
out of it."

"But will you?" Sherry asked, giving Sam a knowing look.
"Breakfast is a free-for-all around here, so make yourself at
home."

Sam helped herself to a cup of coffee and joined them at the
table. "So what's the plan?"

Sherry glanced up at the wall clock. "I'll give Joe a call in a
few minutes. He likes to beat the traffic, so he should be in soon.
And I need to leave for work in about an hour myself." She
smiled at Sam. "Sleep well?"

Sam nodded. "As well as possible." She was thankful that the
drugs seemed to have finally worked their way out of her system.
She had a feeling she was going to need nerves of steel before
this day was over.

Ten minutes later, Sherry hung up the phone after giving Joe
an abridged version of their story. "Joe wants you to meet him
at the office."

"How do we know it's not a trap?" Jake asked, impatience in
every gesture he made. He wasn't a man used to inaction, Sam
knew. And he didn't like someone else making the decisions.

"Trust me, Jake," Sherry said gently. "I know Joe. He isn't
going to do anything except listen to you, if for no other reason
than you are friends of mine."

Jake sighed and raked a hand through his hair. "Thanks, Sher.
I appreciate your help."

"Thank me when this is over."

Jake's smile didn't quite reach his eyes. "You bet I will."

* * *

Jake and Sam arrived at Joe's office at nine-thirty. They'd dropped Sherry off at work and borrowed her car. Now they sat in one of the plush offices of the FBI, waiting for Joe.

"I don't like this," Jake muttered, shifting in his chair.

Sam tucked her hair behind her ear. She didn't like it any more than Jake did, but Joe was their last hope. "Relax. Sherry said we can trust him."

"Sherry trusts me. She's not the best judge of character."

"Well, I am and I trust you. Let's give the guy a chance, first."

"Good idea," a voice from the doorway said. "Long time no see, Jake."

He came into the room, shaking Sam's hand. "I'm Joe Lafferty. Not to be confused with Joe Friday." Even when he smiled he had the serious expression of a cop, Sam decided. But his easy demeanor made her feel comfortable.

"Hi, Joe. Wish we could be meeting under better circumstances," Jake said.

Joe took a seat behind the desk. "Me, too. But let's deal with what we've got."

"I know you've heard what's going on with me. I'm accused of murder."

Joe nodded. "I've heard. Sherry seems to think you didn't do it."

"I didn't."

Sam was reminded of a similar conversation between Jake and her—only she'd been the one professing her innocence. "He was trying to help me."

Joe raised an eyebrow. "I hear you're supposed to be dead."

Jake pulled the newspaper articles and the pictures of Montegna out of his shirt pocket and slid them across the desk. On top of the pile he put the two thugs' wallets he'd confiscated in Key West.

"You've been busy," Joe said, flipping through the wallets. "I can run these names."

"Don't bother. They're Carlos Montegna's boys."

"Montegna? What do you know about him?"

Sam noticed that Joe didn't seem surprised. "He's alive," she said. "And he's after me because of those pictures."

Joe looked through the pictures and then up at Sam. "When were these taken?"

"February twenty-sixth."

Joe nodded. "There have been rumors flying around the department—" He broke off. "It looks like you were in the wrong place at the wrong time."

"What do you know about BOCTA?" Jake asked, adding Manning's wallet to the pile.

Joe sat back in his chair, eyeing them speculatively. "Bureau of Organized Crime and Terrorist Activities. The FBI and CIA know about it. Secret Service knows. But it's not public knowledge."

"What do they do?" Sam asked, feeling a cold chill dance across her skin.

"Their interests are internal. They're an independent entity, policing the government at all levels."

"No one is independent in the government," Jake argued. "Everyone answers to someone."

Joe nodded in agreement. "Sure. But they only report to the highest office. BOCTA is supposed to be the answer to all the dirty politics going on."

"So what does the Bureau have to do with Montegna?" Sam asked.

"My guess would be they cut him a deal. Montegna knew everything and he was supposedly singing like a canary. There are a lot of people who would want him dead."

"The Ortiz Cartel he belonged to was the third or fourth biggest drug cartel in Central America," Jake said.

"First in everything else," Joe added. "Montegna was second in charge. He knows all the dirty secrets."

"And they don't like being crossed," Jake said. "But what good is his word?

"It's more than just his word, from what I've heard. Montegna knew the risks he was taking. He knew what the odds were if he got caught. He's an American citizen. Once we nailed him we could lock him up and throw away the key."

"He must have something BOCTA wants very badly," Jake said.

Joe leaned forward, drumming his fingers on the pictures. "Apparently, Montegna kept records. Detailed records, audio and video." He looked at Sam. "And pictures. Everything's hush-hush now, but from what I've heard, he's got enough information to take down a lot of people."

"And I threatened to ruin that," Sam said.

"Sounds like it. Though, what the hell they were thinking, bringing him to the courthouse, I couldn't begin to tell you."

Sam shook her head. "He was well protected and coming out the back. He wasn't in plain sight for more than a minute. If I hadn't had a telephoto lens, I wouldn't have seen him."

"But you did. And BOCTA needed to keep you quiet." Joe thumbed through his Rolodex.

"It sounds like they're above the law," Jake said.

"Well, they're not." Joe looked at Sam. "You need to call BOCTA. We'll set up a meeting. If there's something dirty going on, we'll take them down." He pushed the phone number and the phone to their side of the desk.

"Who's George Levy?" Sam asked, reading the phone number.

"Assistant director of BOCTA. From what I understand, Montegna was his pigeon."

"I don't like this," Jake said.

"I guess I'd better get it over with." Sam reached for the phone.

"Let me talk to him," Jake said, his hand covering hers on the receiver.

"I can handle this, Jake." His hero tendencies were starting to get on her last ragged nerve.

He must have sensed her aggravation because he pulled his hand away. "Sorry, old habit."

Sam nodded and focused on dialing the numbers but hesitated. "Won't they be able to find us?"

Joe shook his head. "All our calls are blocked. The FBI likes to keep secrets, too."

Sam resumed dialing. The phone rang several times before a pleasant female voice answered. "Name, please?"

Confused, Sam asked, "What?"

"Your name, please?" the woman asked patiently.

"Samantha Martin."

"Contact?"

She assumed the woman referred to the man she was calling. "George Levy."

There was silence on the other end for a moment. "Hold please."

The silence on the other end was interminable. Finally, a man picked up. "Who is this?"

"Samantha Martin. Who is this?"

Instead of answering her question, the man asked, "How did you get this number?"

"A friend. I need to speak to George Levy."

"I'm George Levy. Where are you?"

"Hold on a minute." Sam glanced at Jake, knowing he couldn't hear Levy's side of the conversation. Cupping her hand over the mouthpiece of the phone, she whispered, "He wants to know where we are."

Jake's eyes narrowed. "Tell him we're in north Florida. That's vague enough."

Before she could speak, Levy let out a gusty sigh. "Look, I have a pretty good idea where you are. We had a man at the airport in Key West. We need to meet."

"When?"

There was silence on the other end for such a long time she thought he'd hung up. "This afternoon. Tell me where."

Sam put her hand over the mouthpiece again. "He wants to meet."

"Tell him to fly into the Tallahassee airport on the first available Trans Global flight," Joe said. "Alone. We'll meet him at the gate."

Sam relayed the message.

"Do you have the pictures?"

A chill crawled up Sam's spine. "Yes."

"Bring them."

Before Sam could speak, Jake took the phone from her. "Leave the guns and the hired hands at home, Levy."

"Who is this?"

"You're the man with all the answers—you tell me," Jake said.

"Cavanaugh. You did a number on my man."

"Keep that in mind."

Sam reached for the phone, impatient with Jake and his he-man tactics. "How do we know you won't kill us?"

Levy's voice dropped to a husky growl. "Lady, you don't know what you're involved in or who you're dealing with. I'm your only link to freedom."

"Fine," she said. "We'll be there."

"Tell your boyfriend if he gets out of line, he'll regret it."

The line went dead. Sam looked at Joe, feeling all the color drain out of her face. "We're not really going to meet this guy, are we?"

"It'll be all right," Joe assured them. "We won't let you out of our sight."

"I wish you would, Joe," Jake disagreed. "I'd like ten minutes alone with him."

Joe's expression went cold. "You want him alive, Jake. He may be the only one who can clear your name. And to be honest, if we don't get some answers soon, there won't be anything I can do to protect you."

"Then let's do it."

Sam looked at Jake, hearing the hard-edged determination in his voice. "What are you thinking?"

His grin was predatory. "I'm thinking we're going into the lion's den. And I'm ready to hunt big game."

"I hope this works."

Jake only nodded. He hoped to hell it worked, too. If this was a trap, he wasn't one-hundred-percent sure Joe could get them out of it. "We'll be all right," he said, voicing a confidence he didn't feel.

They'd left for the airport at one and Jake had checked on the incoming Trans Global flight. They sat in short-term parking, waiting for the two o'clock flight to arrive from D.C. Joe Lafferty was in another car beside them while a second car with two FBI agents was parked at the airport exit.

Jake couldn't shake the feeling that they were walking into a trap. He trusted Joe, but if Levy didn't play his hand, Jake would have to turn himself in. And he was willing to bet he wouldn't survive the night in jail. If BOCTA didn't get him, Montegna would. Only time would tell. And judging by the dashboard clock, time was running out.

They left the car at Joe's signal. "I'll be right here. Don't take him too far and don't try any heroics. Just get him to talk."

Jake nodded as he took Sam's arm. "Remember the plan?"

Nerves on edge, Sam only nodded as they found the Trans Global gate. "Got it." She plucked nervously at her shirt. "This thing is uncomfortable."

The "thing" she was referring to was a wiretap Joe had made her wear. He would be able to hear every word of their conversation.

Jake winked. "Hang in there. I'll be happy to remove it personally when we're through." He grinned for her benefit but she didn't return the smile.

"Let's just get this over with."

They didn't have long to wait. A short, balding man came

barreling out of the gate. When he spotted them, his eyes narrowed.

"Where to?"

"We've got a car outside."

Levy had the features of a mild-mannered librarian, but Jake wasn't fooled. He held their lives in his hands. They had to make sure he talked.

Jake maneuvered so that Levy was between them as they crossed the parking lot. Levy didn't seem to notice Joe as he drove past them and stopped just before the airport exit.

"I'm sure you have a lot of questions," Levy said, as he climbed into the front seat beside Jake.

"You could say that," Sam said as she got into the back seat.

Jake gave her a reassuring look. She was strung so tight he was afraid she'd break in half. He needed to keep his cop instincts alert. And in order to do that, he needed her to relax so he wouldn't be thinking about her.

Sam gave him a tight smile. "You seem to know everything about me. How?"

"Since you made it your business to stick your nose into issues that concern me," Levy said, eyeing the packet of pictures Jake placed on the dashboard.

Jake played his first card. "You mean the pictures of Montegna."

Levy swore under his breath. "Yeah." He reached into his pocket and pulled out a roll of antacids. He pinched one off and popped it in his mouth.

Jake slid the pictures over to Levy. "Here. Keep them."

Levy nearly smiled. Then Sam added, "We've made copies. If anything happens to us, those pictures will turn up again. Along with my signed and notarized statement attesting to what's happened to me."

"That wasn't very smart." Levy scowled, thumbing through the pictures.

"We're not concerned with being smart," Jake said. "We're

more interested in staying alive. Now why don't you fix this mess you've dragged Sam into and let us get on with our lives.''

"It's not that easy. You don't know what's at stake.''

Sam's voice was controlled and even. "What is this all about?''

Levy looked at Jake. "You know Montegna's record.'' It was a statement, not a question. "He's not someone to screw with.''

"Last I heard, Montegna was dead,'' Jake answered dryly. He checked his rearview mirror. Joe was two cars behind them. The other agents were in the lane next to them.

"That's the way he wanted it. He wouldn't cooperate unless we could set it up for him to disappear.''

"Why?'' Sam asked, leaning over the seat and closer to Levy. Jake suspected she was trying to guarantee that Joe heard every word.

"Montegna is the key to the largest conspiracy this country's ever seen.''

The hair on the back of Jake's neck stood up. "Don't tell me, let me guess. This has something to do with UFOs.''

Levy ignored him and turned his attention to Sam. "Your pictures threatened to destroy BOCTA's investigation.''

"How?'' Sam asked.

"Montegna has enough evidence to bring down officials at every level of government. From the local beat cop to border patrol to the powers that be in D.C. We're this close—'' he held his pudgy fingers up ''—to busting them all.''

Jake glanced at him. "For what?''

"You name it.'' Levy shrugged, sitting back in his chair. "Drugs, guns, mercenary armies. Organized prostitution, gambling, money laundering, illegal government contributions—the works.''

"What does that have to do with me?'' Sam asked.

Levy went on as if she hadn't spoken. "There are enough crooked officials in his records to fill a prison. And I'm going to bring every last one of 'em down.'' He sighed. "But Montegna's cooperation came at a price.''

Jake exchanged glances with Sam. "What price?"

"His freedom."

"You faked his death and intend to let him get off," Jake said.

Levy nodded. "We needed time. He had ten years' worth of information that had to be sorted, examined, verified." Levy smacked the pictures for emphasis. "The cartel tried to have him assassinated twice in the first month we had him in custody. He never would have survived to stand trial. We made it look like one of the attempts succeeded."

"So it was a setup," Sam said almost to herself.

"I knew it wasn't a good idea to take him to the courthouse. But he had one more deposition to give and wanted one last chance to thumb his nose at the system before he left the country. He'd been undercover for a year and I made sure no one knew anything." He turned and glared at Sam. "Then you and your damned camera showed up and threatened to ruin everything I'd worked for."

The pieces were starting to click into place for Jake. "Who arranged for Sam's stay at the hospital?"

For the first time since they'd picked him up, Levy looked uncomfortable. "That was a mistake."

"Who put her there?" Jake demanded.

"I did."

Chapter 19

"You bastard." Sam clenched her fists in her lap. "How could you do that to me?"

"I did what I thought was necessary."

Jake reached across and grabbed Levy by his tie. "If I were you, I'd explain that comment in a hurry. I think I'd really enjoy making a bloody mess of your face."

Sweat beaded across Levy's brow and his features didn't relax until Jake released him. He turned to look at Sam. "I told you, that was a mistake. I only intended to get you out of the way for a little while. Montegna wanted blood. You were as good as dead on the street."

Sam willed the man to look her in the eye, to see what he'd done to her. "I was as good as dead in that hospital. Why did you leave me there?"

"We use it as a safe house for witnesses. You were an unknown commodity. We had to keep you under control." Levy waved his hand in the air. "I couldn't get you out. I had a dead agent on our hands and everyone asking questions."

"Montegna killed the federal agent?" Jake asked.

"No, Montegna has a couple of very loyal men that split with the cartel when he was brought in. I sent Moreno over to your hotel to clear up this mess but Montegna didn't trust me," Levy said. "He sent one of his men over to take care of you. Moreno had orders to get you the hell out of there."

"If that's supposed to make me feel better, it doesn't," Sam said.

Levy shrugged. "You weren't supposed to get involved. But Montegna's boy had his orders. He killed Moreno."

"Why didn't he kill me?" Sam asked quietly.

"Montegna wanted the film. He was convinced I was trying to double-cross him. His boy was supposed to bring you to Montegna but I guess he couldn't get you out of the hotel without witnesses." Levy ran a hand over his perspiring forehead. "Montegna was livid."

"So you locked me up at that hospital for my own protection?"

"Exactly. When Montegna learned you'd escaped, he sent his men after you again." Levy pulled a handkerchief from his pocket and wiped the sweat from his forehead. "Manning was supposed to keep an eye on you, make sure Montegna's boys didn't get too close."

"Problem was, he got too close to us," Jake said.

"You screwed up when you took out Manning."

"At least he's alive," Jake repeated. "That's more than I can say for Moreno or Greg Tilton."

"Montegna's a loose cannon, unpredictable," Levy said, his voice losing some of its power. "I've had men watching him around the clock for a year now. But we're almost finished with him."

"It was Montegna's goons who killed the people at the diner," Jake said.

"What a bloodbath." Levy thumbed another antacid out of the roll and popped it into his mouth.

"A friend of mine died there." Sam could feel the tension

radiating from Jake—so potent it must be in every fiber of his body. He clenched the steering wheel tighter. "And you framed me for that bloodbath," he growled.

"I'm sorry about Tilton, but it couldn't be helped. If I'd fingered Montegna, he wouldn't have trusted me. He's not someone I want to make an enemy of." Levy edged closer to the door. "I needed a fall guy."

"What you're saying is that you're willing to do anything to keep your little pigeon happy," Jake said, making a U-turn back toward the airport.

Sam felt the wire against her chest and hoped Joe would have enough information to use against Levy. "How did Montegna find us at the diner?"

"Montegna's smart. Too smart. As soon as the call came in that the woman was missing, Montegna knew. He may be dead to the world, but his men still use his connections. When Cavanaugh called Tilton at the police station, Montegna's men had no problem tracking you."

"And you've been after us ever since." Jake's voice was hard, cold.

"It's for your own protection. I have to do whatever it takes to keep this operation running. You were a hassle I didn't need. In the great scheme of things, you're expendable."

Sam pressed her hands against her knees to keep them from shaking. "If we're expendable, why haven't you killed us yet?"

"I don't want you dead, I just want you out of the way until this is over."

"And then what? You'll clear my name, give Sam back her life?"

"You don't get it, do you?" Levy pounded his fist on the dashboard. "This is bigger than either of you. I tried to keep you out of it, but you've made that impossible."

"Well, we're out of it now," Jake said. "I think the press might be interested in hearing what's going on behind closed doors."

"You aren't going to the press. You aren't going anywhere."

"You've kept me prisoner long enough, Mr. Levy," Sam said.

"Montegna is after you. He'll hunt you down like animals unless you let me help you. I can put you into the Witness Protection Program," Levy said. "You'll have new names, new identities. Montegna won't be able to touch you. Believe me, it's a far more generous offer than the one you're likely to get from him."

Jake turned back into the airport parking lot. Sam didn't dare look over her shoulder, but she hoped Joe was right behind them.

"Take your generous offer and shove it."

Levy glared at Jake. "Maybe you shouldn't be making decisions for the lady."

"I'll take my chances with Montegna," Sam said. "At least I know what to expect from him."

Jake had pulled up to the curb, but Levy didn't seem to notice. His face flushed angrily as he turned to look at Sam. "You're going to trust this washed-up cop over me? The only difference between him and Montegna is that Montegna knows better than to bite the hand that feeds him."

"Watch it, Levy. Or I'll show you just what I'm capable of," Jake warned.

Levy tucked the pictures into his jacket pocket. "Fine. It's your funeral." He got out of the car just as Joe Lafferty walked up.

"George Levy, you're under arrest."

Sam and Jake got out of the car.

"What the hell is this all about?"

"It's about abuse of power and corruption," Jake said.

Joe handcuffed Levy. "We heard every word, Levy. Your little game is over."

"You can't touch me." Levy shook his head slowly. "But there's something you should know before you celebrate."

"What?" Sam asked, her skin crawling as he looked at her, his eyes small and evil.

"Montegna managed to slip by us last night. He's out of my control." He smiled. "And he's after you."

Sam didn't think about it. She simply did what she'd wanted to do since Levy had gotten into the car. She pulled back her fist and slugged him.

Joe waved the other two agents off and grinned. "Well, that was fun."

"Thanks for your help, Joe." Jake shook his hand. "Am I off the hook?"

Joe nodded. "We'll want you for questioning. But I think we have enough proof to clear you." He frowned. "But I don't like the idea of you two out on your own. Montegna is crafty. He'll find you."

"What should we do?" Sam asked, rubbing her fingers over her sore knuckles. It had felt good to hit Levy, but her hand was starting to swell.

"I'd like to put you into protective custody." At Jake's protest, Joe held up his hands. "Just for a couple of days, until we can flush Montegna out."

"I can take care of myself," Jake said.

"You're not a cop anymore, Jake. Let us do our job."

"It makes sense, Jake," Sam added. She knew he didn't want to be held captive, even for his own protection. She felt the same way. But this time it was different. This time, it was her decision.

Jake nodded. "All right. Just for a couple of days. But we have to go back to Sherry's to get our stuff. And my dog."

"Fine. Meet me back at my office. I'll give Sherry a call and let her know what's going on."

Joe left them and they got into the car. Once they were coasting down the highway toward Sherry's house, Sam unbuttoned her blouse and removed the wire, wincing as the tape pulled away from her skin.

"Where'd you learn to throw a punch like that?"

Sam managed a grin. "Boxing class."

"Boxing?"

"Yeah. Self-defense for a single woman in New York."

Jake shook his head. "You never fail to amaze me."

"Thanks." The warm glow of his praise washed over her. The words *I love you* were on her lips, but she held back. They were so close to being out of this. Soon enough, they'd part ways. Would her confession make any difference?

"Are you sure you want to go along with this protective-custody idea?"

Sam shrugged. "What choice do we have?

"We've done all right for ourselves so far. I trust Joe, but he's still FBI. There're no guarantees they'll be able to do any better a job of protecting us from Montegna than we can. But if Montegna is out there, we need to get out of Dodge."

Sam knew what he was thinking. Montegna wouldn't discriminate when it came to seeking his revenge. Levy might tell Montegna where to find them. Sherry and Emily would be in his path if he got this far. She shivered. Whatever happened to her, she wasn't going to risk anyone else's life.

"I trust you more than I trust Joe," Sam said finally. "I'll go along with whatever you want to do."

"All right."

They drove into Sherry's neighborhood, the streets empty this early in the afternoon. The car coasted to a stop in front of the house. Jake shut off the engine and turned to her. She didn't like what she saw in his eyes.

"What?" she asked, not at all sure she wanted to hear the answer.

"I want you to leave the country."

"Us, you mean," she said stubbornly.

He shook his head. "No." When she turned her head, he reached over and took her hands. He pulled her around to face him. "Listen to me, Sam. It's the best way. It's the only way to protect you."

"What about you?"

"I'll stay here and work with Joe. We'll catch Montegna and you'll be safe."

Sam pulled away from him, angry and hurt. "You said we'd stick together."

"That was before I knew the score. You'll be safer out of the country."

"Even if I wanted to leave, which I don't, how would I? I don't have a passport or any identification, for that matter. I don't have a dime to my name," she argued.

"I can get Brian or Mac to fly you to the islands. I have contacts who can forge your credentials. You can go anywhere in the world." He paused until she looked over at him.

"No, Jake! I'm not leaving you behind to get killed."

"Please, Sam—"

"Don't ask this of me," she interrupted. "I don't want to lose you. We've come too far. I—I care about you."

She'd been ready to say she loved him, but the words stuck in her throat. She didn't know why he couldn't see it in her eyes. Last night she'd vowed she wouldn't tell him until after this was over, if then. But the thought of leaving him to the mercy of Montegna forced the truth to the surface.

He shook his head in denial. "You hardly know me, Sam. We don't know anything about each other."

She reached across the seat and pressed her trembling fingers to his lips. "I know enough."

It broke her heart that he didn't feel the same way, but it didn't change the truth of her feelings. "I'm not going to run away and let you get killed."

Sam watched the different emotions flit across his face. "I don't know what to say—"

"Say you're not going to run me out of town," she answered lightly, forcing a smile through her pain.

Jake sighed. Reaching over, he tucked a long strand of her hair behind her ear, his fingers lingering on the curve of her cheek. "Oh, Sam."

He didn't have a chance to finish the thought. The driver's door lurched open and the muzzle of a gun pressed against the back of his head. Sam's scream was cut short as her door was yanked open and rough hands dragged her from the car.

Montegna's men had found them.

"Come on, lovebirds. You've got an appointment at the airport." The man's fingers dug cruelly into her arm. Instinctively, she tried to pull away.

"Don't try it," the man said, pressing a gun into her ribs.

Sam's heart leaped into her throat. She tried to scream again, but a large hand clamped over her mouth.

"No tricks."

Jake climbed out of the car and their gazes met. She read the frustration and regret in his eyes before he was jerked toward a white van parked two houses down.

The man holding Sam was the one who'd told her she was going to die. He was tall and thin, but she had no hope of getting away from his iron grip on her arm. Even if she could, the gun in his hand would have discouraged her.

The other man was built like a gorilla—all solid muscle. He outweighed Jake by at least fifty pounds. Sam's pulse pounded in her throat. They were trapped.

It felt surreal to be out in broad daylight, with a gun held to her side. Sam heard a dog barking through the haze of fear as her captor threw her into the back of the van. Her head thudded painfully against the bare metal floor and she groaned.

Jake swore viciously as he was pushed into the van beside her. "Are you all right?" he asked.

Sam nodded as she sat up, holding the side of her head.

The barking of the dog got louder. Sam gasped when she saw Fletcher, his lip drawn back and snarling, jump on the thinner man and bring him to his knees.

"Ahh! Get 'im off me!" the man screamed, beating at the dog's head. Fletcher clung to his back, his teeth ripping at his suit.

Jake took advantage of Fletcher's attack and threw himself at the other man. They tumbled to the ground in a flurry of limbs, the gun flying out of the big man's hand. Sam scrambled out of the van after it, but didn't get far. The thin man managed to dislodge Fletcher and caught her in a flying tackle. She lay on the ground with the wind knocked out of her, dazed.

Pinned beneath the big man's weight, Jake managed to scream, "Run, Sam!"

His voice broke through her haze. She was free. Fletcher hung on to her attacker's leg with a tenacious grip. Sam stumbled to her feet, intent on escape, but it was too late.

A shot shattered the air and a scream ripped from Sam's throat. Frantic, she turned to help Jake but he wasn't the casualty. Fletcher lay on his side on the lawn, still and covered in blood.

Her captor pulled her against his side, his gun pressing against her temple. "I told you, no tricks," he sneered.

Jake still struggled with the other man, oblivious to her. The man holding her yelled a warning and Jake jerked his head around. When he saw the gun pressed to Sam's temple, he froze.

"Make another move and I'll splatter her brains all over the street," her captor said.

Jake dropped his hands in defeat. "Don't hurt her," he rasped, blood streaming from his lip, his eye swollen nearly closed.

The big man hauled his massive weight up from the ground. Searching the lawn, he found his gun. "Let's go," he wheezed, scanning the street.

Jake stood without a struggle, casting one last look over his shoulder at Fletcher. The dog hadn't moved.

Their captors forced them into the van again and quickly bound their hands behind their backs with duct tape. The big man went to the front of the van and took the driver's seat.

"Where are you taking us?" Sam asked, her pulse racing in sheer terror.

The thin man rubbed at his shoulder where Fletcher had ripped his shirt. "Lady, you crossed the wrong man. Montegna wants to take care of you personally."

"Come on, Vinnie," the other man complained over his shoulder. "Before the neighbors call out the SWAT team."

"Yeah, yeah. I'm coming," he said, slamming the van's double doors.

A moment later, the vehicle pulled away from the curb. Sam leaned against the side of the van, trying to keep her balance with her hands tied. Jake sat beside her, blood trailing down his chin and staining his shirt. "I don't suppose you've got a plan."

Jake shook his head. "Not this time."

"I was afraid of that."

Chapter 20

Their captors couldn't hear them above the traffic noise and the partition that separated the body of the van from the two front seats, but Jake wasn't much inclined to talk. He was still kicking himself for letting them get caught.

"I'm sorry about Fletcher," Sam said finally.

Jake felt like someone had punched him in the gut. "I'll kill that bastard if I get my hands on him," he said, but his words lacked conviction. Their odds had dwindled to nothing. And if Montegna's reputation was any indication, Fletcher had been the lucky one.

"They said something about the airport. Why would they be taking us to the airport?"

Jake had been wondering the same thing. "I have no idea. Maybe they're flying us to Montegna."

"It doesn't make sense."

The van turned a corner and Sam pressed against Jake. At any other time he would have enjoyed the feel of her against him. Right now all he could think about was how he'd screwed up.

"Montegna wants his revenge."

"But he's going to all this trouble for the pictures?"

She had a point. Jake struggled to free his hands, but the tape only tightened on his wrists. "Maybe it's more than that."

"But what?"

Jake didn't have an answer. What did Montegna want with them? It was a good bet that he didn't want to have them over for tea.

The van left the highway. They were nearing the airport. Jake's mind ran through all the possible outcomes but his police training overrode any optimism he might have had. Removing the victim from the scene of the crime nearly always ended in a worst-case scenario.

Jake sat shoulder to shoulder with Sam and had to crane his head to look her in the eyes. "Listen, Sam. If something happens, if somehow or other I can manage to distract them, I want you to run. And keep running until you get someplace safe."

He tried to make her hear the urgency in his voice. He didn't care what happened to him anymore. After all they'd been through together, after fighting his emotions, she'd gotten past his defenses. He loved her. Only now it looked like it was too damn late to matter. He'd failed again.

Sam's eyes glittered with unshed tears. "I told you, I'm not leaving you. This doesn't change anything."

"Dammit, Sam!" Jake lowered his voice when one of the men looked back at them. "Don't argue with me now. If we have any chance at all of escaping, you have to do what I say."

He saw the resignation in her eyes a moment before she said the words. "All right."

He felt as if a weight had been lifted from his shoulders— which was ridiculous under the circumstances. But if he could catch a break, Sam might be able to get away. He ignored the nagging voice that asked, what about him? He would make sure Sam was safe.

Or die trying.

At that very moment, the van's engine shut off. The man named Vinnie looked back at them. "End of the line."

They sat back-to-back on the floor, their hands bound together. Sam was oddly comforted by the solid feeling of Jake against her in the darkness. She flexed her wrists and winced. "Now what?" she asked.

"Now we wait."

Sam snorted. How could he be so damn stoic under the circumstances? Their captors had dragged them into some kind of maintenance shack on the outskirts of the airport. Then they'd tied them up and left them without a word. It had been at least an hour, maybe longer.

Sam shifted on the hard floor, trying to get comfortable. The smell of grease made her nose wrinkle. Something scurried behind a pile of discarded tools and she pressed against Jake.

"Do you think they're going to kill us?"

She felt Jake move to accommodate her. "I don't know. Probably."

Leave it to Jake to pull no punches. "Great. So we're just going to sit here and wait for them?"

"Dammit, Sam, I'm trying to think!" he snapped. "And would you quit moving around? You're killing my arms."

"Sorry."

She heard him sigh. "That's all right."

The only window in the building was over a workbench in the corner and was covered with dust and grime, allowing little light to penetrate the dim interior. She craned her neck to look around. Maybe they could find a knife or something to cut the tape.

"Sam!" Jake complained when she twisted beyond his capacity to move.

"I can't just sit here and wait for them to come back. We've got to do something."

She felt his back muscles flex as he tried to turn his head. She could feel his breath graze her cheek, but couldn't quite see him. "Like what?"

"I don't know. Maybe we could get up and push the door open," she suggested.

"And then what? Hop across the fields until we get to the airport? It's at least a half mile."

"Great attitude, Cavanaugh."

"Yeah, well, pardon me for not wanting to make a fool of myself in my last moments."

"Help! Somebody help!" Sam yelled at the top of her lungs until her throat felt raw. Then she fell silent and listened.

"There's no one out there," Jake said mildly.

"Pardon me for not giving up hope." She felt the tears threatening to spill over. "I can't sit here and wait to die. Maybe Joe will find us."

"I wouldn't count on it." Jake shifted slightly and turned his head. Sam could feel his breath stir her hair. "I have a plan."

"You do?"

She felt him nod in affirmation. "I do. Just hang on. We'll get out of this."

Suspicious, she asked, "What's your plan?"

"I'm not telling you."

She strained against her bonds, trying to see his face. "Why the hell not?"

Jake sighed. "You'll just want to argue with me. I don't feel like arguing."

"But—"

"Let's talk about something else," he interrupted.

Sam rubbed her right foot against her left ankle, momentarily distracted by the thought of creepy-crawlies. "What?"

"I don't know—anything you want."

"I want to talk about how we're going to get out of here."

She leaned back, resting her head against the base of his neck. A plane flew low over their makeshift prison, drowning out all sound for a moment. Sam felt the floor quiver beneath her as the aircraft passed. For a moment, she was frozen by her childhood fear of a plane crashing into her house. It was ridiculous, under the circumstances, but that didn't stop her from pulling her head a little lower.

"What was that all about?" Jake asked.

Sam felt her cheeks grow warmer than they already were. "Nothing. Just superstitious."

Amazingly, Jake managed a chuckle. "Do you know what the statistics are on plane crashes of any kind, much less into buildings?"

Sam's leg was beginning to cramp, so she pulled it up under her. "No, I don't know. Do you know what the odds are of getting arrested for a murder you didn't commit?"

"Point taken."

The hum of the plane had faded into the distance, with it landing safely, Sam imagined. She wished she were on a plane right now instead of sitting in the dark waiting for somebody to kill her. If she weren't so terrified, she would have laughed at how desperate she'd become.

"Trust me, Sam. You'll get out of this in one piece."

Sam's throat constricted with unshed tears. She hadn't missed his omission. He would die trying to save her. "I do trust you, Jake."

Just then the door to the shed creaked open and Sam tensed. The doorway filled with the silhouette of a man. She squinted into the bright light. Jake's fingers laced with hers, giving them a squeeze.

"It's about time you showed up to do your own dirty work, Montegna," Jake said.

Montegna's throaty laugh sent a chill through Sam. He moved into the small building, followed by the two men who had brought them here. "Close the door, Vinnie," he said, his voice a rich Hispanic drawl.

The thin man closed the door behind them while Montegna

pulled the cord on an overhead light. The bare bulb cast an eerie light on the mobster as if drawn to his evilness. It was hard to judge Montegna's height from this level, but Sam guessed him to be fairly tall. His dark hair was shot through with strands of silver. He looked like a politician or an actor, but there was a hint of madness in his eyes.

"Sorry about your position," he said, gesturing at the floor. "But it couldn't be helped."

If Sam hadn't known better, she would have thought he cared. He smiled—his even, white teeth reminding her of a shark's. She grasped Jake's fingers tighter and gritted her teeth. She would not let this man know how badly he scared her.

"C'mon, Montegna, get to it." Jake's harsh tone belied their captivity. He sounded in control.

Montegna made a tsking sound. "Patience, Detective Cavanaugh."

Sam could feel Jake's muscles go taut.

"Oh, but you're not a detective anymore, are you?" Montegna propped his foot on a box near the door. Even dressed in casual trousers and a short-sleeved polo shirt he exuded money and power. And violence. "So why did you get yourself involved in my business?"

"You could say I tripped over one of your victims."

Montegna crossed the short distance to them. His glance flicked over Sam, a look of distaste on his face. "The woman. Levy doesn't follow directions. I wanted her dead."

"Even Levy isn't above the law," Jake said.

Montegna puffed up to his full height, arrogance in his cocky grin. "But I am."

"Scum has a tendency to float to the top."

Montegna's foot shot out, clipping Jake across the face. Jake lurched sideways, taking Sam with him. Sam screamed.

"Watch what you say," Montegna said softly, examining the tip of his shoe.

"I'm surprised at you, Montegna," Jake rasped, spitting on the floor. "I thought you paid your boys there to do your fighting."

Montegna watched Jake and Sam disinterestedly for a moment while they struggled to sit up again. "It's hardly a fight, with you down on the floor like a dog, Cavanaugh."

"So let me up and we'll handle this like men."

Montegna squatted beside them, his dark eyes glittering. "That's not my way, Mr. Cavanaugh. You should know that."

"What does that mean?" Sam asked. The man scared the hell out of her, but she wasn't going to be bullied by him.

"Don't ask," Jake said.

Montegna's grin made Sam feel sick. "I'm offended," he said. "You don't know my reputation?"

Sam shook her head.

He leaned over, drawing a finger down the side of Sam's face. The gesture was both mesmerizing and revolting. "I prefer to do things neatly. Cleanly."

Jake jerked against his restraints, causing Sam to gasp in pain. "What you mean is that your victims are never found. And on the rare occasion when bodies turn up, they're unrecognizable to their own mothers."

Sam felt bile rise in her throat at the image that conjured. Montegna's eyes narrowed on Jake. "Not a pretty picture, but an apt description."

"What are you going to do to us?" Sam whispered.

Montegna stood, wiping the palms of his hands across his trousers. "That depends. If you choose to cooperate, you'll simply vanish in a puff of smoke." He waved his hand in the air. "Shouldn't take long for a fire to burn this place down."

Sam trembled. Jake squeezed her fingers, but her hands felt numb. "And if we don't cooperate?"

"I wouldn't recommend that." Montegna snapped his fingers at his men.

Vinnie reached down and pulled a knife from his boot. He passed it to Montegna who examined the blade with the careful attention of a surgeon. "I prefer to do things neatly," he said, drawing the blade across his thumb until it beaded crimson. "But I can make it as messy as you want."

"How did you track us down?" Jake snarled.

Montegna smiled. "At first I thought you must work for Levy. I've never trusted that little runt. It didn't take much to gain the loyalty of some of his men. They've kept me advised of your movements and assure me you don't work for Levy." He leaned in close to Sam. "You simply got in the way."

Sam shook her head. "So what do you intend to do with us?"

"You've insulted my honor, Ms. Martin. You made my men look like fools. I can't have that." He paced the narrow room. The knife blade glinted in the light, sending a shiver of dread up Sam's spine. "And there's always a chance Levy plans to use you against me. I don't intend to let that happen."

"We would no more work for Levy than we'd work for you."

Montegna pivoted on the balls of his feet with catlike grace. "Get them up!" he ordered.

The men hauled them to their feet. Sam stumbled, her legs numb from sitting on the floor. Jake's support was the only thing that kept her from falling.

Montegna stood before her, his dark eyes empty. Soulless. "When I thought you might work for Levy, it was strictly business," he said, bringing the knife up to her hairline and dragging the side of the blade down her face. "But now it's personal."

Sam felt the slightest pressure against her cheekbone. "Please. There's nothing we can do to you."

"No. But there's so much I can do to you."

Sam winced as the knife broke skin, trying desperately to pull away from him. "No!" she gasped.

"Leave her alone, Montegna!"

Jake's words were ineffectual. Montegna's gaze never left Sam's face. "Perhaps I was wrong after all. My men saw you with Levy. Your boyfriend is a detective." Montegna recounted the facts, the knife inching down Sam's face, barely scratching the skin. "Perhaps you work for the cartel instead?"

Sam swallowed hard, forcing her eyes to remain steady on his face. Before she could say anything, Jake spoke.

"She doesn't know anything. I'm the one you want."

Montegna's head snapped up. He walked around to face Jake. "And what do I want with you? Tell me what you know. Now!"

"I'm guessing you don't know the FBI arrested Levy today."

Montegna's eyes narrowed. "You're lying."

Jake shrugged. "Maybe. Or maybe your great deal is about to fly south without you. What was Levy supposed to do? Get you out of the country?"

"I ask the questions!" Montegna roared.

"No deal. Let Sam go and I'll tell you everything."

Montegna snarled in frustration. "You don't tell me what to do! I'll take the woman apart piece by piece and let you watch."

Sam gasped and bit back the urge to scream. There was no doubt in her mind that Montegna was capable of carrying out his threat.

"If you kill her, you'll have to kill me. Then you'll never know the truth," Jake said with a casual nonchalance that made Sam wonder how far he was willing to go.

Sam was sure Montegna would never go for Jake's suggestion. He couldn't let her go. She knew too much.

"Cut them loose," Montegna said with a snap of his fingers.

"But Mr. Montegna—" Vinnie started.

Montegna turned on his man. "I said, cut them loose."

Vinnie took the knife back from Montegna and sliced the tape that bound Sam and Jake together. Sam rubbed at her tender wrists and the sticky residue left on her skin by the adhesive. Before she could relax, Vinnie had her by the neck, his gun pressed to her side.

"Now," Montegna said, addressing Jake. "Tell me what you know."

"I said, let the woman go." Jake's words were slow and measured, as if he were speaking to a child. "Let her go and then we'll talk."

Sam looked at Jake, but his gaze was focused on Montegna. She had no intentions of leaving Jake alone with this lunatic but she wasn't sure what his plan was. The last thing he needed was for her to sabotage his efforts. She kept quiet.

A slow, calculating smile spread across Montegna's face. "Sure, sure. I'll let the woman go. Vinnie, take her out of here."

Vinnie's hand tightened on her arm as he led her to the door. "Jake, no!" Sam struggled to free herself. "I'm not leaving you here."

Jake's face was a calm mask. "Go, Sam. It'll be all right."

Tears fell unheeded. "Jake—"

"Go on, Sam. Please." His features cleared and his cocky grin melted some of her terror. "I can handle this."

"Come on, enough, enough!" Montegna snapped. "Get her out of here."

Vinnie dragged her to the door and threw it open. The late-afternoon sunlight blinded her at first. Vinnie's hand loosened on her arm but didn't let go. Something in the distance caught her eye. At first she didn't understand what she was seeing. But Vinnie did.

"Boss! There are cars coming this way!"

"Run, Sam! Run!"

Sam's first instinct was to follow Jake's order. But Vinnie was too quick for her. "Not so fast."

"Bring her back in," Montegna barked. "Quick! Close the door." He turned his wrath on Jake. "What is this? A setup?"

Instead of answering his question, Jake said, "Give it up, Montegna. You're trapped."

Vinnie dragged Sam back in, pushing her toward Jake. Outside, she could hear the sound of the cars approaching. Montegna went to the door and cracked it open. He cursed under his breath.

Sam looked at Jake. "Who is it?" she whispered.

Jake gave a small shake of his head. "Don't know. The damn cavalry, I hope."

Doors slammed. A voice blared over a bullhorn. "Carlos Montegna, come out with your hands up. You are surrounded."

"It's Joe."

"I have hostages!" Montegna shouted through the narrow gap in the door.

"Come out, Montegna. Let the hostages go."

"Let me go or I'll kill them."

Sam stepped closer to Jake. "What do we do?"

"Sit tight."

Wishing she had half of Jake's courage, Sam wrapped her arms around herself. And prayed.

"You're not going to get out of this, Montegna," Jake said reasonably. "It's Joe Lafferty, FBI. He arrested Levy this afternoon. He'll cut you a deal. You'll be out of the country before tomorrow."

Montegna stalked across the room and grabbed Sam by her arm. Hauling her toward the door, he pointed the gun to her head. "Go," he said, nudging her to the opening in the door. "Eddie, watch him." The big man moved closer to Jake, gun trained. "Vinnie, get over here and hold the door."

With Vinnie propping the door open, Montegna twisted his hand in Sam's hair. "What do you see?"

Sam peered outside. "Three cars."

Montegna yanked her back inside. Pointing his gun through the opening, he fired several shots. The rapid succession of explosions echoed in the small shed.

"Sam, get down!" Jake cried.

Sam crouched down just as a volley of gunfire went off outside. Belatedly, Montegna and Vinnie joined her on the floor. Bullets tore into the walls with dull thuds. Sam crawled across the dirty floor toward Jake. Fighting back the stark fear that clouded his senses, he knelt beside her.

"Cease fire!" Joe yelled. "Cease fire!"

"Let us leave or I will kill the hostages!" Montegna screamed. He looked over his shoulder. "Bring them here."

Jake and Sam were forced to the door. Montegna pulled the door open. "Go," he told his men.

They made a tiny procession, Montegna surrounded by bodies. Sam was in the lead, Eddie behind her. Montegna pulled Jake to his side, with Vinnie bringing up the rear. In tight formation, they made their way to the van.

"Tell your men not to fire, Joe!" Jake called.

Jake surveyed the caravan of vehicles that made a semicircle around the shed. Two unmarked, one sheriff's department. Good, the more witnesses the better. In the distance, two more vehicles approached. One looked like a news van.

Montegna and his men directed Sam and Jake to the back of the van. Montegna climbed in first, followed by his men who pulled Jake in, then Sam. The doors slammed on the half-dozen law enforcement officers.

"Get to the plane," Montegna ordered.

Vinnie took the driver's seat and the engine revved to life. The smell of gasoline immediately permeated the air.

Crouching low in the passenger seat, Montegna roared, "Go!"

The van lurched forward, throwing Eddie off-balance. The big man fell to his knees. Jake delivered a quick uppercut to his jaw. He crumpled silently, the two men in the front oblivious. Jake palmed Eddie's semiautomatic.

"Quick, Sam," Jake said urgently, pulling her to the van doors. "When I say jump, jump, tuck and roll." He cast a look over his shoulder. They had only a minute or two at the most.

Sam nodded. "Ready."

Jake gave the doors a fierce kick and they flew open. "Jump!"

Sam jumped from the speeding van, her body reflexively curling into a tight circle. Montegna yelled behind him, but Jake didn't turn. Leaping from the van, he hit the ground with a painful jolt, rolling to a stop a few yards from Sam.

The van screeched to a halt. Jake got to his knees and braced the gun in his hand. He didn't have time to think, only to shoot. He had to give Sam a chance to get away. The shots ripped the air as he emptied the gun into the van. Then he leaped to his feet and started running behind Sam, reaching for her hand as he passed her. "Come on, Sam! Run, run!"

She stumbled behind him, going down on her knees. Jake looked over his shoulder. Montegna jumped out of the van, his gun pointed at Sam. In that instant, time froze. Jake saw what Montegna intended—he'd kill Sam just on principle.

Jake did the only thing he could. He threw his body on top of Sam's. Montegna fired and Jake heard the bullet whistle through the air before he actually felt it. In the next instant, the van exploded. Flames licked up into the air, and pieces of debris came showering down on them.

Sam pulled away from Jake, looking over his shoulder at the van. "How did you know it was going to explode?"

"The gas," he said weakly, feeling light-headed. "Someone must have hit the fuel tank. I just helped things along."

Sam trembled, her face pale. She was in shock. Wrapping his arms around her, he pulled her close. She was alive and safe. Montegna hadn't taken her away from him. He'd won, this time. "It's over, Sam. It's finished."

"Jake?" Her gaze searched his face. "Are you all right?"

He tried to nod, but his head felt detached from his body. "I'm fine. Just got shot, that's all."

"Jake! Jake!"

He could hear her screaming his name but couldn't seem to form the words to tell her that she was giving him a headache. She rolled him over and he felt the searing pain of the bullet in his back.

"Dammit, Jake. Don't you dare die on me," she cried into his chest. "I love you!"

He wanted to say it had taken her long enough to tell him. Instead, he just smiled and closed his eyes.

Epilogue

In the aftermath of their ordeal, everybody and their brother wanted a statement from Sam and Jake—the FBI, the sheriff's department, the local news media with a feed to the networks, even airport security, wanted information. Joe kept the harassment to a minimum as Jake was taken to the hospital.

Separated from Jake while the doctor looked him over, Sam did her best to tell everyone what they wanted to know. Joe insisted she be examined as well, but she couldn't think of anything right now except how still Jake looked as they wheeled him into surgery.

After what felt like hours, the doctor came out.

"I'm Dr. Goodwin. Are you Mr. Cavanaugh's family?"

"I'm with the FBI," Joe said. "Is he going to be all right?"

"He'll be fine," the doctor replied, his smile reassuring. "He needs rest, and that shoulder will hurt for a while."

Sam sagged against Joe in relief. Jake would be all right. He wasn't going to die.

"We're going to wheel him into post-op now. You can see him for a minute, but then he needs to sleep."

"You go on," Joe said gently. "I'll call Sherry. She'll be worried sick if she hears this on the news."

Sam nodded and followed Dr. Goodwin down the hall. Jake was turned on his side, the stark-white bandage looking out of place against his tanned skin. She stepped close to the bed and laid her hand against his cheek.

"Jake? Can you hear me?" She searched his face for some response. Despite Dr. Goodwin's assurances that he was fine, she wouldn't feel better until Jake woke up.

Jake's eyelids fluttered open and he looked at her. "Where am I?"

"In the hospital," she told him. "They had to take the bullet out of your back."

"I don't like hospitals."

"Too bad. I'm not letting you die on me."

His eyes closed again and her heart skipped a beat. "Jake?"

"I'll be fine," Jake repeated, though his eyes stayed closed. "Sam?"

She leaned close because his voice was so low. "What, Jake?"

"I love you, too."

When Jake woke up, his head hurt, his shoulder hurt and his knee hurt. But the sun was shining and he was alive, so he smiled.

"I was starting to think you'd never wake up. You've been asleep all night." He looked over at Sam sitting in a chair beside his bed. She looked as ragged around the edges as he felt.

He scooted over to make space for her, wincing at the pain in his shoulder. "Come over here and let me take a look at you. How are you holding up?"

She sat next to him on the bed. "I'll survive."

"I guess we're all over the news by now."

"Yeah." Sam smiled. "But this time it's good news."

Sherry pushed open the door. "Can I come in?"

Jake grinned. "Sure."

Joe Lafferty followed her in. "You both look like you've been through the wringer."

"No thanks to the FBI," Jake said. "You were almost too late."

Sam looked at Joe. "How did you know where to find us?"

"One of Levy's men talked. He knew what Montegna was planning. A couple of them had been working for Montegna from the inside. That's why Montegna was able to track you so well."

"What happens now?" Sam asked, reaching for Jake's hand. He did her one better and settled his hand on her waist.

"They'll take Levy in for questioning. Among other things, he'll be charged as an accessory to Greg Tilton's murder as well as his own agent's. We have enough evidence to put him away for a while."

Jake nodded. "He's a power-hungry son of a bitch. He didn't give a damn what Montegna did as long as he got his evidence."

"The case will break wide-open now. I spoke with Mel Patterson, the head of BOCTA," Joe said. "Even with Montegna dead, there's enough documentation to put away a lot of people."

"Montegna's dead?"

Sam nodded at Jake's question. "I didn't get a chance to tell you. The explosion killed him."

"I can't say I'm sorry to hear that." He looked up at Sam and the tenderness in her face was enough to melt his heart. He remembered that split second when he thought he was going to lose her and nothing had mattered but making sure he didn't. "I thought he was going to kill you."

Joe gave him a speculative glance. "You know, we could use someone with your experience and training at the Bureau."

Something—hope, maybe—tugged at Jake. "Thanks, but—"

Joe held up his hands. "Don't make any decisions yet. I'll give you a call next week. We can talk. You don't seem like the type that's cut out for the easy life."

Jake grinned. "Well, a little excitement never hurts. But I'm glad this one is over."

"It's over," Sam echoed, her voice holding a note of disbelief.

"Oh, I almost forgot," Sherry said, turning toward the door. "There's someone here who wants to see you."

"I bet Emily is furious I wasn't there when she got home from school."

Sherry laughed. "Yes, but the little tyrant isn't the only one anxious to see you."

"Then who—?"

Jake's words broke off when Sherry opened the door. Emily stepped into the room, followed by Fletcher. The dog let out a low woof. A white bandage covered one of his rear legs.

"Hey, buddy." He had to swallow past the lump in his throat before he could say more. "Hi, Em."

"Hi, Uncle Jake." He could tell by her drawn expression that she was thinking of her father. For once, the thought of Charlie didn't cause him pain. "Are you going to be all right?"

"I'm going to be fine, kiddo."

Emily smiled. "Good. I want you to come to my next softball game."

"You betcha." Jake reached his hand out to Fletcher. "Hey, Fletch!" Looking past Emily to Sherry, he asked, "He's all right?"

Sherry nodded. "He's got a nasty wound where a bullet grazed him, but the vet said he'd be as good as new in a couple of weeks. The doctor wasn't crazy about letting him in here, but he made an exception."

"I'll take care of him until you get out of here," Emily offered, giving the big mutt a pat on the head.

Jake knew he was grinning like a maniac, but he didn't care. "Thanks."

"I'm so glad he's okay," Sam said softly.

Jake looked up at her, feeling a tender vulnerability he'd never known before. "What are you going to do now?" He heard Sherry, Emily and Joe slip out the door, but he was focused on Sam. Only Sam.

"Well, I need to find out what happened to the rest of my life."

Jake smiled in return. "And I need to get Annie's van fixed before she nails my hide to a barn door."

"I need to get my job back." Sam hesitated before going on. "Or find a job somewhere else." She brushed a tear away. "And I have to finish reading my father's letters. I want to get to know him."

"And I have to square things with Brian and Mac before they nail my hide to a hangar door," Jake added.

"I have to find a place to stay until this mess is straightened out, and buy some clothes of my own."

"You can stay with me." Jake laughed. "As soon as I can get them to let me out of here."

"Are you sure? You can get on with your life now. You've got a lot of plans to make, with Joe's offer and all."

"I want you with me, Sam."

"I thought we hardly knew each other."

He ran his fingers over her lips. "Did you mean what you said last night?"

She nodded. "When I thought I might lose you—"

"I felt the same way when I thought Montegna was going to kill you, Sam."

"You saved me."

He shook his head and smiled, a joy he'd never known before replacing the dull ache he'd carried with him for so long. "I didn't think about it, I just did it. I wasn't going to let you get away so easily. I love you, lady."

Sam returned his smile. "I thought we hardly knew each other," she said again.

"Good point." Jake was quiet for a moment. "What's your favorite color?"

"Green."

"And what do you like for breakfast?"

She grinned. "An onion bagel with cream cheese."

He pulled her down beside him and tucked her hair back from her face. "Are you a morning person or a night owl?"

She turned her mouth into his palm and pressed a lingering kiss there that set his blood on fire. "Definitely a night owl."

He swallowed hard. "And how do you like to sleep?"

"Naked," she said, leaning forward to kiss the straight edge of his jaw. He couldn't have loved her more if he'd known her all his life. "With you."

As his mouth descended on hers, he murmured, "That's all I need to know."

*   *   *   *   *

Based on the bestselling miniseries

A FORTUNE'S CHILDREN *Wedding:*
THE HOODWINKED BRIDE

by BARBARA BOSWELL

This March, the Fortune family discovers a twenty-six-year-old secret—beautiful Angelica Carroll *Fortune!* Kate Fortune hires Flynt Corrigan to protect the newest Fortune, and this jaded investigator soon finds this his most tantalizing—and tormenting—assignment to date....

Barbara Boswell's single title is just one of the captivating romances in Silhouette's exciting new miniseries, **Fortune's Children: The Brides,** featuring six special women who perpetuate a family legacy that is greater than mere riches!

Look for *The Honor Bound Groom,* by Jennifer Greene, when **Fortune's Children: The Brides** launches in Silhouette Desire in January 1999!

Available at your favorite retail outlet.

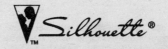

This March Silhouette is proud to present

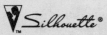

SENSATIONAL

MAGGIE SHAYNE
BARBARA BOSWELL
SUSAN MALLERY
MARIE FERRARELLA

This is a special collection of four complete novels for one low price, featuring a novel from each line: Silhouette Intimate Moments, Silhouette Desire, Silhouette Special Edition and Silhouette Romance.

Available at your favorite retail outlet.

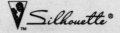

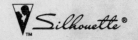

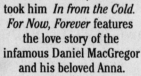
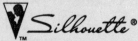

Silhouette Romance proudly presents an all-new, original series...

Loving The Boss

Six friends dream of marrying their bosses in this delightful new series

Come see how each month, office romances lead to happily-ever-after for six friends.

In January 1999—
THE BOSS AND THE BEAUTY by Donna Clayton

In February 1999—
THE NIGHT BEFORE BABY by Karen Rose Smith

In March 1999—
HUSBAND FROM 9 to 5 by Susan Meier

In April 1999—
THE EXECUTIVE'S BABY by Robin Wells

In May 1999—
THE MARRIAGE MERGER by Vivian Leiber

In June 1999—
I MARRIED THE BOSS by Laura Anthony

Only from

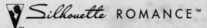
Silhouette ROMANCE™

Available wherever Silhouette books are sold.

INTIMATE MOMENTS®
Silhouette®

COMING NEXT MONTH

#919 THIS HEART FOR HIRE—Marie Ferrarella

Given the threats against him, Logan Buchanan knew he had no choice but to hire private investigator Jessica Deveaux, but seeing her again only reminded him of how much he'd once loved her. Now it was up to Logan to prove he'd changed, before someone took away his one last chance for happiness.

#920 THE FUGITIVE BRIDE—Margaret Watson

Cameron, Utah

FBI agent Jesse Coulton was having a hard time believing beautiful Shea McAllister was guilty of doing anything illegal on her Utah ranch. As he worked undercover to discover the truth, Jesse desperately hoped she was innocent—because the only place she belonged was in his arms!

#921 MIDNIGHT CINDERELLA—Eileen Wilks

Way Out West

After being accused of a crime he hadn't committed, Nathan Jones was determined to put his life back together. And when he met and fell for his sexy new employee, Hannah McBride, he knew he was on the right track. But then their newfound love was put to the test and it was up to Nate to prove that he was finally ready for happily-ever-after.

#922 THE DADDY TRAP—Kayla Daniels

Families Are Forever

When Kristen Monroe and her nephew Cody knocked on his door, Luke Hollister knew his life would never be the same. As she hid from Cody's abusive "father," Kristen shocked Luke with an incredible secret. And the longer they stayed, the more Luke fell in love—with the woman he desired and the son he'd always wanted....

#923 THE COP AND CALAMITY JANE—Elane Osborn

Bad luck seemed to follow Callie "Calamity Jane" Chance everywhere. But when she met sexy detective Marcus Scanlon, she knew her luck had changed. He was hot on the trail of suspected catnappers, and Callie was his only witness. Once the culprits were nabbed, would Callie accept Marcus's proposal—for a disaster-free future?

#924 BRIDGER'S LAST STAND—Linda Winstead Jones

Men in Blue

Detective Malcolm Bridger never thought he'd see Frannie Vaughn again after their one memorable night together. Then Frannie got mixed up in his current case. Suddenly Malcolm was falling for this forever kind of girl, and their near one-night stand was slowly becoming a one-*life* stand.